GW00871558

AGENT OF PROPHECY

The Prophecies Series - Book 1

M.A. ROTHMAN

Primordial Press

ISBN: 978-0-9976793-4-2

ALSO BY M.A. ROTHMAN

Technothrillers: (Thrillers with science / Hard-Science Fiction)

• Primordial Threat

• Freedom's Last Gasp

• Darwin's Cipher

Levi Yoder Thrillers:

• Perimeter

• The Inside Man

• Never Again

Epic Fantasy / Dystopian:

• Dispocalypse

• Agent of Prophecy

• Heirs of Prophecy

• Tools of Prophecy

• Lords of Prophecy

Trimoria

CONTENTS

MY LIFE FOREVER CHANGED

eath awaits you. That was the only thing Arabelle remembered from her dream when she woke to her father poking his head into her tent.

"Good morning, my heart," he said. "You shouldn't sleep the day away."

Arabelle groaned and stretched under her covers. "But my bed's so comfortable."

Her father normally indulged her love of sleep; at times she wouldn't get out of bed until midday. She was spoiled, but hated to admit it, even to herself.

"I'm sure it is, but it's travel day—and a beautiful one at that. I'll send Maggie in to help draw you a bath and get ready."

He pulled his head from the tent, and one of her guards called out for her maid.

Travel days were the one day Arabelle couldn't lie in bed all day. When the caravan was on the move, she had to move with it.

And unfortunately that happened often; at least every couple of weeks her people would uproot themselves to travel from one village to another within Trimoria.

Maggie came into her tent a moment later, saw that she hadn't budged from underneath her covers, and frowned.

"Lady Arabelle, you must get ready. You can't keep your father waiting. You're supposed to break your fast with the Sheikh. Besides, the men can't pack your tent until you're out of it!"

Maggie, at twenty, was only three years older than Arabelle, but the way she mothered her, you'd think Maggie was twice Arabelle's age. Arabelle's actual mother had died giving birth to her, and sometimes it seemed like Maggie was trying to fill that hole in her life.

As Maggie poured steaming water into a bath from a series of lidded jugs that had been placed just inside the flap of her tent, the scent of roses filled the air. Grudgingly, Arabelle climbed out of bed and got ready for her day.

Arabelle bounced comfortably on Logan, her dappled gray stallion. Her father had handpicked him for her eighth birthday, and she'd loved the horse ever since, taking him out for a run whenever she could talk her guards into escorting her—which was not as often as she liked. Even though she'd always promise to not cause trouble, she'd inevitably forget and would let Logan race as quickly as he would take her. Her guards would yell and fume because they couldn't keep up.

She didn't do this on purpose, exactly—it was just that the exciting possibility of a few moments of actual freedom was... irresistible. The thrill of speed, the exhilaration of the wind through her hair.

Arabelle patted Logan on the neck. "I promise I'll take you running soon, and we'll go as fast as you can take me."

He nickered and bounced his head up and down with approval.

To anyone who observed the migration of the caravan, it would look like an entire city was on the move. Father had once told her that they had approximately nine hundred and fifty wagons. Arabelle had asked about the mess they must leave in their wake with so many people, but her father had explained that the enigmatic blink dogs took care of that.

"If it weren't for the scavengers like the vulture and the blink dog, the trash and spoiled foodstuffs would indeed become a burden to us all."

Blink dogs really would eat anything—Arabelle had witnessed that herself. They were called "blink dogs" because they could blink out of existence, only to reappear as much as fifty feet away from where they had been. The popping sound that accompanied these disappearances could often be heard near the back of the wagon train, along with their unusual high-pitched laughs.

"Ahem, Princess?" Someone pointedly cleared their throat next to Arabelle, and she turned to find Roselle, her personal tutor, riding beside her. "You can't escape your lessons, dear. Even when we're in transit."

Arabelle always enjoyed talking with Roselle. Roselle was

easily the oldest person Arabelle knew, but she was vibrant, fun, and full of entertaining and educational stories. Arabelle loved hearing about history's adventures, even though she could never be involved in such things herself.

"What's today's lesson?" she asked.

"I thought it might be good to talk about the First Protector, and the lessons a princess might gain from such a man."

"The Protector responsible for the demon wars?"

Roselle made a clicking noise with her tongue. "Bah! Dear child, you need this lesson more than I realized." She sighed. "You know that your father, as Sheikh, rules all in his domain." She pointed ahead of the caravan. "But who is charged with the safety and enforcement of the laws in the town of Aubgherle?"

"Throll Lancaster!" Arabelle said excitedly. "He's the town's Protector. I met him once. If I recall correctly, his wife is named Gwen."

"Very good, Princess. I'm always impressed with your memory. And what does it mean to be a Protector?"

"Protectors catch thieves and organize groups of rangers to defend against slaver raids."

A deep voice boomed behind them. "Yes, my dearest, but that is only the barest essence of what a Protector is."

Arabelle's father rode up beside her, wiped the sweat off his shaved head, and recited a passage from some tome he'd likely read ages ago.

"Only the best among us could strive to emulate the sacrifices the First Protector made to save the people of Trimoria. Zenethar Thariginian, King, and the First Protector of Trimoria, sacrificed all that he was in the final battle against the demons.

4

With this altruistic last act, he raised the barrier that keeps us safe even today."

Roselle murmured, "May his sacrifices never be forgotten."

"My flower, the Protectors are intended to do all that you said, but they are selected as men who epitomize the virtues demonstrated by the First Protector. They are a force of good in this chaotic world we live in. Any Protector would be willing to lay down his life for the well-being of the people he is charged with protecting."

Arabelle pulled lightly on her reins to keep Logan from outpacing the others. "So the lesson for me is to keep in mind all that the Protectors have done, and all that they continue to do in service of their people? I should consider such sacrifices a part of what I should do for our people?"

"It's a start, my dearest. Always keep in mind that our people depend on us to lead them—and thus we must do whatever is necessary for their welfare. It's our sacred obligation, even if it feels onerous at times."

"And the people love you for it, my Sheikh," Roselle said, bowing her head with respect.

Father smiled at the old woman, then turned back to Arabelle. "One day, you and your husband will lead this caravan. You'll have responsibilities that are hard for you to imagine. It's about time you give such things serious thought, my dearest flower. I won't be around forever."

The princess felt a growing anxiety as she wondered whether she'd ever be ready for such responsibilities.

Suddenly she was struck by a question that hadn't occurred to her before. "So, the dream that everyone shares of the demon's destruction, and the man on top of the hill—that's the First Protector? It really did happen?"

Her father gave her a look of incredulity. "You thought that was a simple dream?"

Arabelle shrugged. "I suppose I never gave it much thought. What about the barrier he raised? If it isn't just a story, then where is it? How is it that I've never seen it?"

"You can't approach such things, Princess!" said Roselle. "It's too dangerous."

"But I don't even know what the barrier looks like or where to find it. How can I avoid it if I don't know anything about it?"

Her father chuckled softly. "That's a good point. As I'm sure Roselle has taught you, the Trimoria that we know today is but a small portion of the continent our people traveled across long ago, before the demon wars. Today's Trimoria is defined by the barrier: an impenetrable wall of mist that runs along its perimeter. No person who has ever entered the mist has returned."

Arabelle's thoughts had already led her to another question. "Why doesn't Trimoria have a king anymore?"

"The line has run out," Roselle said with a sigh. "In my grandfather's day, King Harold Thariginian still ruled. But all his descendants met an early demise, and we have since been left without a royal house."

"Is that when the wizard Azazel came to power?"

"L-let's not discuss Azazel, please," Roselle stammered.

"But the First Protector was a wizard, too, right?"

"Yes," her father responded. "He was also a great warrior and a king."

"Okay, but if wizardry can be used for good, such as by the First Protector, why is it outlawed by Azazel?"

Her father suddenly looked uncomfortable and a bit pale.

Roselle cleared her throat. "Why don't we move to a more pleasant topic? Let's discuss the relationship of our people to the city dwellers of Trimoria."

But as her teacher droned on, Arabelle wasn't listening. She was too busy wondering what had caused her father's strange reaction.

———

Arabelle was allowed to go anywhere she wanted in the caravan, but her father did have a couple of rules that she was never supposed to break. The first was never to leave the confines of the caravan without letting him know. The second was to keep an escort with her wherever she went.

She broke both of those rules today.

It happened after the caravan had set up camp alongside the forest east of Aubgherle. Arabelle was familiar with the area, for Aubgherle was a larger town, which meant they would sometimes stay here for a month at a time—and during those stays, she took advantage of every opportunity to lose her escorts and wander into the woods. She relished the solitude she found deep in the forest.

A heavy mist blanketed the valley with silence as she crept through the trees, looking for her elusive quarry. Her father didn't believe in the existence of elves. Most people didn't.

Arabelle knew better.

Not only had she spied glimpses of them many times before, but on rare occasions one of the younger elves had actually stopped to talk to her. Some of them couldn't speak Trimorian, but some could. They were a lovely race of beautiful people, but they completely mistrusted most humans.

She secretly aimed to earn their trust.

It was very early in the morning, the sun barely promised its arrival with its peach-colored bloom on the horizon. Now, as she tiptoed along, looking for the paths that the elves sometimes left, a high-pitched gurgling roar shattered the silence and a green-scaled, lizard-like creature the size of a large dog burst through the foliage.

The creature gave Arabelle a sinister stare that sent shivers up and down her back. It was unlike anything she'd ever seen or heard of in Trimoria. Its baneful yellow-and-black eyes glared at her as it growled menacingly. Then it scratched the ground with its claws, unfurled a set of wings, and gathered itself for a leap.

Suddenly a series of gray blurs whizzed by. The creature made a coughing sound as it sprouted a pair of arrows from its chest.

An elf appeared out of nowhere and struck the monster in the neck with his sword, nearly decapitating it with a single stroke. The creature's twitching body pulsed streams of blood as its snake-like eyes closed for the last time.

The elf turned to Arabelle. "Are you hurt?"

She felt a wet burning on her chest. She looked down and saw two steaming holes in her traveling clothes. The creature had spit something at her just before the elf killed it. The world blurred, tilted suddenly, and the ground came rushing up to meet her.

"Arabelle, you are not well."

She tried to open her eyes but couldn't.

I can't move.

"You are not paralyzed. You are simply unconscious."

I don't feel unconscious. Wait... how did you know I thought I was paralyzed?

"My name is Seder, and you are being taken care of. We have time to speak in this manner. Speak with your mind—I will hear you."

Are you an elf? Can elves read minds?

"No, I am not an elf. I am... something else. Think of me as a spirit. Now listen, for I'm going to tell you a story that involves you. It is time you must shoulder a great responsibility."

Will I get to see more of the elves?

"I promise you that from this moment forward, your relationship with the children of the woods will change forever."

Then tell me!

"This tale begins many thousands of years ago. The Creator made me and my world and gave me a brother named Sammael. While Sammael enjoyed creating chaos wherever order existed, I enjoyed making order out of chaos. We were a matched pair.

"We learned that there were other worlds with more of the Creator's children, but that Sammael and I were different than most of the Creator's children. We could reach across the distances to these other worlds, whereas those in other worlds evidently could not.

"My brother felt the need to sow his chaos in these other worlds. I have always known that I am here to balance the actions of my brother. If my brother ever managed to achieve influence in a world without my balance, the results for that world would be disastrous.

"That is what is happening here. My brother has found a way to send a significant part of his essence into your world. He wants to tear the land you call Trimoria apart, and I am trying to keep that from happening. I have foreseen the need for you to be a part of my plans."

How can I possibly help? I'm only a girl. I don't even know how to swing a sword.

"The threads of destiny have woven themselves about your family, and they are especially knotted around you, Arabelle, Princess of the Imazighen. I wish I could make your journey easier, for you will suffer greatly. However, it is through this suffering that you will learn much about yourself and who you are meant to be."

What am I supposed to do?

"Survive."

Survive?

"The fate of all you know rests on your survival. Just look within for what you need. You have it within you to accomplish almost anything. But... I will grant you one additional skill that will aid your journey. When you awake, you will be able to locate any living creature you envision.

"Now relax. I am going to release you into consciousness.

Remember, the fates of your people and your land lie in your hands."

———————

Arabelle opened her eyes to find a wizened elf standing over her.

"Welcome back to the living, miracle child," the elf said with a smile. "You should be dead."

Dead? Why would I be dead?

The elf didn't respond, and Arabelle realized she was still talking with her mind. She tried again, aloud this time.

"Why would I be dead? I merely fainted after… after an elf dispatched that hissing monstrosity. What was that thing, anyway?"

The old elf helped her sit up. Her body ached, and her muscles screamed in protest at the movement. Only then did she realize she was wearing no clothes, and her body was slathered in a pungent ointment that smelled of pine resin.

She covered up quickly. "Where are my clothes?"

The elf retrieved her clothes from a table beside him. As she dressed, her muscles aching, he explained.

"You were attacked by a creature that we thought had long ago gone extinct. A corrupted dragon, or, as some of the history books call it, a "demon-kissed dragon." Unlike the dragons of common stories, these dragons are unable to think logically. They are creatures of pain and suffering, and live only to eat, kill, and sow chaos. They rarely grow large, because inevitably their blind quest for destruction leads them into the path of a larger predator. But they need not size; even a hatchling such as the one you encountered is quite deadly. These dragons can attack with both claw and spittle. You were hit with some of the latter, and the creature's poison seeped through your skin."

Had Arabelle not been the victim of this event, she wouldn't have believed it. *A real dragon?*

"So this… salve that's all over me. Did it cure me?"

The old elf looked somber. "I'm afraid it didn't. The poison that infected you is still within you, trying to paralyze you, and no known cure exists. But I searched my library and discovered a way to delay the onset of the symptoms. The key is to ensure that the poison is never allowed to settle in one spot for too long. If it does, it will crystallize, and muscle paralysis will ensue. Once that happens, it's only a matter of time before it impacts your ability to breathe, and then you will most certainly die."

Arabelle took in a shuddering gasp. "I'm going to die?"

"Not if you don't want to," another voice proclaimed. A second elf walked into the room. She recognized him as the one who'd rescued her from the beast.

"This is Castien," said the older elf. "He's the one who brought you to me. He is our master of the sword, and was tracking the beast. Unfortunately it got to you before he got to it."

"Thank you for saving my life," Arabelle said. "For now," she added. She still couldn't believe she'd blithely just been given a death sentence. *I'm going to die.*

Castien smiled and put his hands on Arabelle's shoulders. "Not just for now. As long as you don't stop moving for very long, you can survive as long as you wish."

"But that's impossible. I have to sleep sometime, don't I? I should be dead already!"

"And you would be, except I've been moving your limbs regularly to prevent the onset of symptoms. Tell me: Do you want to live long enough to be useful to your people?"

A million thoughts rushed through Arabelle's head, but only one mattered. "Of course I want to live!"

"Good. Because it's not impossible. We have old records of elves who have survived for many decades with such a poison— by never sleeping for more than a couple of hours at a time. You'll learn to sleep, wake up to flush your muscles with blood by vigorous movement, sleep some more, and repeat the process. Like all new things, it'll be difficult at first, but you'll do it. Because if you don't, you'll die. It's as simple as that."

Arabelle looked down at her chest. "All that from being spat upon?"

Castien walked to a table in the corner of the room and returned with a sword—or the remains of one. He held it up in front of her. "Do you see the pitting of the metal, and how it looks like portions of the blade have been melted?"

She nodded.

"This was the sword I used to kill that infernal beast. Its blood ate right through the metal. So you can imagine the power of the beast's venom."

Arabelle rubbed at her ribs. "Okay. I need to stay active. I need to learn how to sleep for only two hours at a time. And I need to stay alive. For my father's sake as well as Seder's."

The elder elf's eyes widened. "Did you say Seder?"

"She probably worships him, Eglerion," said Castien.

13

"I don't worship him," Arabelle said. "In fact I'd never heard of Seder before he talked to me."

Now both of the elves looked at her with incredulous wide eyes.

"Seder talked with you?" Eglerion said. "What did he say?"

Arabelle related the conversation she'd had with the mysterious voice that called himself Seder. Eglerion's eyes grew wider with every word.

When she was done, he turned to Castien. "Castien, you must guide her in your special skills. I'll clear this with Xinthian, but this young lady *must* be given a chance to serve out her obligations to Seder."

Arabelle was confused. "Xinthian?"

Eglerion rested his hand on her shoulder. "Xinthian is the eldest of our people. In the absence of our queen, he is the authority in Eluanethra, our home."

Castien chuckled. "Don't let Eglerion fool you. He is nearly as old as Xinthian and holds the same authority."

Eglerion shot a severe glance at the sword master before returning his attention to Arabelle. "For Seder to have spoken with you…" He shook his head. "In truth, I was not aware that he spoke with humans, so his message must be of great import. He is a spirit of great power and an agent of good for my people. I would trust his message implicitly."

It was left to Castien to escort Arabelle back to her caravan. As they walked through the misty forest, Arabelle had questions. Lots of them.

"Why do your people hide from humans?"

Castien gave her a long look. "I would have the name of the human I am sharing elven secrets with."

Arabelle felt herself blushing under the gaze of her rescuer. "Arabelle."

"Arabelle, nothing I share with you can be shared with others. Do we understand each other?"

"I understand."

"You ask why we hide from humans. It's because, while most humans are kind and well-meaning, there are those among you that we won't tolerate."

"Do you mean Azazel?"

Castien nodded. "Him, and those who follow him. Though that's a topic I can't discuss further; some secrets are not mine to give. Suffice it to say that the elven people and the humans are not enemies, but it's best that we maintain distance between our two people. For now."

They neared the edge of the woods, and Castien stopped.

"It's approaching midday, and you can find your way from here. Meet me at midnight at this spot, and we'll begin your training. And if you value your life, don't go to sleep before then."

Arabelle looked up into Castien's almond-shaped eyes and admired his close-cropped blond hair and characteristic elven ears. His appearance was simultaneously foreign and beautiful.

She felt uncomfortably warm standing so close to him.

Suddenly it struck her how much she owed this courageous elf, and the morning's events came rushing back. She'd almost died. She was still going to die. It was all too much. Her throat tightened and tears flowed unbidden, and on an impulse she wrapped her arms around Castien's waist, buried her face in his chest, and sobbed.

She felt a comforting hand on her back. "Arabelle, I promise to arm you with the knowledge you need to survive. I can't promise you it'll be easy, but it'll be a life—make of it what you can."

She choked back tears and looked up at her wondrous rescuer. "Thank you for saving my life."

Castien stepped back and put his hands firmly on her shoulders. "Don't let my efforts go to waste by dying now. Your burden is heavy, but you have it in you to be something special for your people and possibly for all of Trimoria. Tonight, your lessons begin."

AN ORPHAN'S LIFE

W hen Grisham woke up in the darkness sometime after midnight, his first thought was: *It's officially my twelfth birthday.*

There was no one else who cared anymore, but Grisham still felt good that he'd made it to another birthday in this strange world.

And he was blessed to be lying on a cot with a roof over his head—even if that roof was over the dormitory of a Cammorian orphanage packed with other cots and other orphans. Any time one of the human children complained about the sleeping arrangements, he would recall a darker time, during the first year after his father's death, when he wandered the streets of Cammoria and slept under piles of rat-infested garbage to prevent himself from freezing.

He was lucky to have this cot. He vividly remembered the

day he was first allowed into this dorm and given a thin blanket. He'd been shocked at his good fortune.

He rolled over onto his side and closed his eyes. *Twelve years old.* Not bad, considering.

Soon he fell into a restless dream-filled sleep, reliving the moment when his life had been turned upside down.

Grisham's people were known as the Ta'ah. The Ta'ah lived deep underground, where they were protected from the dangers of the world above. Mostly protected. Even deep within their tunnels and caves, hunting parties occasionally encountered a stray demon from the surface, or worse, one of the dreaded priestesses of Lilith.

Still, it was much preferable to the aboveground, where almost all life had been eradicated, all signs of civilization destroyed. It had been centuries since their people had ventured into that cursed world. Why would they, when they could stay safe within their homes thanks to the magicks of the elders?

But for Grisham, the safety of home was not to be. For the seers of their people had said that Grisham and his father were destined to carry a treaty across the great barrier to the Tharig-inian king.

To Grisham, the thought was unimaginable. He couldn't even begin to picture what the outside world might be like. The elders had assured him that aboveground life on the other side of the barrier was much safer than it was here, but Grisham was still wary and afraid.

It was this mission that now brought Grisham and his father to a hidden chamber on the lowest level of the Ta'ah's underground home. Only those with the permission of the elders were allowed on this high-security level.

A mirror stood against one wall. Grisham had heard of this device only in ominous whispers, and was surprised to see that it looked like an ordinary mirror, five feet tall and six feet wide, within a metal frame. The only thing slightly remarkable about it was that the frame was marred by a series of indentations, each about the size of a fingernail.

Two elders had accompanied them to the chamber. The elders withdrew glowing gems from their robes and placed them into chosen indentations on the metal frame. After a moment the glow in the gems faded, and tiny lights appeared on the frame, flickering on and off in a series that moved around the mirror, gradually moving faster and faster, as if a single light were moving in a circle around the frame.

Grisham shivered, unable to hide his nervousness.

Dad put his hand on Grisham's shoulder. "Don't worry. I've been through such traveling devices before. There's no pain."

The two elders stood at the sides of the traveling portal, eyes closed, and hummed. The flickering of the lights increased, and soon their rotation was moving at such a speed that the individual lights blurred into a solid circle of light framing the mirror. The circle pulsed, flaring brightly into the infrared, and the reflection in the mirror melted away, showing a scene from the world above.

For the first time in his life, Grisham saw the sun.

Dad gave his shoulder a squeeze. "Are you ready?"

Grisham looked around the room one last time. The elders now swayed back and forth, chanting, their eyes still closed. Crackling energy swirled around the chamber, making his hair stand on end.

He nodded. "I'm ready."

He and his father stepped forward together.

Grisham felt only a moment of vertigo, and then he was there, his ears popping due to the change in pressure. A chill breeze met his face, and he breathed in the unknown smells of a new world. He looked behind him and saw no sign of the cave or the portal.

He had actually traveled through the portal—and through the barrier.

"We have no fear of demons here?" he asked.

His father wrapped an arm around his shoulder. "No, my son. The Thariginian king protects us within his barrier. And now we proceed with our mission. Find the heir to the Thariginian king, and help him to reunify our two peoples."

Grisham would never have imagined that the citizenry of a protected land could present as great a danger to them as the demons from outside the barrier. But he soon came to learn that even here within the barrier, he and his father weren't safe.

Their troubles began when Grisham's father lit a fire with a wave of his hand—a simple weave of magic. They had thought they were alone, sheltering in an abandoned barn, but it turned out the magic had been seen by a human hidden in the loft above.

That human shouted in alarm, darted from his hiding spot, and ran outside. Grisham and his father were fortunate to have moved along before black-clad soldiers came to investigate.

At the time, they were naïve about this new land and its restriction. They had no idea why the brief show of magic had caused such a stir. Only later did they understand why. It turned out that the land within the barrier was ruled with an iron fist by a wizard named Azazel. The people of Trimoria suffered under the yoke of his tyranny because he was the last remaining wizard within the barrier—having wiped every other practitioner of magic from existence—and he wouldn't hesitate to incinerate an entire village to enforce his rules. The one they'd violated was that magic employed by anyone other than Azazel himself was banned—and those who practiced it were sentenced to death.

So even the simple act of using magic to light a fire was enough to catch the attention of the soldiers known as Azazel's enforcers.

Unfortunately, it wasn't easy for them to hide among humans. To the people aboveground, who'd never seen a Ta'ah, they looked like dwarves—but dwarves rarely mingled with humans, which meant one adult dwarf and his child were easy to seek out.

They managed to survive only due to Dad's skills in weaving illusion. When they stood still, he could make them completely invisible, and when they moved, the same illusion could bend the light around them to make them appear to be several feet from their actual location. Many a crossbow bolt would have gone through them were it not for this trick of the light.

Grisham and his father fled the populated areas, taking refuge in a cave in the mountains. Grisham much preferred the cave to the aboveground anyway. Looking at the clouds and the sky made him dizzy.

How can these aboveworlders get used to a limitless ceiling?

Still, Grisham waited near the entrance as he waited for his father to return from foraging for food. Dad had cast a weave of protection across the entrance before leaving, which would make Grisham invisible to any humans or creatures who might happen to pass by.

But as Grisham would soon find out, the weave didn't disguise his scent.

A giant soldier emerged from the trees, stepping into the clearing just outside the cave. He barely resembled a normal man. He towered two feet taller than most men, and a pair of canines jutted from his lower jaw. He sniffed the air, then turned his yellow eyes in the direction of the cave.

Grisham froze, his heart pounding in his ears.

The giant sniffed again, growled, then started walking purposefully, menacingly toward the cave.

Grisham didn't know what to do. The cave was shallow; there was nowhere to hide and nowhere to run. He could only stay still and quiet and hope that somehow this human-like beast would turn aside.

Then, from out of nowhere, a blast of electrical energy knocked the beast off his feet, and Dad's voice shouted, "I warned you to stay away from me and my kin!"

Grisham's father stepped out from among the trees, advancing on the soldier. He threw another searing bolt that sent the soldier into spasms. Electricity arced up and down the soldier's body, and he bellowed in agony.

Dad pulled his arm back to send a finishing blast.

But he never finished that weave, for at that moment he was engulfed in a torrent of flame.

Grisham stifled a scream.

Another human appeared, this one draped in a red robe, a smirk on his face, wisps of smoke rising from his fingertips. A dozen crossbow-wielding soldiers were at his back, all in the familiar black armor with the red insignia on their chests. Azazel and his enforcers.

Grisham's heart threatened to beat out of his chest. He wanted to run to his father, but could only look on in horror.

The crackling flames subsided. His dad was still alive. But his beard had been burnt away and his skin was bright red and raw.

"You survived!" the wizard said with a laugh. "Most impressive." In his hands he accumulated a crackling black ball of energy. "I've never met an anvil-banger wizard before. Of course, where there's one, there are bound to be others. Don't worry. I guarantee you I'll dig all of your dwarven brethren out of their holes one by one if I have to."

Dad kneeled, and Grisham sensed he was gathering his strength to send a killing blast. But then he paused, turned in Grisham's direction, and yelled, "He who knows when to fight and when not to fight will be victorious!"

He dove to the cave entrance, just in front of the weave of

protection, and shot a furious blast of energy at the overhanging cliff wall.

The mountain shuddered, and Grisham was thrown backwards. A crack opened in the cave wall behind him, and at the same moment, the cliff came tumbling down directly on his father—sealing off the entrance to the cave and crushing the life from the only family Grisham had.

Grisham woke with a start, soaked with sweat despite the chill in the air.

"You have that dream again?"

It was Wat, who had the cot next to him. Wat was one of his few friends at the orphanage.

Grisham nodded. "Unfortunately."

Wat sighed wistfully. "I wish I had memories of my parents. The matron is the closest thing I've ever had to an actual mother or father."

"I'd rather not talk about it," Grisham said. It had been three years since the death of his father, yet it still felt like only yesterday. The seers had been so wrong about his destiny. His fruitless mission had ended with his father's death, as had Grisham's hopes of returning home.

"Why don't you accompany me on a hunt today?" Wat said. "Us dwarves need to look out for each other. You know as well as I do that there's no chance a dwarf will ever get adopted in this city."

Grisham started to shake his head. Wat meant well, but

Grisham couldn't allow himself to depend on anyone's companionship. Especially Wat, who wouldn't even be in the orphanage much longer. He was seventeen, and would soon be forced out to make room for younger children. He would have been forced out sooner if not for the matron's kindness. Luckily, he'd already achieved a miracle for an orphan dwarf: he'd made friends with the local librarian and had earned an apprenticeship at the city library.

"Come on, Grish. What do you say?"

Grisham looked up at his friend. When Wat was gone, Grisham would be the only "dwarf" in the orphanage, and any semblance of his heritage or people would have walked out the door. Perhaps he should seize his opportunities while he still could.

"Yes," he said. "I'll join you on the hunt."

Wat's smile brightened the room. "Excellent! I have hope for you yet. I'll borrow a bow and we'll try to get some nice fat hares. It'll be fun. You'll see."

———

Wat was the only person in Trimoria Grisham felt he could talk to. His father's death had taught him early on that he could trust no one here, and so he hadn't. In fact, he hadn't exchanged more than a hundred words with anyone other than Wat in three years —and even he and Wat didn't talk much. If he didn't have Wat, he would truly have nobody. As he strode through the woods with his friend outside Cammoria, he was glad he'd come.

Wat crouched to pick up some rabbit dung. He hefted it in his hand, then dropped it with a nod. "It's fresh. They must be around here somewhere."

Grisham scanned the grassland, but saw no hints of wildlife. When it came to hunting, Wat saw many things that he didn't.

But Grisham did see that something was going on with his friend. Wat's aura was fluctuating between white and red, and whenever he looked over at Grisham, it turned a deep purple.

"Wat, is something wrong? You don't look right."

Wat looked over at him. Purple yet again. "What do you mean? I look like I always do."

"No, you look purple when you look at me. You've got something to say, but you don't know how to say it."

Wat furrowed his bushy eyebrows. "I look purple?"

"Your aura, I mean. I can tell you're preoccupied with something."

Wat opened his mouth, paused, closed it again, and stroked his braided beard. "Grisham, you're looking at my aura right now?"

The look on Wat's face told Grisham he might have just made a giant mistake.

"Don't you… don't you see auras?"

Wat shook his head. "No, Grisham. Nobody sees auras."

Grisham broke into a cold sweat. *I'm an idiot. Seeing auras is probably something only the Ta'ah can do. Now I have to run away again before—*

"Don't worry," Wat put his hand on Grisham's shoulder and gave it a light squeeze. "I'll never tell anyone."

His aura was pure white as he spoke those words. White was the aura of truth. Wat believed what he was saying.

Grisham let out a shaky sigh of relief.

"But Grish… this is definitely something you should keep to yourself. If anyone knew, they might report you to Azazel's black-armored scum."

Grisham nodded. "I will. I just—can we just forget I ever said anything?"

"Forget what?" Wat said with a grin. He leaned in. "But hey, if this thing I've already forgotten about gives you an advantage, use it. You'll need every advantage you can get. Just don't let anyone know you're using the thing I've forgotten."

"I don't even know what you're talking about," Grisham said, smiling.

"Neither do I!" said Wat.

They both laughed.

A wolf howled in the distance, and Wat looked up sharply. "That's not good. We'd better head back to town. I wouldn't want to be out here and run into a pack of wolves."

"We won't run into them. Those wolves will be busy eating for a while. Didn't you hear his howl? He was calling his pack to tell them he just got a kill."

Wat stroked his beard and furrowed his eyebrows again.

Grisham realized he'd messed up somehow. "What did I do now?" he asked.

"You understand wolf-speak?"

"I mean…" Grisham paused. He'd never really thought about this before. "I wouldn't say that. It's not like I've ever had a conversation with a wolf. But I sensed what that wolf said."

Wat smiled. "A word of advice from an older and wiser of our kind. Don't admit that to anyone, either. It's no wonder you've kept so silent since I met you. Keep that up. These kinds of things, they might make people believe you can do... you know."

"Magic?"

"Yeah."

As they walked back toward the town gates, Grisham was quiet. He was busy replaying everything he'd ever said to anyone, and realizing just how many times he'd *almost* asked an innocent question that could have gotten him killed.

I can't trust anyone. Not ever.

Back in town, Wat went straight to the library, so Grisham returned to the orphanage alone. As he passed through the outer gate, the matron called his name and waddled over to him, beaming.

"Young Grisham! I found someone who seems interested in adopting a dwarf. Can you imagine the good fortune?"

So many questions popped up in Grisham's mind at once that all he could muster in response was, "Uh ..."

The matron handed him a parchment. "I knew you'd be thrilled. You are to meet the young couple in an inn called the Drunken Crow. And please, Grisham, try to show them how intelligent and kind you are under that sullen exterior. Win them over, then have them put their mark on the parchment. I'll then put my mark on it as well, and the contract will be complete. You'll have a family, Grisham. Isn't it wonderful?"

Grisham stared dumbly at the tightly rolled parchment in his hands, sealed with wax. He was still stunned by the news. "What's this couple like?"

"I'm afraid I haven't met them; they used a courier to make the arrangements. It all seems *very* promising though. Oh, I will miss you, my silent little boy." She grabbed Grisham's shoulders, turned him around, and nudged him forward. "Get going before they have a chance to change their minds. I'm sure it's meant to be."

Grisham stumbled to the inn in a fog. Adopted? Truthfully, he'd never seriously considered the possibility that it might actually happen. No one in Cammoria would adopt a dwarf.

He was so lost in his thoughts that he barely noticed the seedy character watching the inn from an alley, his aura full of ominous black and red streaks. Nor did he notice that the streets were oddly empty.

If he had, perhaps he'd have been on his guard. As it was, he stepped across the threshold, felt something hard hit the back of his head, and collapsed as darkness washed over him.

LIFE AT HOME

As Arabelle returned to the caravan, a thick, heavy mist had settled over the fields. The moisture settled on her skin, and she could barely see a few feet in front of her. She mostly found her way by following the sound of griping.

"How can I set out my goods if I can't see my customers—or know if someone's about to steal from me?"

"Curse the maker of this mist. It's the damnedest blanket of fog I've ever encountered. I can't lead my sheep to pasture in this stuff. I'll lose them all!"

Arabelle heard running footsteps only a moment before someone plowed right into her, knocking her to the ground. For a moment she feared she'd been attacked, then she saw it was only a young girl who'd collided with her, and she, too, had fallen to the ground.

"Of all the stupid…" the girl groused. "What are you doing out here? It's supposed to be an empty field."

"Why in the world were you running when you couldn't see where you were going?" Arabelle replied, rubbing her arm. It felt like a bruise was going to form there.

The girl must have only now realized just whom she'd run into, for her eyes widened and she gasped. "Princess! I'm so sorry! My sister and I were playing tag. I was running away from her."

Arabelle smiled. "It's all right. I know you, don't I? You're Madam Mizmer's daughter?"

The young girl nodded. "Yes, milady. My name is Zoe."

"I don't remember seeing you in the cook tents often. Your sister always said you were off playing with the sheep."

Zoe scrunched up her nose. "Mum tried to make me learn to cook last year. She said it was my place to do such things. But when I saw what Mum did to make mutton stew, I ran out of the tent screaming."

Arabelle suppressed a laugh. Blood and meat had never given her pause, but she knew some girls were squeamish about such things. "What do you do then, if not cook?"

Zoe wiped the grass from her pants and shirt. "Now that I'm nine, Pa lets me go with him to take care of the sheep and goats. But we can't do that in this fog, so he said Alexandra and I could play."

Arabelle realized that she might be able to use this girl, and the fog, to her advantage. "Zoe, I'll forget you slammed into me if you do one little thing for me."

Zoe squinted suspiciously. "You doing something sneaky?"

Arabelle's cheeks burned. "I've been wandering around outside the caravan today…"

31

Zoe gasped and looked around. "Where are your escorts? You aren't supposed to be without them, are you?"

The princess put her fingers up to her lips. The girl could afford to be a bit more discreet. "I snuck away from them. I don't like having them follow me around all the time. But I was thinking, if anyone asks if you've seen me, could you say you've seen me at odd times throughout the morning in different parts of the caravan? Father gets so worried, and he would feel better if he thought that I'd stayed around the caravan. I'll already be in trouble for sneaking away from my guards, but I don't want him to worry too much."

Zoe chewed on her lip, then finally nodded. "I won't say a word. But if anyone asks, I'm pretty sure I saw you looking at apples soon after I broke my fast, and another time I saw you looking at silken head wraps." She winked. "I can be sneaky when I need to be."

"Thank you." Arabelle gave the girl a hug.

A booming voice exploded from behind her. "There you are, Princess! Where have you been? I've been looking for you all morning. The Sheikh wants to speak to you."

It was Tabor, one of Arabelle's guards, scowling as usual.

Before Arabelle could respond, Zoe spoke. "I'm sorry, sir." Her face turned bright red, and tears rolled down her cheeks. "My puppy died. One of the wagons crushed him while in the mists. The princess helped me bury him." She paused long enough for a racking sob before adding, "Don't be mad at her. It's all my fault."

Tabor's expression softened. "Well... I..."

Arabelle was astonished—and impressed—by the girl's

ability to switch emotions so quickly. She hugged Zoe again. "I'm so sorry about your dear puppy. I'm sure you'll feel better soon."

She pulled back a bit, her back still to Tabor, and mouthed the word *Thanks*.

Zoe smiled ever so slightly as she turned and disappeared into the mists.

"My heart, you made me worry about your safety. You know you aren't supposed to be about without an escort."

Arabelle and her father were sitting cross-legged in her father's tent, waiting for their midday meal. Arabelle bowed her head in shame.

"We have nearly a thousand tents in our caravan," her father continued, "and not all of them belong to our people. There are those who wouldn't respect who you are, my dearest."

"Yes, Father."

Arabelle had heard this lecture many times. Her father would repeat how their family held a great responsibility, and that she was the jewel of their people.

If only he knew the truth. That she was now destined to die from a poison nobody could cure.

The serving women brought in several large plates of food for the two of them to share. One plate held Arabelle's favorite skewered meats, nicely charred on the outside, pink with juices on the inside. Another held a variety of vegetables on a bed of pearl-shaped wheat pasta, and a third contained freshly baked flatbread, along with a bowl of fragrant spiced olive oil.

It was a wondrous bounty, and Arabelle felt a pang of guilt.

Not everyone eats nearly as well as I do.

When the serving women had departed, her father resumed his lecture.

"I can't bear the thought of losing you, my precious flower. You're all I have, since your mother died giving birth to you."

"Yes, Father."

Her father sighed and took a bite of the flatbread. "Did you know your mother foresaw her own death?"

Arabelle looked up with surprise.

"I can see I haven't. Has Roselle not told you about our people?"

"She's told me that the Imazighen have forever wandered the lands as free people, separate from others, and—"

He waved her off. "Yes, yes. I'm talking about the seers. Every once in a great while, an Imazighen will be born with the ability to see visions of the future. Your mother was plagued with these visions since childhood. Some good. Some bad. And just before her death, she foresaw many things."

"Did she foresee anything about me?" Arabelle asked.

Her father looked at her kindly, but she could tell that tears threatened to pour forth. "Yes, my heart. She saw a great confusion within you. A great possibility of danger in your life. She made me swear to keep you safe. She also told me that you may be the key to true freedom for the Imazighen. So you see, your safety is more important than you realize."

Arabelle liked learning about her mother, but these visions

were frightening. Confusion? Danger? Was it possible her mother had foreseen what happened today? The poison?

"What did she mean, the key to freedom?" she asked.

Her father shrugged. "Her visions were not always as clear as I, or she, might have liked. However…" He scooted closer to Arabelle and whispered in her ear. "In these same visions, just before her death, she saw a danger to Azazel. The nature of the danger was unclear. It involved demons, elves, and the barrier. Perhaps. As I said, some visions were less instructive than others."

"Does Azazel know of this danger?" Arabelle whispered back.

Father shook his head. "Not from your mother, that is for certain. She despised that evil wizard for binding our people into working with him. Our people might have been destroyed altogether had my grandfather not agreed to escort his scum around Trimoria."

Arabelle frowned at the mention of her people's shame.

Let the slavers take Azazel and all of his minions to the coldest pits of the Abyss.

"Did she see anything else about me?" she asked.

"Only what I've said. I'm afraid you won't have an easy life, my heart. But you will lead our people to salvation." He smiled at her, his eyes welling with tears, and when those tears ran down his cheeks, Arabelle's throat tightened with emotion. In private, her father's emotions were always on the surface, something he shared only with her. It was something that warmed her from within, the bond they held to each other was unlike any she'd ever likely know. He was the one man she could trust.

He took a deep breath and let it out slowly. "She truly loved you, you know. She knew she would die in childbirth, and yet she felt nothing but joy at the idea of bringing you into this world. I only wish she could be here to see what a wonderful young woman you're becoming."

Arabelle smiled through her own welling tears. "I wish she could be here too."

After lunch, Arabelle sat at the carved wooden desk in her tent, Roselle hovering over her shoulder. Her teacher was trying to get her to work on her math, but Arabelle had other ideas. She wanted to learn about the elements of her mother's visions.

"Roselle, how much do you know about Azazel, the demon wars, and the barrier?"

Roselle's wrinkled face transformed into a look of shock. "Princess! It is wholly inappropriate for a young woman to concern herself about such things."

A surge of anger rushed through Arabelle, making the blemishes from the dragon venom burn. "If you can't teach me about the topics I feel are important, maybe I need to find another teacher!"

As soon as the words left her mouth, she regretted them and said. Where had that sudden anger come from?

"I'm sorry, Roselle, I didn't mean—"

It was too late—Roselle turned with a huff and marched out of the tent, saying, "I'll be sure to tell the Sheikh about this, Princess."

It was two hours after lunchtime, and Arabelle walked through the caravan, Tabor keeping pace with her, a silent, heavily-muscled shadow. She was pleased to see that the mist was thinning; people were finally setting up their stalls and getting ready for business.

She wasn't wandering aimlessly, though; she was searching for Maggie, her handmaiden. Unfortunately, during the day Maggie ran errands, which meant she could be almost anywhere.

A ruckus sounded ahead of her, accompanied by a clash of metal against metal. Curious, she walked toward the sound. In an open space between several of the wagons and tents, she found several of her father's guards training.

Tabor put a hand on her shoulder. "Princess, perhaps you should not see this? It could get bloody."

She waved dismissively. "I'm not a little girl, Tabor. I can deal with a bit of blood."

She watched the proceedings with interest. It wasn't a usual training session—it looked more like an actual fight. One of the guards was squaring off against a very short man wielding a mace and shield. No, not a short man—a dwarf.

She nudged Tabor. "What's happening here?"

"In order to take a position as a guard in your father's employ, one must first prove oneself a competent fighter. Evidently this dwarf has chosen to compete for one of the open positions."

"Did you have to prove your worth like this?"

"Aye, Princess. Though that was a very long time ago."

"And who did you upset to get cursed with the job of watching me?"

Her tone was teasing, but Tabor frowned. "I upset no one. I had the great honor of being your mother's protector. And prior to your birth, I swore to her that I would keep you safe from all physical harm. I honor that oath every day."

At hearing Tabor speak of her mother with such reverence, Arabelle felt tears well in her eyes. She looked at the man with a new appreciation for his devotion and duty.

"I'm sorry, Tabor. I know I'm horrible, sneaking around and hiding from you."

"It's expected, Princess. Your job is to be who you are. My job is to prevent mischief from occurring to your person."

The man's obvious dedication made her feel all the more guilty about the deadly secret she was keeping—the one that would force her to slip away from him again tonight. She had to meet Castien. She couldn't sleep until she learned whatever it was he'd be teaching her.

At that moment the dwarf swung a vicious blow at the soldier's unprotected knee. The man might have been limping for life had it landed, but before it could connect, the dwarf shoved the soldier with his shield so hard he literally flew out of the ring.

The crowd cheered.

The soldier who was running the contest raised a white flag. "The winner is Oda the dwarf." He turned toward Oda. "Do you have a clan?"

Oda belted his mace and smiled. "Of course. I be a Rockfist." He walked over to his opponent and helped him up. "You be needin' to learn to use yer shield properly," he told the soldier. "If

I'd not pulled back with my mace, your knee would be useless till the day you died. I won't be havin' that on me conscience."

Tabor called out to the man with the white flag. "Khalid, hire that man. He may be short in stature, but he is tall where it counts, in honor and skill."

Khalid's eyes widened as he met Tabor's gaze, and he bowed his head. "Yes, sir. Thy will be done."

"Why does that soldier hold you in such reverence?" Arabelle asked.

Tabor clicked his tongue dismissively. "I am the lead guard in your father's employ. Who else would be trusted to watch over his wife and then his daughter?"

"How is it I never knew that?"

"Only the weak and foolish need to talk about who they are. I believe a man's actions speak much louder and more truly than a man's voice."

A new pair of contestants entered the ring, and a murmur rippled through the crowd. One of them was a man she recognized: a soldier with huge muscles and he was gigantic. Everyone called him Ogre; Arabelle didn't even know his true name. And yet for once, this giant of a man wasn't drawing the attention of onlookers. Instead the crowd was focused on his opponent, a tall, handsome young stranger expertly flipping a yew staff in a blur of practiced circles. His shoulder-length honey-blond locks, brilliant blue eyes, and chiseled features caused many a sigh of appreciation from the women in attendance.

"Who is this applicant?" Arabelle asked her guard.

"Princess, that young man is one of the Nameless."

39

"Nameless?"

Tabor shook his head. "I'm quite certain Roselle has told you this. You need to apply yourself to your lessons."

Arabelle rolled her eyes. "Consider this one of my lessons then. I'm listening."

"A Nameless is a wanderer who has no familial ties— not to the caravan, not to Trimoria's towns, and not, in the case of a dwarf, to any clan. Most Nameless are not fit for decent society and remain in hiding—or become a victim to the slavers."

"Why would a man like that be applying for a job in my father's guard?"

"I would guess he's trying to better his lot in life, Princess. But if that's his goal, he will have a tough time of it. Nameless have earned their bad reputations, and it takes much to overcome such a stigma."

As the young soldier removed his cloak, Arabelle stared. In addition to his perfect features, he was trim and well-muscled, too.

A raven-haired girl at the edge of the ring waved a red rose at the Nameless. Arabelle recognized her—that was Madam Mizmer's eldest daughter, Alexandra. The sister of the girl she'd run into that morning. Arabelle decided to go over and say hello.

"Oh, Princess, how nice to see you," Alexandra said as she approached. "Are you here to see Hassan too?"

"Hassan?"

Alexandra blushed. "Isn't he just gorgeous? He only arrived last week, and already every girl I know has her eye on him."

Arabelle had to agree, the man was undeniably handsome. As he continued his warmup, his blond hair fluttered in the wind, and Arabelle found herself unconsciously running her fingers through her own dark hair, as if to compare.

How juvenile and ungracious to be jealous of a boy's hair.

"He's only seventeen years old, so my Pa won't forbid me talking to him," Alexandra gushed. "But my Mum says, 'No chance I'll let you ruin your life chasing a Nameless soldier around. Especially one who's deformed.'"

"Deformed?" Arabelle said. "Are you kidding? He looks perfect." As soon as she said that, she felt her face heat up, betraying the unaffected look she'd been maintaining.

"He *is* perfect," Alexandra agreed. "But look—he has six fingers on each hand. Not that I mind. Would you not talk to someone just because he has a couple extra fingers?"

Arabelle studied the blond warrior's hands from afar. He really did have six fingers on each hand. In a way, she found it a relief to know that this perfect specimen of a man had at least one imperfection.

The time came for Hassan and Ogre to square off—Hasson twirling his staff, and Ogre wielding a blunted broadsword. Thought Hassan was a good six feet tall, Ogre nevertheless towered over him.

For a moment the two men circled, studying each other's moves. Then, as if both responding to the same cue, they lunged, their weapons connected, and Hassan was thrown back, nearly stumbling out of the ring. He had to scramble to recover his balance.

"If that Nameless tries to meet strength against strength," Tabor murmured beside Arabelle, "this will be a very short contest."

Hassan skipped closer to the giant soldier and lunged once more with his staff. Alexandra squealed with fright; it looked as though the object of her affections had stretched himself too far. Ogre clearly saw the same opening, as he chopped viciously at Hassan's exposed flank. But somehow Hassan used his momentum and staff to vault past the giant, whose sword crashed harmlessly into the dirt where Hassan had just stood.

Without giving the giant a chance to recover, Hassan swept his staff at the back of Ogre's knees, sending him hard onto his back. Hassan spun and positioned the business end of his staff mere inches from Ogre's face. The big man's eyes crossed as he stared at it.

Khalid raised a white flag and called an end to the match.

Alexandra squealed, as did all the women who'd gathered to watch. "Oh, Princess, he won, he won!"

When Khalid tossed Hassan a brown tunic with the mark of the caravan on it, Alexandra was even more excited. "They're actually going to let him work with the caravan soldiers! He's going to stay with us!" She looked at herself, then up at the princess. "I have to change. I can't let him see me again in this plain frock!" With a quick curtsey, she scurried away.

Tabor shook his head. "Please, Princess, promise me you'll never allow yourself to be so swayed by a man's looks."

Arabelle laughed. "Don't worry. Father has made it clear that he will arrange things for me when the time is right. I trust him."

Tabor grunted his approval. "Smart girl. Your father is a wise man, and it would be a better world if all children were as attentive to their parents as you are to yours."

Not finding Maggie in the caravan, Arabelle decided she must have gone into the Aubgherle marketplace. There was really no need—everything one could need was available in the caravan—but Maggie always got excited when they approached Aubgherle. She must have told Arabelle dozens of times that the town was the center for the best silk weavers in all of Trimoria.

With Tabor and his men shadowing Arabelle's every step, she searched for the silk merchants—with no success. Getting frustrated, she finally decided to make use of her escort.

"Tabor, do you know where the silk merchants are?"

He relayed the question to his soldiers, and one of them nodded and took the lead. He took them through a throng of people haggling over merchandise, clearly knowing the area well. Arabelle should have asked the guards in the first place, but she'd had no idea any of them would know anything about silk.

Suddenly, Tabor put his hand on her shoulder and firmly pulled her behind him. Arabelle knew better than to argue, but she did peek over his shoulder to see what the issue was. Just up ahead, a man was being pulled away from a stall by one of Azazel's black-garbed enforcers. He screamed in protest. "You can't do this! I did nothing wrong!"

The people in the marketplace quickly stepped back to give the soldiers in black some room. Those that were too slow were punched or kicked, and were at risk of being dragged along with the protesting man.

"Tabor, why do they allow—"

Tabor shushed her with a stern look.

Soon the soldiers were out of sight, and the man's screaming was replaced with the normal sounds of marketplace banter. Their forward motion resumed, although now Tabor maintained a protective hand on Arabelle's shoulder.

Arabelle eavesdropped on the chatter as they walked.

"I wish the Protector could do something about Azazel's men," said a woman in a bright dress.

A bearded merchant responded. "Don't hope for such things. You don't want Aubgherle to have the same fate as Ilonia, do you?"

Arabelle looked up at her guard. "Tabor, can I ask you something?"

"Of course, Princess."

"What happened to Ilonia?"

Tabor sighed. "Princess, your hearing is too keen for your own good."

"Tell me. Please?"

"I will answer, and then we will have no further discussion on this topic while in this town. Agreed?"

"Yes."

Tabor leaned in close and whispered. "Ilonia was utterly destroyed by fire in my grandfather's time—and that fire is attributed to Azazel's wrath. Azazel, it is said, is centuries old, and there is nothing anyone can do against that wizard's might. The ashes of Ilonia remain as evidence that if one were to stand up to him, even a Protector, it would not end well. Now, no more of this talk. It's dangerous. If you want to know more, please consult your father."

"Thank you for telling me the truth, Tabor. Too many people try to hide the facts from me."

"I'll never lie to you, Princess. However, some truth isn't mine to give."

The lead guard stopped in front of a stall with many bolts of brilliantly colored silk. Arabelle didn't see Maggie, but she decided it was worth asking the merchant if he'd seen her. As she explained who she was and described what Maggie looked like, a wide smile appeared in the tangles of the man's beard.

"Yes, milady, she was here, and a very good customer. She bought many things for you that I arranged to deliver to your father's caravan." He looked up at her escort of soldiers and hastily added, "But the delivery left only moments ago; we could intercept it if you would like to look at it first, milady."

Arabelle waved off the suggestion. "I'm sure it's fine, I just want to find Maggie. Did you see where she went?"

The merchant looked relieved. "As a matter of fact, I saw her following after a man who passed by as we were completing the transaction."

"What did this man look like?"

"He wore the mark of the caravan. Fair-haired, a long staff. Handsome, I suppose. He was heading in the direction of the weaponsmith."

Arabelle groaned. So Maggie wasn't immune to Hassan's charms either.

Thanking the merchant, she turned to Tabor. "Tabor, do you know where the weaponsmith is?"

"Yes, Princess, but don't you think it's likely that your handmaiden has returned to the caravan by now?" He nodded toward the sun, which was dropping toward the horizon.

"You're probably right. But let's check the weaponsmith before heading back. I can't miss her; I must talk to Maggie before nightfall."

My life depends on it.

TRAINING ASSASSINS

Kirag stood guard in a hidden alcove high above his master's throne, armed with a dragonbone crossbow loaded with a poisoned damantite bolt. His normal responsibilities were to stop any physical attacks on Azazel and to lead his army of enforcers. But today's instructions were simpler. While Azazel was outside inspecting the shipments of grain, Kirag was to allow no one into the throne room apart from the guards stationed there. In fact, if anyone else even tried to enter, they were to be killed instantly.

One of the things that had earned Kirag advancement was his patience. He was able to remain unmoving for well over a day waiting for the appearance of his quarry. He also never let things startle him. Startlement was a sign of weakness, and all weakness had been beaten out of him by his mother when he was barely of an age to speak.

The door into the throne room flew open, but it wasn't an

intruder. It was Azazel himself, yelling at the guards to leave immediately. They scrambled toward the door. Kirag did not. He knew he was expected to remain at his station.

Azazel glanced up at him, his eyes flashing with a fiery glint, and acknowledged the soldier's existence with a nod. Then he ascended his throne and waited.

Soon the smell of burning sulfur wafted up to Kirag's nostrils, and a mist formed in front of the throne. In moments the mist coalesced, taking the shape of a woman.

As leader of Azazel's enforcers, Kirag was more than comfortable with magic—but this magic made him uneasy, for one reason alone: it seemed not to originate from his master. Kirag had almost never witnessed magic performed by anyone other than Azazel himself.

Well, except by my own mother, he thought.

But that was a secret that Kirag kept strictly to himself. He didn't like to even think of the dark magic his mother had practiced on her victims those many years ago.

The woman before the throne spoke. *"Caution, Azazel."*

She was petite, with long blonde hair, brown skin, and ears that indicated elven ancestry.

Azazel stood. This, too, made Kirag uneasy. "What do you mean, Ellisandrea?"

"I have foreseen danger. Look for strangers to Trimoria. They threaten all that we have achieved."

"Strangers?" Azazel repeated. "But there is no such thing as a stranger to Trimoria. Thanks to that fool Protector, we're surrounded by an impenetrable barrier."

"I cannot see where they are from," the woman said. *"But*

they are not from Trimoria, and they do not belong here. Find them, or they will jeopardize all for which we have strived."

"I'll have my men seek out the strangers and bring them to me," Azazel said.

This remark only added to Kirag's discomfort. He knew that barrier well. He first encountered it when he was five years old and living with his mother in the mountains. He'd grown fond of a wolf puppy that had begun following him, but he knew he had to keep it a secret from his mother, or she would step on it, or torture it, or worse.

Naturally she found out about it. And when she saw him playing with the young wolf, she snatched them both in the air, one in each hand. She carried them high into the mountains, to a place he'd never explored, and there before him stood a strange gray wall of mist.

She shook Kirag by the scruff of his neck. "Barrier. Things go. Never come back. Do not cross."

She lightly tossed the puppy away from the barrier. As always, the puppy came scampering back toward Kirag with its tongue lolling out, ready to play.

Mother pointed to the puppy. "See? It return."

She picked up the puppy again, and this time she tossed it into the gray mist.

Kirag waited, expecting his wolf to return. It never did.

Mother nodded. "No return. Dead wolf. Lesson learned. Stay away."

Kirag hated the memory. Hated what his mother had done. But he'd learned the lesson his mother had taught. Had learned it well.

Nothing survived the barrier.

Which was why he looked down at his master in the throne room with disbelief. *How can Azazel so readily accept that strangers have come through that mist?*

Azazel addressed the elven witch once more. "What would you have me do with them when they are found?"

"They must be killed."

"It will be my pleasure, Ellisandrea." Azazel stepped toward the apparition and caressed her cheek. When he spoke again, it was in a whisper, and Kirag had to strain to hear. "When can we meet again, my love?"

My love?

Azazel never took such a tone. With anyone. Weakness, supplication, submission—these were entirely foreign to Kirag's master. Which meant this Ellisandrea must be unimaginably powerful to make his master act so.

"Soon. Do what you must, and all will be as promised."

The woman faded, as did the acrid smell.

Azazel stared into empty space for a moment. Then he stalked to the door and flung it open. "Attend me!" he called down the stairs. "I have tasks for all of you!"

As armored footsteps approached, Azazel looked up. "Kirag, I know you heard everything. I expect you to lead this mission. From now on, this is your only goal. You will focus on nothing else. Ellisandrea has powerful premonitions, and I assure you, what she tells me is undeniably true. There *are* strangers in Trimoria. Or will be. Her understanding of time isn't like ours; these events might be happening now, or they may happen a year from now. That will make your mission all the more challenging. But you must not fail me."

Kirag nodded. "Yes, Master."

The other soldiers entered the throne room and took their appointed positions. Azazel turned to them.

"I have a mission for you all. Kirag will lead you in this…"

Kirag paced the mustering grounds while the soldiers poured out of Azazel's tower and stepped into formation. His task was simply defined, but difficult to execute.

He had no idea where these strangers would show up, when they might show up, how many they would be, or what they looked like.

To someone without his background, this might seem like an impossible task. But he had a few ideas. First, he needed to increase the number of Duos in his retinue of assassins.

Looking over his soldiers, he felt a moment of disgust. They were so small and uncoordinated. *Humans.* His own heritage was much more complicated. His grandfather had been a dwarf with magical powers, and his grandmother had been an ogre. In fact, his mother blamed her father for enchanting her mother and producing her, and this was the source of her deep-seated disdain for all dwarves.

Kirag didn't know his father, but he believed his father was human, for his mother had many times complained to him how weak human males were and how she had accidentally killed several of them in his making.

Despite, or because of, this mixed heritage, Kirag towered over the gathered soldiers. He was nearly eight feet tall and weighed half again as much as the largest of them. He'd yet to find a human that provided a contest for him when it came to a fight.

"I'm taking you to one of my training camps!" he shouted to the assembled men. "You'll all be given the rank of Grubs. Today, you're barely worthy of guarding a cesspool. But with training, skill, and luck, you will survive to become members of Lord Azazel's Black Talons. As a Talon, you will have earned the black leathers of Azazel's enforcers—and the honors that go with them."

He paused to let that sink in.

"If anyone isn't willing to undertake the training, leave now."

Most of the soldiers stood motionless, staring stoically forward. Only two soldiers left the ranks. Kirag pulled two daggers from his vest and whipped them at their receding forms. The blades whistled through the air and buried themselves into the men's spines, such as they were.

Kirag watched with satisfaction as the two men collapsed, dead.

"Lesson number one. You are in Azazel's employ. You have been given an opportunity to advance. Don't insult him by not giving your best effort."

The second lesson came that evening. They had set out from Azazel's tower immediately, but as the sun dipped to the horizon, Kirag gathered the troops around him.

"We have another half day's travel before we arrive at the training camp. As you know, slavers travel throughout the plains of Trimoria seeking those who are unaware and unprepared. Part of being in Azazel's employ means that you are never caught unaware."

The men looked at each other uncertainly.

"Set up for camp, but instead of a camp for twenty soldiers, create a single campfire for three. Elect three among you to stay at this camp and attend the fire. The rest of you, create cold camps one hundred yards away. Make your selections now."

The soldiers argued about cold rations and quarreled over who would have an opportunity to remain at the campfire. They settled their disagreements by drawing lots, and once they established the warm and cold camps, Kirag assembled them again.

"The men in the warm camp will need to remain alert through the night. Slavers usually attack in the early hours before dawn. You can easily imagine that a campfire with three soldiers will seem a tempting target."

The soldiers who'd won the privilege of attending the warm camp now looked down at their drawn lots with regret.

"Men, we have two distinct advantages. First, the slavers will not expect more than a dozen soldiers pouring out of the inky blackness of the night. Second, they are slavers. This means they are trying to take you alive, not kill you."

Kirag smiled. "*We* don't have the same restrictions. I expect you to kill them. Settle in for the night, and be prepared."

The camp was quiet, but the tension could be felt on the wind. Kirag watched from his chosen observation point. The campfire would be visible for many miles, and he was confident it would attract slavers. They were like fleas on a blink dog—they seemed to be everywhere.

Tonight would be the soldiers' first test as Grubs. He'd given them the strategy. It was now their job to execute.

Kirag stretched his senses to hear anything out of the ordinary. One of the men in the cold camps had developed a snore. But within moments, the snore stopped rather abruptly. Maybe the other men in that group weren't complete idiots after all.

Hours passed, the night deepened, and still Kirag stood watch, sensing, listening.

Just prior to the coming of dawn, he heard the crack of a twig. His superior night vision—another benefit of his mixed heritage—revealed six human-shaped silhouettes sneaking past, followed by a seventh outline that hulked over the others.

Great, an ogre. These soldiers aren't prepared to fight an ogre.

As the humans formed a circle just outside the firelight, the ogre stood back from the group. Kirag slowly pulled his sword from its scabbard and crept toward the giant.

The six slavers moved as one, throwing nets on top of the three men at the warm camp. Instantly, the war cries of the soldiers from the cold camp echoed through the darkness, and they fell on the attacking slavers.

Before the ogre could react, Kirag slashed his greatsword

across the tendons behind the ogre's right knee, separating them with a sharp series of snaps. The behemoth collapsed on his useless leg, and Kirag rammed the tip of his sword into the ogre's now-exposed neck, pressing down with all his weight. Blood fountained from the wound.

The ogre slammed a fist into Kirag's chest, sending him flying through the air and struggling to breathe. But Kirag was not dissuaded. This wasn't his first time fighting an ogre, and certainly not the first time he'd been hit by one.

He laughed as the ogre attempted to stand. The behemoth was too stupid to realize that he'd already been defeated. As he looked down at the useless leg now disobeying him, blood continued to pulse forth from the precisely placed wound in his neck. *That* was the death blow.

Sure enough, in moments the ogre sagged and crumpled, never to rise again.

Over at the warm camp, the soldiers were celebrating. All six slavers lay dead or dying.

They've done well.

As the bedraggled collection of Grubs approached the outskirts of one of his training camps, Kirag noted the dim reflections of light signals from guttered lamps. The Grubs had been spotted by the camp scouts. And these novice soldiers seemed to have no idea.

Kirag smiled as he hung back to let the troops continue down the path. A valuable lesson was about to be reinforced.

Be ever vigilant.

They emerged from a mountain pass, revealing campfires a half mile away. And in the dry expanse that separated the Grubs from the camp were the telltale signs of disturbed soil.

Again, Kirag saw this, but the Grubs did not.

The soldiers quickened their pace in anticipation of the possibility of a warm meal. It was only as they reached the trap that a few of them spotted the unnatural ripples in the terrain and hesitated. But only a few; the vanguard marched ahead, oblivious.

One of the more alert men in the rear called out a warning, but at that very moment a resounding crack broke the air and a half dozen men screamed as the ground underneath them collapsed. Clouds of dust exploded out of the hole, and then a shroud of silence fell.

Kirag walked to the edge of the hole with the rest of the men. The soldiers who had fallen were now impaled on sharpened wooden stakes that gleamed with fresh red blood.

"Vigilance," Kirag said. "If you aren't looking for things out of the ordinary… if you ever trust that you are safe… you *will* die."

A collection of black-clad Talons trotted toward them. The Talon in the lead had a pair of obsidian daggers tucked in his leathers and wore a necklace with the hourglass symbol of Azazel.

He halted before Kirag and saluted. "Lord Kirag, welcome to the training camp— "

"I am not lord anything, fool, and don't forget it. It's Kirag or sir. Next time you call me lord I'll test out your daggers on your hide."

The soldier blanched. "Yes, sir!"

"Your name is Glendale, correct?"

"Yes, sir!"

"I've brought you some new Grubs to train. After today's training, I'll have a special mission for the Grub who proves himself. You and I will talk first thing tomorrow morning. I want to hear what you think about these Grubs and get your recommendations."

Glendale saluted. "Yes, sir! I will put them through their paces!"

"They are yours to do with as you will, I'll be back in the morning for our talk."

Glendale turned to face the soldiers. "Gather up! You will address me as sir. You will *never* call anyone of rank by their name. Forgetting yourself will earn you ten lashes."

As Glendale continued with his instructions, the Grubs looked at each other nervously.

Kirag took the opportunity to scout out tomorrow's path. As he moved away, he heard Glendale's voice behind him. "You have lots of bleeding to do before you die or qualify to wear your leathers. Get moving!"

Kirag carefully avoided the traps on the approach to the camp. It was a couple of hours ahead of the rising of the sun on their second day in camp. One of the Talons perched midway up the cliff nodded down at his superior, alert even to Kirag's stealthy intrusion.

Good.

He continued to move softly, stealthily, as he approached Glendale's tent. The lead trainer, too, was not taken by surprise.

"Good morning, sir. I can hear your approach."

Kirag grinned. "Glendale, if you weren't alert, I might have entered your tent and slit your throat."

The soldier lifted the flap of his tent and waved him in. "I don't doubt it, sir."

Kirag chuckled. "I suppose the throat-slitting will have to wait. Let's talk about the Grubs."

Glendale struck flint on steel and lit a small fire, and he and Kirag sat cross-legged on opposite sides. "What would you like to know, sir?" Glendale began. "They are undisciplined and out of shape. But most of them have some promise and should survive the training."

Kirag scratched at his freshly shaved face. "You said *most* of them. I presume some of them are likely untrainable then?"

Glendale nodded.

"No concern. I need a Grub today that you don't mind losing. An untrainable would be fine for that."

A smile crept across Glendale's face. "Garog's your man. He's large and strong, but stupid. I don't believe he can be trusted as a Talon, and I would never want him in my Duo."

"Garog it is. Lead me to him."

Glendale led Kirag through the Grubs, left to sleep as they could on the bare ground. There was no stealth now, and the men scrambled out of the way, clearing the sleep from their eyes.

But their target was not so quick to wake. In fact he

continued to snore, rather loudly, oblivious even as his visitors walked right up to him.

Glendale kicked Garog's feet. "Wake up, Grub!"

That woke him. The soldier bolted upright, banging his head on the wagon he'd slept beneath, and looked up at the two men standing over him.

"Sir?"

Glendale snapped his fingers in the man's face. "Don't look so dazed, it's an embarrassment. Kirag has a special mission, and you've been chosen to participate."

Garog looked at Kirag with frightened eyes. "Y-yes, sir."

Kirag looked the man up and down. "You are dressed adequately; you will not need anything else for this mission. Follow me."

He turned and walked back through the camp without even looking to see if he was being followed. But he certainly heard Garog's clumsy scrambling behind him.

Yes, this one would do nicely.

It's time to visit Mother.

———

Daylight broke through the clouds as Kirag walked a treacherous trail etched into the side of a cliff, Garog was huffing behind him. Kirag knew this path well; he had run up and down it thousands of times in his youth. It was remote, far from civilization, but that was just how his mother liked it. She was very ogre-like in her need for solitude.

Which was probably best for everyone, considering her

tendency toward violence. Kirag had learned early on to avoid her except at meals. Even other ogres avoided her. They thought she was crazy, as she spent much of the day muttering to herself or talking to creatures that he was fairly certain weren't there. Not that Mother cared; even if they allowed it, she would have refused to be a part of an ogre tribe.

And now Kirag had to risk his mother's fury once more. It was the only way he could think of to approach Azazel's impossible task of finding unknown strangers who could be anywhere in Trimoria at any time. Mother had the uncanny ability to see distant events that hadn't yet occurred.

But she rarely entered one of her trances without first having exerted herself in some extremely violent manner. Which was why Kirag had brought the Grub.

He wasn't entirely sure if Mother was aware of her trances. They just… happened after particularly violent outbursts. The first time Kirag observed one, he had been the object of that outburst. He had made the mistake of asking Mother if he could have any brothers or sisters. After she beat him to within a glimmer of unconsciousness, she fell into a stupor, only partially aware of him, and he learned of this strange power she possessed, though he never spoke to her of it afterward.

Now, as he crested the cliff, he saw the cave that had been his childhood home. He knew his mother was inside—it was rare that she would be hunting at this time in the morning, and besides, he detected her scent.

He turned to watch Garog dragging himself to the top of the cliff. The Grub was clearly exhausted, despite his size and strength, and looked utterly bedraggled. Kirag sneered in disgust. The man was a waste of flesh.

Kirag held a finger to his lips in a sign to remain silent, then pointed to the cave. "I lived in that cave as a child."

Garog squinted at the cave, then looked at Kirag stupidly.

"Within that cave is a chest that has a special weapon," Kirag continued. "It is in the deepest section of the cave, and I don't believe I can squeeze into that section anymore. Go in there and drag that chest out here."

Garog nodded with a sly, greedy smile.

He found a suitable stick, tied a cloth around its end, and lit it with some flint and steel. Then, holding his torch aloft, he crossed the distance and entered the cave.

Kirag strolled after him and waited outside. Within seconds he heard Garog's cry of alarm and his mother's familiar bellow. Then came ripping noises, and Garog's last gurgling breaths.

Kirag stepped into the cave. The torch had guttered out after falling from the brute's hands, but his eyes quickly adjusted to the darkness. His mother knelt before Garog, or what was left of Garog. Parts of him were scattered about. But Mother now remained still, her lips moving, her eyes darting back and forth.

It had worked.

"Mother, Azazel has asked me to find strangers who don't belong in Trimoria. Where do I look for these strangers?"

Mother's eyes closed, and spittle frothed at her lips. She swayed silently.

Soon a light emanated from within her. She stopped swaying and blinked rapidly. "Trouble from the Imazighen."

She swayed again. The light brightened. She stiffened. "The elves," she growled. "The elves are trouble."

More swaying. Now the light took on a sparkling effect. "The swamp," she said. "Trouble from the swamp."

And with that, the light dimmed and disappeared. An inky blackness filled the cave, and Mother shivered and collapsed, asleep among the offal.

Kirag crept from the cave. He hadn't learned much, but it was something.

At least know he knew where to look for these strangers.

LEARNING ELVEN SECRETS

Arabelle wore a billowing robe and kept her hood raised as she was escorted to Maggie's tent. Her handmaiden was stitching some of the silks she'd bought for her mistress earlier.

Maggie looked up and smiled widely. "Oh, Princess! I found some superb material today. I should be able to finish a couple of new dresses for you by the end of the week."

Arabelle gave her friend a knowing smile. "Did you find Hassan?"

Maggie blushed brightly. "Hassan? What do you know about him?" Her face fell. "Oh—you aren't looking at him too, are you? Do you think your father would approve?"

The princess snorted with laughter. "No, Maggie, I'm not interested in Hassan. However, if you are, I believe you might have some competition. It seems many of the girls have their eye on him."

Maggie leaned closer. "I know, but I have an advantage."

"Oh?"

"I overheard Hassan in the market today talking with a weaponsmith about needing a proper sheath for his staff. Evidently he's having trouble finding one, since so few people regularly wield a staff as a weapon. So…"

Maggie opened the chest at the foot of her bed and pulled out some boiled leather strips that had been woven into a belt with a tubular sheath attached. She proudly showed Arabelle how the belt wound around her waist and demonstrated how the sheath had an inner lining of silk to prevent the staff from getting stuck.

"I've been saving these leather pieces and scraps of silk, and I was able to put my weaving skills to good use. So, what do you think?" She looked at Arabelle hopefully. "If I present him with something that nobody else has, he must look at me favorably, wouldn't you think?"

Arabelle had never spent much time studying the ways of attracting boys, but she couldn't fault Maggie's logic. She smiled. "I think so."

Maggie's face lit up. "I'll present it to him tomorrow, then!" She put the belt and sheath back in her chest. "Oh, but Princess, did you need something?"

"Yes, and it's very important." She gestured for Maggie to sit on the bed, then sat cross-legged in front of her and held her confidante's hands. "Maggie, you need to swear on your life and honor that you will tell nobody about this."

Maggie looked curious, but nodded. "I swear, Lady Arabelle. I would never betray your confidence."

"You cannot even tell my father, Maggie. You must take this secret to the grave. Lives are at stake. Do you understand?"

Now her faithful handmaiden looked worried, but she nodded solemnly. "I swear upon all that I hold sacred that I will keep what is said tonight secret, and will never again mention it to any living soul."

Arabelle breathed a sigh of relief—and then told Maggie all about the events of this morning. The encounter with the poisonous dragon. The rescue by the elf. When Arabelle lifted her blouse to show her the blemishes on her ribs and the bruised and mottled skin that surrounded it, Maggie gasped. When she told Maggie about the poison, and what she would have to do to survive, Maggie burst into tears.

My poor emotional friend.

"I know it's hard, Maggie, but I'm going to fight this, and I need your help. I've arranged to meet with one of the elves, who'll teach me how to live with this poison. I'm to meet him tonight at midnight. But neither my father nor Tabor would ever allow me to travel to the woods alone."

"Lady, I'll do what I can, but how can I possibly get you to the woods unseen?"

"*I* can't visit the elves unseen, but you can."

"I don't understand."

Arabelle grinned. "We're going to exchange places. You will leave here wearing my robes, go to my tent, and sleep there tonight. I'll stay here in your tent, and leave later in one of your traveling cloaks. Nobody will take notice of my comings and goings, because they'll think I'm you."

Maggie shook her head. "But milady, I—I can't. What if Tabor asks me a question on the way to the tent? I can't exactly pretend to be a mute."

"Actually, you can." Arabelle smiled again. "Call Tabor in right now. Tell him I have a sore throat and need a honeyed tea to soothe it."

Maggie smiled in understanding and called in the princess's guard. Tabor poked his grizzled face into the tent and grunted when Maggie made the request. He turned to someone outside. "Ahmed, fetch a honeyed tea for the princess."

Maggie smiled. "Thank you, Tabor. I believe it would be best if Lady Arabelle doesn't speak anymore tonight. After she enjoys her tea, can you please escort her back to her tent?"

Tabor grunted again. Apparently he was a mute this evening too.

When the tea was served and Tabor had withdrawn from the tent, Arabelle and Maggie exchanged clothes—and a conspiratorial look.

"Congratulations, Maggie," Arabelle whispered. "You're now a mute princess."

Maggie smiled.

———

After Maggie left with Tabor, Arabelle counted backwards from one thousand, allowing plenty of time in case anything were to go wrong. She was anxious as she finally stepped outside, but as she had hoped, nobody was watching. She was a handmaiden, not a princess, and was free to go where she pleased.

Soon she was outside the caravan and crossing the fields that bordered the woods. She wasn't sure exactly where on the edge of the forest she was going to meet Castien, and she didn't remember exactly where she'd parted from the elven sword master. She would just have to walk along slowly and hope that he could find her.

As she walked, her eyes followed a rabbit hopping through rows of corn growing in the field, passing by several voles burrowing under the ground. They—

Wait. How was she seeing these creatures? The moon was covered by clouds, and it was very dark, yet the rabbit was clear as day to her eyes. And the voles…

The voles were *underground.*

Excitement coursed through her veins as she recalled her conversation with the mysterious Seder.

When you awake, you will be able to locate any living creature you envision…

Could this be what Seder meant?

An idea struck her, and she closed her eyes and brought to mind an image of Castien. The distinct cut of his jaw, the elven shape of his ears. She didn't see him like she had the animals, but as soon as she pictured him, she *sensed* him.

She knew where he was.

Arabelle began jogging in his direction, and the feeling of him became stronger. She ignored the outlines of woodland animals—they were everywhere, now that she was aware of them—and focused only on Castien. Soon it felt like she could almost hear the elf's heartbeat.

She stopped suddenly. Her sense told he was right here, but…

She looked up. The smiling elf was sitting on a branch above her.

"Good," he said. "You have a strong woods sense. I'm quite surprised to find that in a human. Especially one as young as yourself."

A blush burned Arabelle's cheeks, and she decided not to tell him about Seder's gift.

The elf hopped down from his branch. "Time for the most important lessons of your life. Follow me."

He led her through the woods, and with her newfound night vision, Arabelle was able to easily track his movements. He shined with a preternatural glow—a different hue than that of the animals. Still, following him was not easy. Whereas he lithely ducked and dodged the branches and thorns that reached out and grabbed at them, she staggered along clumsily and seemed to get her robe snagged on everything. By the time they stopped, Arabelle was sure she looked like a mess.

Castien knelt near a bush and pointed.

"Do you see this leaf shaped like an anvil? It's hard to see the colors in the dark, but this is a green leaf with thin red filaments running through it. In the old language, these are called *Tishkakh* leaves; I'm not familiar with what humans call them. These leaves can be used to make medicinal teas that soothe bad dreams."

"Okay. So I should make this tea and drink it?"

The elf shook his head. "No. Everything I'm showing you is a tool. For now, you must only learn what I'm telling you."

"But—"

Castien held up his hand. "Let me complete my answer before you ask another question."

Arabelle waited silently.

"Good," said Castien. "You aren't nearly as impatient as I feared. As for the leaf—you shouldn't be drinking teas made from this. Dreamless sleep will not be useful for you. And although it is customarily used to soothe bad dreams, if you steep enough leaves into a tea and make it very strong, the person who drinks the tea will not remember anything that transpired in the last several hours. This is extremely useful when you need someone to forget a recent event—perhaps if you've been seen by someone you don't want to be seen by."

"If that happens, how would I get them to drink a tea I brew? It seems impractical."

The elf chuckled. "Excellent question, young one. It *is* impractical. But this leaf can also be dried and powdered, making it very potent. A small inhalation of this powder will have the same effect as an entire cup of tea. More, and it can be a lethal weapon."

Arabelle suddenly understood. Castien wasn't only teaching her how to survive the poison inside her; he was teaching her how to survive, period. She'd never had a reason to attack anyone in her life—but now… now her life was going to forever be very different. The thought made her stomach tie itself up in knots.

"If you find yourself in a situation where you might use the powder," Castien continued, "I strongly suggest that you wear a mask so as not to inhale it yourself. It will leave you unconscious for hours—which in your case, is a death sentence. You must always, *always* remember the poison that courses through your veins."

Arabelle nodded. "I'll have Maggie create me a mask, just in case."

Castien's expression turned stern. "This *Maggie* must not learn about anything I teach you."

"I understand."

Over the next two hours, the sword master led Arabelle through the woods, teaching her many lessons. He proved to be as talented an herbalist as he was an expert with weapons. She learned which barks could be used to help with pain, which plants could be chewed to help one stay awake—particularly useful for her condition—and which saps were deadly poisons and could be used to coat blades or arrows.

Castien pulled a shimmering dagger from a sheath belted to his waist. "Have you used a dagger before?"

"Only at mealtime."

Castien handed her the dagger hilt-first and smiled. "First rule: keep the pointy end away from you."

Arabelle gripped the leather-wrapped handle. She was surprised how comfortable it felt in her hand. A pale moonlight had filtered through the clouds and the forest canopy, making the blade shimmer with reflected light.

The next hour was spent in learning about the proper use of a dagger—for both offense and defense. These lessons were more difficult than the herbalist lessons, but in some ways more satisfying. Holding the dagger made Arabelle feel powerful.

At the end of the hour, Arabelle tried to give the dagger back to Castien, but he waved it away.

"Consider it a gift from me to you. Keep it near you and practice all the time. I have taught you the basics, but you will need to practice, practice, practice. When you think you are doing well, practice some more. Your life should consist of sleeping, eating, and practicing."

Arabelle looked at the dagger dubiously. "Castien, I'm grateful for the lessons. But I thought you were going to teach me about not sleeping. I'll never need a dagger or a tea if I die in my sleep."

Castien looked up at the sky. "There is time. We are at least three hours from sunrise. We shall start now."

"Great. Do I make a tea? Chew some bark? What do I do?"

The elf laughed. "No. You practice. No plant is needed—only willpower and habit. As you go to sleep, you must concentrate on accessing your body's internal time. If you know you must wake in an hour, you will wake. Now try it."

"What? Right now? Just… go to sleep and wake up?" A chill of fear rushed through Arabelle.

Castien gave her a comforting smile. "I'll watch and make sure nothing goes wrong. But try to convince yourself I'm not here. Tell your body that it must do what is necessary."

With that assurance, Arabelle lay on a bed of moss at the base of a tree, wrapped her robe tightly around her, and concentrated on the impossible task of falling asleep for exactly one hour.

When Arabelle opened her eyes, it was still night, but she could tell that time had passed. The sounds of the forest had changed, and Castien was sitting on his heels watching her from a different position. That, plus her stiff neck, told her that she must have slept.

"How long?" she asked.

"You slept for ten minutes shy of one hour. *Very* good for someone who has never had to wake themselves before."

Arabelle felt the warm pride of accomplishment. "I did it!"

Castien stood. "I knew you could. Now stand up and move around. You must ensure that the poison is circulated so it does not crystallize."

The sword master pushed her through various silent drills that had her thighs burning and her arms feeling like limp noodles. It was all the more difficult because she felt the fuzzy-headed exhaustion from lack of sleep.

Will I be able to do this forever?

Castien explained the schedule that she must follow. "Two hours of sleep followed immediately by one hour of vigorous practice. No exceptions. Over time you will learn that your body only truly requires four hours of sleep a night. Continue this, along with your blade practice, and not only will you be safe from the poison, you will hone yourself to a fine edge."

"You speak of me as if I were a weapon."

Castien smiled. "Young lady, you *will* be a weapon. One that, I suspect, many will underestimate."

Arabelle felt the dagger sheathed under her robe and smiled as she thought about what people would think if they knew what she'd done tonight.

Castien looked to the horizon. "You need to get back to your home soon. Dawn's approaching."

"Can I visit you the next time the caravan is in this area?"

"You can seek, and I might *let* you find me again, young princess." Castien pulled a worn leather-bound book from his tunic and handed it to her. "This guide lists uses for many common plants. Study this as well, for I doubt human scholars have written much on such things."

Impulsively, Arabelle hugged her elven tutor. "Thank you, Castien."

He returned the embrace and whispered something in a language she didn't understand. Then he added, "Live well, young Arabelle. Prove your worth to yourself and fulfill your destiny."

The first rays of light were just breaking over the horizon as Arabelle slipped into Maggie's tent. She took off her robe and climbed under the covers to catch up on some much-needed sleep.

It seemed like only seconds later when Maggie shook her. "Lady! Lady! Wake up! You mustn't sleep, remember?"

Arabelle groaned, stretched her limbs, and felt a strange numbness in her extremities. That brought her wide awake in an instant. Her blood ran like ice as she realized what had almost happened. *How could I have already been so careless?*

She quickly leapt from the bed, stomped her feet, and clenched and unclenched her fists to quicken her blood's circulation.

"How late is it?" she asked.

"It is just after dawn. Oh, Lady, I was so worried about you.

We never discussed how we were going to get me out of your tent without raising suspicion. I'm afraid I might have angered your guards."

"Quick," Arabelle said. "Give me my robe and put on yours."

They quickly donned the proper garments, and just in time. Maggie was still adjusting her robe when the tent flap opened and Tabor stuck his head in.

"Princess! Why didn't you wait for an escort? We have talked about this."

"I'm sorry, Tabor, but I needed to talk to Maggie right away, and I knew since it was still early, it would take time for the escort to assemble."

Tabor grumbled and glared at Maggie, as if this were all her fault. The handmaiden looked at her feet, unable to meet his gaze.

"You girls are up to something, and I do *not* like it. I will have to tell your father about this incident, Princess." He pulled his head from the tent for only a moment before sticking it back in. "Your escort is waiting outside, Princess. Please try to behave." And he disappeared once more.

Arabelle turned to Maggie. "See? It's all fine."

Maggie still looked uncertain. "Tabor seemed awfully angry."

"Tabor is always angry." Arabelle waved dismissively. "Now I need to return to my tent. I have so much to do. Can you inform my father and my guard that I'm going to be staying in my tent today? Blame the 'sore throat' from last night if you like. But nothing too terrible; I don't want visitors."

"Are you sure that's all I can do, Lady?"

"Oh, you *can* do something else for me. I need a new outfit. Something that allows me to blend in—so no silk. Maybe black, or dark gray. Just… ordinary clothes. And I need to be able to exercise in it."

Maggie looked excited. "Of course! That sounds like a fun project." She fingered her own robe, noticing the damage Arabelle had done to it last night. "It seems I will need to find you a durable cloth, as well."

"Oh, and one more thing. I need a mask—a tagelmust. It needn't be made of the same material, but I want to be able to wrap it around my head and cover my mouth."

Maggie giggled. "Lady! Only your eyes will be visible. You will look like my grandmother."

"I have my reasons," Arabelle replied with a smile.

"I will get to work on it right away, milady."

Arabelle hugged her. "Thank you, Maggie. And Maggie… while we're alone, you can just call me Arabelle."

Maggie pulled back and shook her head vigorously. "Absolutely not, Lady. It would be improper."

Her response saddened Arabelle, but she understood. The Imazighen had held her family as their unquestioned leaders for countless generations. Centuries ago, they had ruled a vast land that was now forbidden to them by a magical barrier, and though all that was left of that kingdom now was their vast caravan and its people, her family was still revered. It was her ancestors who made sure to keep their people together, their culture alive, through the centuries—even through the great demon wars. And it was said that one day her family would lead the Imazighen back to their lost lands.

Arabelle gave Maggie another hug. "Regardless of what you call me, dear Maggie, know that I love you."

She turned and left the tent before Maggie could see the tears that blurred her vision.

Arabelle spent the next ten hours in her tent, doing brutal courses of exercise interrupted by short stints of anxiety-ridden sleep. It was tiring—physically, mentally, and emotionally. She could hardly imagine doing this every day, and every night, of her life. And yet she had no other choice.

It was late in the afternoon when she sank into the flower-scented hot water that Maggie had prepared. She'd gained a total of four more hours of sleep since this morning—which, according to Castien, was all she needed. And that was on top of the sleep she'd foolishly gotten in Maggie's bed this morning. Yet still she was tired.

Maggie began cleaning up after her, and as she picked up her mistress's clothes, Arabelle's new dagger fell out.

The maiden's eyes widened. "Is that from—"

"Yes," Arabelle cut in, "and we need not talk about it. Please put that in my chest for safekeeping."

Maggie put away the dagger, holding it with two fingers as if it was going to burn her.

"Is it almost time for dinner?" Arabelle asked. "I'm very hungry."

"Yes—I believe Madam Mizmer is roasting fowl tonight.

Will you be dining with your father, or are you staying in your tent?"

"Lay out my clothes to visit with my father. I have a few things to ask him."

Arabelle's muscles ached fiercely, and as Tabor escorted her to her father's tent, she had to work hard not to let it show. Apparently she was unsuccessful.

"Princess," asked Tabor, "what ails you?"

Arabelle gave Tabor her most innocent look. "What do you mean? I'm sure you've heard I was feeling a bit tired today."

Her guardian crinkled his nose. "Don't pretend with me, Princess. I've seen enough lame horses and injured soldiers to recognize physical pain. You're being very cautious with your stride. So I ask again, Princess, what ails you?"

Arabelle gave a dramatic sigh and tried to appear guilty. "You're right, of course. This morning when I raced to Maggie's tent, I accidentally tripped on a stone and turned my ankle. It isn't serious, but I'm trying to be careful to ensure that it doesn't get worse."

He shook his head. "Foolishness." He knelt and examined Arabelle's ankles. "No swelling. Would you like me to carry you?"

Arabelle stepped back. "Don't you dare! I'll die of embarrassment."

"I very much doubt that, Princess."

"I'm fine, Tabor. I just need to stretch it out."

Tabor smiled. "As you wish."

As they walked, a pair of Azazel's enforcers came walking in the opposite direction. Enforcers weren't often seen in the caravan, and Tabor put the flat of his hand on Arabelle's back and hurried her along. But as they passed the two black-leathered soldiers, she caught a fragment of their exchange.

"Looking for strangers in Trimoria. What do you think that means?"

"I don't know. Just keep your eyes open for anything out of the ordinary. Last thing we want is for Kirag to accuse us of inattentiveness."

As the strands of conversation faded, Arabelle wondered what that was all about.

LIFE AS A SLAVE

As Grisham's wits returned to him, his head still throbbing, he found himself shuffling along a dank underground corridor. A metal collar had been snapped around his neck. Humans shuffled both in front of him and behind. All of them had collars around their necks, and each of those collars was connected by a chain to a single, massively thick chain that ran the length of the marching line.

The truth hit him harder than the blow he'd suffered to the head. *I've been taken by slavers.*

A deep bellow sounded from far behind him. Only after hearing it a third time did he understand the words. "Go or bash head. Go now!"

The human in front of him grumbled, "Damned ogre. I wish someone would bash *his* head in."

Another voice replied. "You'll need a very large club to even tickle that beast. Just shut up before you cause us trouble."

They marched quietly forward from then on. Grisham had no idea who was leading; he could only see the man directly in front of him. He knew only that the passages turned and twisted, and his Ta'ah senses told him that they were sloping ever deeper beneath the ground.

At one point he heard a chanting coming from a cross corridor, and he realized with surprise that the words were in the old language. His father had insisted that he learn it, even though he grew up speaking Trimorian, yet this was the first time he'd heard the old language spoken since he'd crossed the barrier.

On another occasion, they crossed a passage lined with purple flames that reminded him of the forbidden passages from his youth. The humans muttered, cursed, and quickened their pace to get past it, and Grisham wondered if the underground world here held the same dangers that he had known on the other side of the barrier. Demons. Followers of Lilith. Perhaps something even worse.

After what seemed to be hours of stumbling through the underground, they arrived in a large cave, and Grisham saw for the first time the ogre that had been bellowing at them from behind. The thing was easily six feet wide, heavily muscled, with two large teeth jutting up from his lower jaw, and he stood twice again as tall as the largest humans, who were already twice again as tall as Grisham. When he stood straight, he was at eye level with the ogre's knee.

The behemoth pointed at a pile of picks and hammers. "Take. Bash rock. No bash rock? Me bash head!"

Grisham scrambled to grab a hammer small enough for him to wield. It was terribly worn and its head was pitted.

"Bash rock!" the ogre bellowed.

Grisham followed the lead of the other prisoners and began slamming his hammer against the wall of rock ahead of him. He didn't know why; he didn't spy any veins of ore or signs of unusual minerals. But he certainly wasn't going to ask. The rules here had been made clear enough: Bash rock, or bash head.

He worked like that in silence for a long while, wondering if this monotony would ever end. If they would get food, or water, or even a short break. Then he felt the vibrations of the ogre walking up behind him.

"Puny dorf bash tiny rocks."

Grisham turned and saw the beast pointing at a pile of debris that some of the others had excavated from the wall. Apparently this target was deemed more suited to his "puny" efforts.

He moved toward the pile, the chain on his neck resisting as it dragged the heavy main chain behind him, and began mindlessly hammering on the stones. His arms and shoulders were burning from the effort, and his stomach growled. But Father had long ago taught him how to focus on a task to the exclusion of all else. By concentrating on his work, he distracted his mind from his body's complaints.

He didn't pause until he felt a hand on his shoulder. And as soon as he stopped working, his needs came rushing back: thirst, hunger, and throbbing pain.

Behind him stood a grizzled human with a kind, wrinkled face. The man actually smiled as he handed Grisham a bowl of gruel. "Food is served." He hitched his thumb toward a trough. "This time, I bring you a bowl. Next time, you need to move quickly before these vultures eat it all."

Another human, a teenager, shook his head. "Nicholas, if the dwarf wants to bang on rocks all day, let him. He's going to be one of the first to die anyway. Might as well leave more food for us."

Nicholas turned to the teenager. "Best watch yourself, Grappa. You'd do well to remember that down here you're just a slave like the rest of us. This young dwarf worked harder than you on your best day, and he's half your size." As he spoke, his aura included large streaks of red and white—anger and honesty.

Grisham was surprised and grateful that this stranger had defended him. "Grisham," he said. "My name is Grisham."

The man and held out his calloused hand. "Pleased to meet you, Grisham. I just wish it were under better circumstances. My name is Nicholas."

Grappa spat on the ground and mumbled, "Dwarf-lover."

Grappa's aura was filled with streaks of red, yellow, and black. The first two, anger and cowardice, were common human traits, but it was rare to see tinges of black, which usually mean a person has evil intent.

I will have to stay away from that one.

Nicholas invited Grisham to sit with him to eat. As the older man scooped gruel into his mouth with two fingers, he said, "Best eat before it gets cold. It's not good when it's warm, but I promise you that it's worse when it's cold."

Grisham shoveled the pasty substance into his mouth. His gag reflex tried to kick in, but he suppressed it. There were oats in it, he tasted that, but beneath that something was off and very sour.

Nicholas scratched at his beard. "So tell me your story, young sir. How did you end up getting captured by the slavers?"

"Well, I live in the orphanage in Cammoria and—"

"Ha!" Grappa interrupted. "A dwarf *and* an orphan. A two-time loser!"

Nicholas grabbed the boy's chain and yanked on it, pulling the teenager closer, then cuffed the boy on the back of his head. "Mind your manners or you'll regret it."

Grappa scowled and backed away. The black in his aura flared.

"Let me guess," Nicholas said to Grisham, ignoring the interruption. "You got an offer to be adopted, it was arranged for you to meet your future parents somewhere, and something happened."

"How did you know?"

Nicholas clicked his tongue. "Ptah! Many an orphan has come here, and your tale isn't uncommon. These slavers target those who are helpless or foolish, but they especially like those who won't be missed."

Grisham felt bad for the matron at the orphanage. *She* would miss him. He could always tell she truly cared for her charges, and she had been expecting him back with the signed parchment. He couldn't imagine what Wat might think.

"How did you get caught by them, Nicholas? You don't seem like an easy target."

Nicholas sighed. "I wish I could say I put up a struggle, or did something valiant and lost. But no. I was a hired soldier for a caravan, and I'd just gotten my month's wages, and it was the first anniversary of my wife's death. So of course I got roaring drunk. I went into the forest at night by myself, and the slavers scooped me up as I slept in front of my campfire. Clearly, I deserved my fate due to sheer stupidity."

"I'm sorry to hear about your wife, and your misfortune."

The man smiled. "She was a good woman, but she'd been sick for a long time." He stretched his arms. "Relax and stretch for a bit; that ogre won't be back for at least a couple hours. We must take whatever rest we can, when we can, for the ogre certainly won't tolerate resting in his presence."

"Can I ask one more question?"

Nicholas lay down on the ground. "Certainly."

"What are we doing down here? What good is it to break these rocks? What are we mining for? I see no veins of ore."

Nicholas chuckled. "I heard more than one question in there." He yawned and closed his eyes. "Nobody knows what we're doing here. All we ever do is dig, dig some more, and sort through broken rocks. We're never told what we're looking for, nor are such questions tolerated."

"I'm sorry, one more question, and you don't need to answer if you're going to sleep, but is the ogre the only slaver here, or are there others?"

"Oh, there are others. The ogres are the muscle. There are also some humans that work for them, but the one you don't ever want to meet is the elf priestess. I'd rather not speak of her. Let's just say she and Azazel would be a well-matched pair. Both are evil to the core, and frighten me for many of the same reasons."

Anytime Grisham heard the wizard's name, his thoughts turned to the day his father had sacrificed himself for his sake.

Grisham lay on the ground and closed his eyes. *And look at what I've accomplished for all his sacrifices.*

———

Grisham's vision was consumed with a field of white. From within the whiteness, a voice echoed in his mind.

"Grisham, all is not lost. Your mission is not complete."

He found himself unable to move, not even to open his eyes. He began to panic.

"Do not be afraid; I am here. To all who watch, you are asleep. Simply think your thoughts, and I will receive them."

"Who are you?"

"I am Seder, and our time is brief. Listen carefully, and remember. Your hardships have been many, but I will provide you with what you need to complete your mission."

"Mission?"

"Your destiny is to bring your people out of self-imposed isolation. You must find the Thariginian king and, as the representative of your people, strike an agreement with him."

"But Seder, there *are* no longer any Thariginian kings in Trimoria."

"Not all is as it seems, young Grisham. Soon, a Thariginian will be discovered. You will meet with him, I promise. You will complete the first step of your destiny."

Grisham felt a spark of hope. If Seder said it was possible, then it was possible. "That means I escape, right? How?"

A moment passed in silence and the field of white shimmered.

"Be patient. Some events must occur before your escape is possible. I have unlatched powers that were hidden deep within you—powers that are rarely seen within your people. They will emerge slowly. In the meantime, pay careful attention to what things look like. And Grisham... always avoid the influence of Lilith."

Seder's voice faded, the field of white dimmed, and a scene unfolded in Grisham's mind.

A dozen black panthers enter a wide passage into a mountain cliff. The tunnel is symmetrically constructed, with clear signs of dwarven workmanship.

The lead cat roars. "We have arrived, lizard lords."

From deeper within the tunnel comes the sound of claws scraping against stone, and the ground vibrates from the movement of a heavy creature. The cats hiss in fear and shrink back.

Sparks and hints of flame flash in the dark of the tunnel, then a giant, scaled head appears.

A dragon.

The dragon's claws spark against the stone as it moves forward on thick muscular legs. It's sixty feet long from its snout to the end of its tail, and its armored black scales glow with hints of red.

A grinding voice erupts from deep within the dragon's chest. "Changeling, you have arrived as promised. We must now await my brother. He is late, as always."

A thud outside the cavern announces the arrival of another creature of tremendous size. A blood-soaked snout appears at the cave's opening. *"I heard that, sister. Can I help it if I was hungry and you said I wasn't allowed to eat the swamp-cat creatures? I blame my tardiness on you."*

Smoke billows from the first dragon's snout. She growls in exasperation. "Males," she mutters.

She turns back to the cats. With the exception of their leader, they cower between the two beasts. "It is now time. You understand that once my brother and I pierce the barrier and you cross over, we have no way to retrieve you. You will be stuck."

The lead cat yowls his understanding.

The female dragon turns to her brother. "It is time."

LIVING WITH THE CURSE

Arabelle took her training very seriously in the weeks after leaving Aubgherle. In the process, she discovered that Castien's exercises had a valuable side benefit. Not only did they allow her to live with the poison her body carried, they also made her stronger. She was beginning to understand why Castien had referred to her as a weapon, and she wanted to be a powerful one.

After all, the elves and Seder seemed to believe she was meant for something more than survival, and indeed, she felt like she was meant for something more. She just hoped she wasn't deluding herself.

She also practiced every day with the dagger as well, though of course this too had to be done within the confines of her tent. The one time Maggie walked in on her practicing, the poor girl looked like she was going to faint.

The one skill she could practice anywhere was the ability she had now started calling her *inner sight*. Any time she wanted to find her father, she would simply visualize him, and her senses would point her in the right direction. It worked for Castien, too. Though the elven sword master was now many days away, her senses would carry her to the edge of the caravan, and she would stare into the distance, knowing that if she could miraculously fly in the direction her senses told her, she could travel in a straight line to him.

But strangely, Arabelle's inner sight didn't work well on other people—only those two people. If she tried to find someone else, her senses gave her no response at all. It was as if everyone else didn't exist. It was worrisome; she had to learn how to fix this so she could use the skill as intended.

And then... she did. It turned out the problem was a simple one, if embarrassing. Arabelle realized that she rarely paid much attention to what people truly looked like. So when, for instance, she visualized the merchant who sold her favorite pastries, her inner picture would be incorrect, or incomplete, and thus her inner sight provided no response.

It troubled her to realize that she hadn't even been looking at the people in her life. Had the merchant always had a missing tooth? Had Tabor always been quite that scarred? Arabelle was especially ashamed when she realized she was misremembering Maggie's eye color. It was then that she decided that she must invest time in improving her attention to detail.

And when she did, her inner sight improved. She pictured the pleasantly plump and jovial face of Madam Mizmer, and found her in the market, haggling over a melon. She pictured the dwarf, Oda, and found him at the stables grousing about the size of the horses. She would never again need to search the caravan for

Maggie. And of course she could find Tabor if she needed to, though he was almost always at her side.

"Princess," Tabor said one day, "you seem to be changing."

Arabelle looked up innocently. "Am I?"

Tabor cleared his throat. "Yes. You seem more energetic, you walk with a much smoother stride, and you seem more comfortable with yourself. I also believe you've lost some weight."

Arabelle felt a flash of anger. Her clothes were indeed more loose-fitting than they used to be, but how dare he comment on her appearance? She breathed in and out slowly to calm herself. "I'm the same as always," she said.

She thought she saw a flicker of sadness on Tabor's stern face. But he merely said, "If you say so, Princess. I must be mistaken."

That evening as Arabelle readied for bed, she was still thinking about Tabor's remark. The truth was, he was right. She *had* changed—much more than she'd realized.

She pulled up her skirts to examine her legs. They were lean now, with sinewy muscles that hadn't been there before. When she flexed them, she could see every fiber move and ripple. The same transformation had occurred in her arms. She could see the muscles, feel the inner strength there. It was a good feeling, a powerful one.

But, as much as she hated to admit it, she was now thinner than most. Far thinner than she'd ever been before. Was it visible in her face, too? Was she gaunt and sickly looking? She could have called for Maggie to bring a mirror, but she already knew the truth. Although she was stronger than she'd ever been in her life, she was also losing too much weight, and in order to stay healthy, she needed to do something about that.

She reached for the basket of fruit on her nightstand, and a realization dawned on her. Maggie had only started leaving fruit for her... maybe a week or two ago. Could that be the handmaiden's subtle way of suggesting her lady eat more?

She grabbed a cluster of red grapes and popped them in her mouth one by one until she'd eaten them all. Certain her stomach couldn't hold another bite, she tucked herself into bed, instructing her brain, as always, to awake in two hours.

She wondered if her sleep would be dream-filled. She'd noticed that her improvements in observation in the waking world had also transferred to her dream world, and oftentimes memories of their details would stick with her for days afterward.

That, too, might be useful. The Imazighen believed that dreams could be used to tell one's future. Arabelle was dubious —she was fairly confident that her most recent dream, about eating dirt, had no special meaning—but was open to the possibility.

She closed her eyes, and she did in fact fall quickly into a dream.

She walks through a field of flowers, their scents floating on a warm breeze. Suddenly the field blinks from existence and is replaced with a lake.

A rumbling approaches. A large metal box on black wheels

travels, without horses, toward the lake. It stops at the water's edge, and a door on the giant box opens. Four people emerge, talking and laughing. Their clothes are strange. They pull some rods from another door in the box, line up along the shore, and begin fishing.

Two are teenagers—both boys—and the others seem to be their parents. The smaller brother catches a fish and holds it up for everyone to see. The mother then pulls a small black box from a bag and places it against her forehead. Everyone smiles, and the box emits a flash of brilliant white light.

Soon the larger brother catches a fish as well, a much larger one, and the strange ritual with the small black box is repeated.

As the larger boy turns, Arabelle sees his face, and his brilliant smile, and she finds herself blushing. She feels a kinship with him, and his blue eyes possess a kindness that draws her in. She steps forward to talk to him.

And the dream fades away.

Arabelle woke from the dream soaked with sweat. As she replayed the dream in her mind, it made no sense—like most dreams. But that boy…

Arabelle gasped. When she thought of the boy, her inner sight awoke, pointing her in the boy's direction. Was this a real person? Had she dreamt about a stranger she had never met?

And that wasn't the strangest part of it all. Thus far, her inner sight had always been correct. Sometimes it didn't activate at all, but when it did, it never failed to point her in the right direction. But now…

She looked in the direction where her senses had pointed her. She was staring straight up at the ceiling of her tent.

Arabelle devoured the spiced lamb resting on a bed of Madam Mizmer's special rice dotted with dried fruit, then tore into a piece of flatbread.

Across from her, Father laughed. "My heart, I'm so glad to see your appetite has grown. I knew you would come around."

"Come around?" she asked.

"Oh, nothing. Tabor is worried for you, is all. First he claimed you were hiding an injury, then that you were too thin! I told him his skills lie in assessing soldiers, and horses, and to leave the health of my daughter to me." He stopped himself. "But don't let Tabor's comments bother you. You're a growing girl, and your body is changing. It's natural to gain or lose weight. And I know you would tell me if you were unwell or injured."

Arabelle felt a prick of guilt. "Father," she asked, "am I too thin now?"

He looked at her appraisingly, then pressed his finger to her forehead. "My dove, the beauty of a princess lies within. Just eat when you're hungry and let nature take care of the rest. If you listen to your body's needs, you will not be led astray."

His kindness and understanding only made Arabelle feel more guilt over the lie she was about to tell. But she was determined to do it—to clear a path for her to take the actions she felt were necessary for her growth.

"Father," she said hesitantly, "there's something I've been

wanting to talk to you about."

"Anything, my heart."

"Well, I've been having frightening dreams lately. The same ones over and over again."

Father set his food aside, and his expression was serious. "Dreams are not to be ignored. Come, tell me everything. Together we'll determine what is best."

<hr />

When Arabelle had completed her lie, her father twirled his mustache around one of his thick fingers.

"These dreams *are* concerning," he said thoughtfully. "Always the same dream of being attacked, with no escort to protect you. This could be an ordinary nightmare, fears of the day creeping into the night. But for you to keep having the same dream... yes, it suggests a vision. And the other detail, about you defending yourself with a dagger... it's most interesting. Perhaps this is the heart of the message your vision is trying to convey. A warning, and an instruction. Telling you what skill you will need to possess."

Arabelle nodded silently. Her father was interpreting her made-up dream precisely as she'd intended, but that only made her feel more guilt for lying.

He stood. "Wait here, my dear. It's time you receive something."

He walked across the tent and rummaged through a chest. It took him some time to find what he was looking for, as it was buried at the bottom. Finally he let out a grumbled, "Aha!"

He stood holding two items: a supple leather sash with loops in it, and a small wooden box. He sat down with Arabelle again.

"My daughter, these belonged to your mother. And now they belong to you."

He handed Arabelle the box first. It was polished to perfect smoothness and embossed with colored stones. Inside were two daggers, their blades a shiny black, their handles wrapped in gray leather.

Her father nodded toward the box. "The handles are bound with the skin of a man-eating fish. That skin won't get slippery even when coated with blood."

"I've never heard of such a fish."

"Nor should you have. These daggers are from a time before the demon wars, before the barrier. If those fish still exist, they live in the vast oceans that we no longer have access to."

Arabelle had no words for how beautiful the daggers were. She touched them gingerly. "Mother carried these?"

Father chuckled. "As a matter of fact, when I first encountered her in the market, she almost skewered me with one of them. Your mother was always full of surprises."

"Like what?" Lately, Arabelle had been feeling increasingly hungry for knowledge about the mother she'd never known.

Father twirled the end of his mustache again, looking pensive. "Well... did I ever tell you that your mother wasn't the first woman I was betrothed to?"

Arabelle's eyes widened with shock. "No! How can that be?"

Father reclined against some pillows. "My parents had me betrothed at birth to a daughter of a very close friend of theirs. I grew up with her, played with her as a child. We became close.

And then one day, there was a riding accident. She fell from her horse and died. I was in mourning for a long time. I remember thinking that I would never recover from such sadness. But then I met your mother."

"And that was when she tried to stab you."

He laughed. "Precisely. I was walking in the marketplace on the outskirts of Cammoria when I saw the most beautiful girl I'd ever laid eyes on. I completely forgot myself, boldly approached, and asked her name." He pointed at the daggers in Arabelle's lap. "She pulled her weapon on me."

"That seems a bit extreme."

Her father rubbed at one of the thick rings on his fingers, the one that had been a wedding gift from Arabelle's mother. "I… may have approached more assertively than I intended. And it nearly started a riot. Her father was a wealthy merchant, so she had many escorts, and when she pulled her weapon, they all drew their weapons as well. I, too, had an escort of course, and when they saw all the blades arrayed against me, they too showed their arms. It was a tense moment. But I held up my empty hands, and your mother stared at me for what seemed like an eternity. Then she gave me the greatest gift I have ever received: her brilliant smile. I was hers forever after."

"So you chose who you married?"

He scratched at his chin. "Yes and no. Your mother swore that she'd seen me in her dreams even before we met, and she knew that we were destined to marry. So it's more true to say that your mother chose me. Or fate did. But it's also true to say that I very much begged my father to make arrangements with her parents."

Arabelle smiled. She wondered why she hadn't asked more about her mother before now. Truly her parents had been in love.

Father pointed again at the daggers in Arabelle's lap. "In any case, I think she would be proud for you to wield her daggers. But… you must make me a promise."

"Of course, Father."

"I want you to train with Tabor. I trust him to be careful with you."

Arabelle felt the warmth of victory spread through her. She set aside the box, leaned forward, and wrapped her father in a hug. "I would be honored to train with Tabor, and wield Mother's daggers. Father, thank you so much. I'll be very careful."

He hugged her tightly, then held her at arm's length. "I know you will. But I ask one more thing. Keep this training secret. You will have an advantage if people underestimate you."

She smiled. "Nobody expects a princess with claws, eh?"

Father slapped his knee and laughed. "Exactly right. Now go get Tabor. Let's break the news to him together."

Tabor threw a kick at Arabelle's ankle, and she dove at his legs, attempting to touch him with her finger. Instead she merely flopped unceremoniously into the spot he had just vacated.

She glared up at her escort, now her trainer. Tabor was *really* old—even older than her father, and he was nearly forty. Yet the man moved like a snake, and no matter what she tried, she wasn't able to tag him.

She rose to her feet and stalked him as if he were her prey, waiting for him to grow inattentive or weary. But somehow, Tabor never got distracted. Not even for a moment.

Wiping a sweat-soaked strand of hair from her face, she crouched in an attack stance, feinted to his left, and dove for his right. Again she landed in the dirt, and this time Tabor poked her in the back of the head with a thick finger.

"Princess, I'm afraid you just received a mortal wound." He chuckled merrily. The old man was enjoying this.

Arabelle got up and wiped the dust from her clothes. "Fine, I'm dead now. But you're supposed to be helping me get better. What am I doing wrong?"

"Honestly, you're doing more right than you know. But it's unreasonable to expect that you'll catch me unaware, or be faster than me, after only a few weeks of work. I've been training at hand-to-hand combat for more than thirty years, and without being overly modest, I'm one of the best there is. You won't beat me, Princess. But in trying to do so, you're learning."

She sighed. He was right, of course. "So what am I doing right?"

Tabor's face brightened. "Now *that* is the right question to ask. You're learning to observe your opponent. You've been watching my feet instead of my hands—"

She dove at him suddenly, leading with her extended finger, but he simply stepped backwards and tapped her on the top of her head.

Tabor actually roared with laughter, and he had to wipe tears of amusement from his eyes. Yes, the old man was enjoying this *far* too much.

Arabelle dusted herself off and continued the conversation as if her last failed attack had never happened. "Well of course, Tabor. You can't exactly stab someone without moving your feet or adjusting your stance. You've fooled me once or twice by moving your upper body while your feet were planted in another direction. That always turned into a feint."

Tabor's look of amusement melted into one of appraisal. "If only my soldiers had half your intelligence, Princess. You're correct. Watch a man's feet. They don't lie." He shook his head. "You know, when your father first told me he wanted me to train you, I felt sorry for you. But now?" He broke into a broad grin. "I feel sorry for your future husband. You're very smart and very tough, for a princess."

She smiled despite herself, trying to ignore the *for a princess* qualifier.

Tabor rubbed his chin. "In fact... I've never had a woman soldier in my employ, but if I had watched you sparring in this way, and you weren't the princess, I wouldn't dismiss the idea as impossible."

Now *that* was a solid compliment, and Arabelle beamed.

She stretched her arms and legs. "Ready for another round?"

Tabor pointed both of his index fingers at her and smiled. "Be careful, I'm armed with two fingers now."

Arabelle now spent her days working out with Tabor and her nights working out to Castien's prescribed exercises. The dagger work was excellent for developing her observation skills and reaction times, whereas Castien's workouts helped her build inner strength and muscle control. One thing both workouts had in common: they always left her physically exhausted.

But she was also cognizant of Castien's other lessons, and was determined to become more knowledgeable about the uses of plants. She had already read the volume he'd given her, but thought there must be more knowledge to be had.

She started, perhaps foolishly, by asking Maggie if she knew of any plants with medicinal uses, such as those that might help someone with bad dreams. Naturally Maggie took this to mean that Arabelle herself was having bad dreams, and she immediately kicked into full-on mothering mode. But once Arabelle convinced her that she was merely curious about the subject, Maggie pointed her to Madam Mizmer. Evidently the cook had once apprenticed to an herb-woman.

As Arabelle approached Madam Mizmer's cooking stalls, her mouth watered at the delicious scents that wafted her way. The roasted meats and pungent spices filled this portion of the merchant's quarter.

Madam Mizmer, a portly woman with hair always tied up in a cloth headdress, was busy yelling orders at her harried staff when Arabelle arrived.

"Hurry up, Alexandra! We need those vegetables chopped for the soldier's stew, and make sure they're chopped evenly this time! I'll not be hearing that some of my vegetables aren't cooked properly."

"Yes, Mother." Poor Alexandra looked up meekly from her vegetables and gave Arabelle a wan smile.

Madam Mizmer didn't reserve her shouting for her own daughter. As she stirred a pot, she shouted at several other helpers. "Stop dawdling! You girls have only two hours until the merchants come for their midday meals! And Keena, watch the spicing this time. Not everyone enjoys the burn as much as you do."

Only then did the head cook notice Arabelle. She greeted her with a look of concern. "Princess? Is there something wrong? Was your morning meal improperly prepared?" she shot an accusing look at poor Alexandra.

Arabelle shook her head. "No, nothing like that, Madam Mizmer. Your meals are always delightful. I came to ask about something else. I was told you once apprenticed with an herb-woman?"

Madam Mizmer fanned herself. "Oh my, that was ages and ages ago, my dear. Most of my herb knowledge is now applied to the cooking arts, not the healing ones. Does something ail you, Princess?"

Arabelle wondered how to approach this. She'd learned with Maggie that she couldn't just blurt out what she was after. No one would believe that a princess merely wanted to learn; they would all assume something was wrong, and try to help.

But as she gazed over at Alexandra, madly chopping away at a seemingly endless pile of root vegetables, she was inspired.

"Madam Mizmer, in truth, I was hoping to learn how to cook from you. I know it's something that a mother normally teaches her daughter, but…"

The woman raised a hand. "Say no more, dear." She waddled from behind the stall and put her arm around the princess's shoulder. "I can only imagine how difficult it must be for you. My own mother died almost ten years ago, and it still seems like only yesterday. Things must have been very hard for you never knowing your mum, never having her around to teach you the things of mothers and daughters. Rest assured, I will gladly teach you anything you want to know."

"Well, I was thinking, could you just teach me some of the basics? Maybe start with something simple that I could serve my father. Maybe… tea? Eventually I could move up to a stew or bread. Do you think I could learn all that?"

Madam Mizmer smiled. "A smart girl like you can learn anything you set your mind to. Come."

She shuffled toward an adjoining tent and led Arabelle into its dark recesses. Apparently this was where she kept many of her dried goods, as a huge variety of plants hung from the ceiling to dry.

"What kind of tea do you like most? I have many to choose from, and each one has its own trick to extract the most flavor."

Arabelle looked at the bewildering assortment of plants. "Do you have any teas that help with bad dreams?"

The rotund lady gave Arabelle the same look that Maggie had. "My dear, are you having nightmares?" She clucked. "Well of course you are. Not to worry, I have something just for that."

She plucked a branch with crispy leaves from one of the strings that crisscrossed the tent. "If you crush one of these leaves in steaming water—not boiling—and drink it quickly just before you close your eyes, you will have a dreamless sleep. It's important the water is just hot enough to be steaming. Too hot or too cool, and the leaf's effectiveness will be diminished."

Arabelle examined the leaf. She had to suppress a smile when she saw that it was anvil-shaped and green, with tiny red filaments streaking through it.

Exactly the leaf Castien showed me.

"Thank you, Madam Mizmer. I'm sure this will help. Can I have a supply of this?"

"Of course, my dear. But use only one leaf for your mug. I wouldn't want you to get sick." She waved for Arabelle to follow. "Now, tea you can start on immediately, but stews and bread… we'll have to work our way to that. I think the next step for you is vegetables. I'm sure Alexandra could use some help there."

Arabelle forced a smile. "Of course, chopping vegetables sounds… just wonderful."

Alexandra giggled. "When I woke up this morning, I never dreamed that I'd be sharing my chores with you, Princess."

Arabelle laughed as she chopped. "I can't say that I saw this coming myself."

They weren't the only ones. Before long, Alexandra's younger sister came running into the tent, her eyes wide. "Princess! Mum came by and told Pa you were chopping vegetables with Alexandra! I didn't believe it, but here you are!"

Arabelle smiled at her former co-conspirator. "Hi, Zoe. Yes, your mother is helping me learn how to cook. How are things going with the sheep?"

Zoe jumped up on a stool and kicked her bare feet. "One of the ewes gave birth to a pure white lamb with pink eyes today!

My friend Henna says that's a good omen. Pa says there's no such thing as omens."

Alexandra smile deviously. "Hey, maybe Mum will bring the pink-eyed lamb for us to stew."

Zoe crinkled her nose. "Ew, gross. Maybe she'll mistake Hassan for a sheep and *he'll* be chopped up for the stew."

Alexandra's cheeks reddened. "You leave Hassan out of this!"

Zoe stuck out her tongue at her sister, then waved at Arabelle. "Bye, Princess. Pa needs my help with shearing. I just wanted to see if you were really here, chopping vegetables with my sister. That's weird." She shook her head, hopped up, and padded away as quickly as she'd arrived.

Arabelle chuckled. The girl definitely spoke her mind.

She turned to Alexandra. "So... Hassan? How are things going there?"

Alexandra stuck out her lower lip in a pout. "Mum's been keeping me so busy I can barely get away to even be seen. But he did look directly at me once when I passed him on the street. He was with the other soldiers and couldn't really stop to talk, but I know he would have if he could."

Arabelle couldn't imagine being so obsessed over a single look from a boy. Unless... well, she supposed if it were the right boy.

Her thoughts wandered to the boy from her dream, the one with the sparkling blue eyes and brilliant smile. Her inner sight again tried to tell her that he was somewhere directly above her. She wished she could talk to Seder and ask why that was happening.

"I heard a rumor that Hassan now wears a new fancy braided belt for his staff," Alexandra said.

"Oh?"

The girl nodded as she continued to chop at her vegetables. "Yes. And they're saying it was given to him by a girl." She chopped harder, and Arabelle began to pity the vegetables. "Do you think that's true? It can't be true. I would know if Hassan had eyes for anyone but me."

Arabelle held back a smile. Maggie must have finished her project.

Good for her.

Before she was forced to figure out how to answer Alexandra's question, she was rescued by the return of Madam Mizmer, leading a freshly shorn sheep toward the stall.

"Looks like it's time for the main part of the stew," she said.

The next day after dinner, Arabelle had some different training in mind. But first, it would involve ditching Tabor.

She told him that she was interested in buying some new clothes, so he escorted her to the textile tents, which were filled with both pre-woven clothes and the raw materials to sew practically any clothing one might need.

"You can wait out front," Arabelle said to her escort. "It will probably take some time for me to try things on."

Tabor panned his gaze over the vast tent, as if looking for threats. There was no one there but vendors and buyers, haggling over clothes. Finally he nodded at Arabelle and stepped outside to wait.

Arabelle went to a curtained changing area and stripped off her robes. Underneath she wore the dark-gray outfit Maggie had prepared for her. She pulled the matching headscarf from her bundle and wrapped it around her head, leaving only her eyes visible. The veil was common among her people, especially among the older women, and even the men would wear a tagelmust, which was nearly identical in style, when facing the dust of travel.

Finally she removed her slippers, wrapped them in her robe, and set them neatly in the corner. She'd found that her slippers would make a sound that her bare feet would not, and for tonight, she wanted maximum stealth.

When she walked out of the dressing area, nobody gave her a second look.

Now came the real test. Tabor.

She took a deep breath and walked purposely toward the exit, maintaining a steady gait. She dared not even glance at Tabor as she left the tent, for she was certain he would somehow recognize her. She just kept on walking, taking several turns through tents, wagons, and stalls, then stopped and turned.

She had done it. No one was following her.

Her goal for the evening was stealth and observation. She intended to spend the next half hour seeing how much she could observe without being noticed. She walked on the balls of her feet as Castien had instructed, and practiced walking in the twilight's shadows.

She followed some soldiers tasked with maintaining peace in

the caravan. Men like this were trained to be alert, scanning the spaces between the tents, looking for anything out of the ordinary. But she applied the skills the elven warrior had taught her, using the shadows to her advantage. She found that keeping perfectly still was the most difficult part. Every time she did it, her leg muscles would quickly begin to ache.

But it worked. Even when a soldier looked directly at her, in her dark clothing, in shadow, and remaining as still as a rock, his eyes would pass over her without stopping. Arabelle felt a thrill at the accomplishment. As a princess, she never went anywhere unnoticed. Being invisible was a freedom she'd never before felt.

She was still following the soldiers around, seeing how close she could get, when a young red-haired soldier arrived with an announcement. "Kirag has arrived!"

One of the other soldiers responded with a cautioning tone. "Stay far away from that one, Ephraim. You don't want to gain the attention of Azazel's right hand. He's nearly as deadly as the wizard himself."

The young soldier replied in a whisper that Arabelle could barely hear. "He's calling all of Azazel's soldiers together for a meeting near the center square."

"May they all freeze in the coldest recesses of the Abyss," spat the other.

As the soldiers moved along, Arabelle decided to spy on another target: this Kirag. She'd heard of the man—he was said to be a giant, and meaner than a snake—but she'd never laid eyes on him.

She crept into the shadows that surrounded the town square in the evening. Not a merchant was to be seen; even those who were normally active at this hour had apparently chosen to close early. But the town square was far from empty. Two dozen of Azazel's black-clad enforcers stood at its center, facing a man who was incredibly tall—a good two feet taller than any other man around him. Oversized canines protruded from his lower jaw, and the yellow of his eyes gave him the look of something… inhuman.

This was Kirag.

"Within the next week," he was saying, "I will be sending Duos to various parts of Trimoria to continue the search."

"What about the slavers?" asked one of the soldiers.

Kirag laughed heartily, then fixed the soldier with a cold stare. "If a slaver takes you, you aren't worthy of the uniform you wear. There are more Grubs in training. They will gladly replace not only the Duos I am sending out, but any of you who choose to fail me."

The soldier who'd spoken seemed to shrink before these words.

Kirag was about to say more, then stopped and sniffed the air. "I smell flowers. If I find that one of you has the scent of a woman on you, I have some special missions that will remove that stink quickly. You must be an idiot to think you can do your job while reeking of such scents."

Arabelle quickly crept back toward the clothing tent. She'd learned at least one valuable lesson tonight.

I have to tell Maggie to stop putting scents in my bathwater.

HUNTING FOR STRANGERS

K irag sat at his desk in the tent that the Talons who were stationed with the caravan had set up for him.

His mother's visions had given him some directions in which to look, but he'd need as much manpower as he could get. He'd left Glendale with instructions to assemble Duos from the Grubs as soon as they were qualified. The training master had been supplied with as many of Azazel's specially made amulets as he might need.

Few people even knew that these amulets existed. And even if they did, there was no blacksmith in Trimoria who could create one without Azazel's assistance. They were made of damantite, and only Azazel's powers were sufficient to melt the metal so that it could be cast into amulet form. Damantite held a deep black color when forged, but when the light struck it at an angle, it shone with hints of red.

That last feature made them unable to be duplicated. Not that many would try, but there were plenty of fools in the world, and occasionally someone would try to pass himself off as one of Azazel's Talons. A fool might, with effort, re-create the Talon's blackened armor with Azazel's red hourglass insignia on the chest. But he couldn't re-create the amulet.

Kirag smiled as he remembered one such fool. He'd done his research—he had an exact replica of the armor, and he even knew about the existence of the amulets. But he didn't realize that these amulets weren't simple painted iron creations.

After Kirag apprehended the false Talon, Azazel had the impersonator's entire family brought before him—grandparents, cousins, infants, everyone. Forty-five people in total were assembled that morning in front of Azazel's tower, with everyone in Cammoria gathered to watch. Azazel held a black sparkling ball of energy in his hands as he pronounced the penalty for impersonating one of his agents.

Death.

But it was worse than that, because the punishment was not given only to the perpetrator, but to his entire family.

Azazel incinerated the whole lot of them. Not all at once. He started with the infants, children, then the elderly, then the women. He saved the impersonator for last.

Kirag still occasionally found himself fondly recalling that morning.

The guard at his tent announced a visitor, and Kirag waved him in. It was Isaac, the local regiment's lead enforcer, wearing the customary black leathers of a Talon. No impersonator here.

He was middle-aged and clean-shaven, with hard gray eyes. Two obsidian daggers were tucked into his belt.

Good. This soldier has earned enough trust to have been sent on missions and has managed to return with success.

Kirag nodded his greetings. "Tell me what you've done to earn those daggers."

The man touched the handle of one of the daggers and smiled with a gap-toothed grin. "I earned these nearly a decade ago, sir. Lord Azazel had gotten information that twin boys were born in a remote village. I was told these boys were to be destroyed by any means available. I was the second Talon sent to this village."

"Why the second? What happened to the first?"

"The villagers saw him approach and ambushed him. He was returned to Cammorian headquarters with two broken legs and stripped of all clothes and weapons."

"What happened upon his return? What did your chief do?"

The soldier sneered. "The disgrace was killed and left for the vultures. My chief sent me to finish the job. The villagers were expecting an assault and were prepared to fight. So I snuck into the village on a moonless night, threw oil-soaked rags onto the homes, crept back out, and shot flaming arrows onto the roofs.

"Once all of the inhabitants were busy fighting the fires, nobody gave a thought to the two babes, except their mother, who held them both in her arms. My final arrow passed cleanly through both children."

Ruthless. Good.

"Tell me about the ceremony where those were made. Who attended?"

The man looked nervous. "I was told that the only people to whom I can speak of the dagger ceremony are the chief enforcer or Lord Azazel himself. But as you are now the chief enforcer, I suppose it's all right.

"Lord Azazel asked me for my Talon's daggers. He dropped them to the floor and turned them into slag with but a moment's application of his immense power. The chief enforcer retrieved a form for a dagger and placed within it a sparkling metal I didn't recognize. Lord Azazel poured a powder over the form and applied his prodigious mystical power. Even with my eyes closed, the brightness was blinding. The daggers that I now carry were the result."

Kirag nodded. The daggers were true, as he assumed they would be. He had, once, encountered a Talon who had lifted his daggers from another. That man's fate was even more enjoyable than the one that had befallen the impersonator.

"Isaac," he said, "I have a task for one who can be trusted to not fail."

The soldier straightened. "I will succeed or die trying. What is the task?"

Kirag grinned at the man's earnestness. "You are to find some strangers who don't belong in Trimoria. I can't tell you what they look like, where they are, or how many they might be. But this caravan provides a good base of operations for a search. Azazel has ensured that the Imazighen travel throughout most of the wasteland and the surrounding towns. As you travel with them, I need you to send out scouting missions and keep an eye out for anyone who seems out of place. When you find them, question them as to their origins. Extract information by whatever means is necessary, and log whatever you learn so I can go over it at a later date. But do not cause strife within the caravan. We don't need an uprising. Keep your work quiet."

Isaac nodded. "I'll do what I can."

Kirag leaned over his desk and growled. "Yes, you will."

It was two weeks later when Kirag paid his first visit to Isaac's new interrogation tent. It was secluded, a mile from the caravan, so as not to be widely known. That was good, as the coppery tang of torture was evident even from outside, and the inside... the inside was far worse.

He found Isaac going through the pockets of some blood-soaked clothing.

"Have you learned anything?"

The soldier tossed a ruined shirt into the fire and wiped his sweaty hair from his eyes with a blood-encrusted hand. "As a matter of fact, we have a name." The soldier pointed to a dead naked man on the ground before him. "I had to torture him for nearly thirty minutes, but he talked. There's a stranger in the caravan, recently arrived, but already employed as one of the Sheikh's soldiers. Nobody knows his history. They call him Hassan, although they say he is one of the Nameless."

"Find him, and extract all information he can provide. He may be of interest, or he may be no one. These caravaners call everyone a Nameless if there's no one who can vouch for them."

"Yes, sir."

As he turned to leave, two Talons dragged an unconscious caravaner into the tent. Isaac rubbed his hands together, smiled menacingly, and set to work on his latest subject.

A GREATER EVIL IN THE TUNNELS

Day after day, and then week after week, Grisham worked in the rock mines. That's what he thought of them as: rock mines. Because all they were mining for was rock. He survived by keeping his mind focused on the job, banging with single-minded purpose, the sounds, the smells, and the pain fading from his consciousness.

When it was time to drink, he drank. When it was time to eat, he ate. Sometimes Nicholas would sit with him. Other times he would catch Grappa staring at him surreptitiously. But for the most part, he was alone—as he had been ever since his father's death.

Apart from a few hours each "night"—he couldn't be sure of the days in here, but his stomach told him they were being fed once a day—the brutal ogre taskmaster watched them almost constantly. Occasionally, however, he would disappear briefly for some errand or another. Or perhaps to relieve himself.

It was during one of these moments that Grappa finally acted out against Grisham, as the Ta'ah had long known he would. The ill-tempered teen paused in his work, walked over to Grisham, and took a swing at the Ta'ah with his pickaxe.

Grisham just barely jumped out of the way, and the pick sparked against the spot where he'd been standing only seconds before.

"Grappa!" yelled Nicholas, scrambling between them. "What in the seven levels of the Abyss do you think you're doing?"

Grappa sneered. "That dwarf is already mindless. He seems to *enjoy* slavery. Why defend him when all he does is exactly what's asked of him?"

Nicholas stalked toward the young bully. "You will leave Grisham alone, or I'll make sure you're in no shape to do anything. We each deal in our own way with what has become of us. Don't make things worse."

The ogre's crunching footsteps echoed in the cave, and anyone who'd been distracted by the incident quickly turned back to their work—including Grappa. The punishment for slacking, even for a moment, was brutal.

The ogre reappeared, and this was one of the rare occasions when he brought company. Two men in slaver garb walked in behind him, dragging a wooden chest toward the far end of the cave.

The ogre turned to the slaves and bellowed, "Move back. Boom."

Grisham was yanked backward by the collar as the other slaves raced away from the chest. Apparently they understood what was happening much better than he did.

The two slavers pushed the chest into a crevice in the wall of the cavern. When they could push it no further, one of the slavers struck flint against metal to light a rope that was trailing from the blackened chest. A bright spark caught on the rope, sending flickering shadows throughout the cavern. Then the slavers, too, ran from the chest.

A whoosh pierced the silence, followed by an explosive pressure wave that blew everyone off their feet.

Grisham lifted himself up off the floor. His eyes stung, but apart from that and the ringing in his ears, he was unharmed. He gave a small prayer of thanks to the one above. Some were not so fortunate. He looked around and saw that two men had been killed by flying debris.

While the ogre went to examine the results of the explosion, the human slavers disconnected the two dead slaves from the main chain and dragged their remains away.

Grisham turned to Nicholas, who had a slight trickle of blood dripping down his forehead. "What do they do with the dead?" he whispered.

Nicholas shuddered. "They're fed to the megapedes."

Grisham knew of these beasts. Megapedes were armored creatures that could eat through stone as rapidly as a person could walk through a pool of water. The Ta'ah back home avoided them even more than they avoided the demons. The megapedes didn't seek out the Ta'ah, but if they happened to come across one, they wouldn't hesitate to fight.

The ogre stomped back to the center of the cavern. "Bash rock, or bash head." He looked directly at Grisham and pointed at all of the scattered rocks. "Puny dorf. Lots bashing."

Grisham picked up his hammer and went back to work with the rest. But as he did, he heard a muffled gasp to his left. Grappa. The surly teen was carrying his pickaxe in his off hand, while the other hand lay limp at his side. As he returned to work, he could barely swing his pickaxe.

He'd been injured in the explosion. And now he had to hide that fact or he would be sent to the megapedes with the others.

I can't live with myself if I don't try to help him.

Grisham moved closer to Grappa and whispered, "Do you want to trade? I think I can wield the pickaxe and you could wield the hammer with one arm."

Grappa's face turned red with fury. "Stay away, vermin! I'll have no—"

"Bash!" the ogre yelled from across the cavern.

Grisham scurried back to his puny rocks. As he worked, he cast glances toward Grappa, who continued to have difficulty swinging his pickaxe one-handed.

Unfortunately, the ogre noticed too.

The taskmaster stomped toward them. "Bash good!" he bellowed in Grappa's ear. His voice was so loud that it even hurt Grisham's ears, several feet away.

The ogre watched Grappa a moment more, then reached out and lifted the teen's limp arm.

Grappa screamed in pain.

The ogre responded by slamming the boy's head against the wall.

For a moment, silence fell across the cavern like a shroud. Then the ogre stomped his foot and shouted, "Bash!"

Everyone immediately went back to work, trying to ignore

the human slavers disconnecting Grappa from the chain and dragging him off to the megapedes.

After Grappa's death, the slaves grumbled more frequently about escape. Grisham wanted to escape no less than anyone else, but despite his Ta'ah roots and his familiarity with underground passages, he was utterly lost down in these mines. They'd taken too many turns and had passed through too many tunnels that all looked exactly the same. Even if he and the other slaves could escape the chains, they'd never escape the mines themselves.

Nicholas agreed with him, except for one part. "Grisham, if you ever get a chance to escape, don't worry about anyone else. Take that chance. If anyone can do it, it's a 'dorf.'" He chuckled. He'd been calling Grisham that lately in mockery of the ogre. "Besides, most of us are resigned to dying down here. I've been here so long I barely remember any other way to live. You don't deserve that fate. Promise me, if you find a chance, you'll take it."

Grisham promised. "What's the penalty if you're caught escaping?"

Nicholas shrugged. "I don't know. Megapedes, probably. You never know, they might just stick you back on the chain and it wouldn't matter at all."

Only two days after that discussion, Grisham thought he might have the chance to find the answer to his question. When the ogre departed after the evening meal, there was a commotion at the far end of the chain, and one of the slaves raised his pick and smashed it down on the chain that bound him. It took a few blows, but he snapped through it, then scrambled away and disappeared into the passages, hopefully to his freedom.

Nicholas sighed and bowed his head in prayer. "May luck guide your feet."

Grisham laid his head on the ground and he too hoped for the escapee's welfare. As his eyes closed, he wondered whether he would ever find the courage to do such a thing.

Grisham was woken by the bellow of the ogre. "Wake! Move!"

He and the rest of the slaves scrambled to follow the ogre's directions. As the ogre herded them out of the cavern, Grisham couldn't help but wonder why.

Did the ogre even notice the missing slave? Or the broken chain?

Was it that easy?

As they moved in a line through various passages, Grisham heard the sound of screaming as if someone was being tortured. He hoped that poor soul wasn't the missing slave. Maybe it wasn't that easy after all.

Eventually they passed through a tremendous arched entrance guarded by two other ogres and stepped into a cavern vastly different from all the others.

At its center was a giant rectangular building, thirty feet high, maybe sixty feet wide and long, constructed of white stone. Dwarven construction, Grisham thought. Along the front of the building stood a series of pillars etched in runes that Grisham couldn't read, and the two huge doors between the pillars had no handles.

Statues stood throughout the rest of the cavern: dwarves, elves, humans, ogres, giants, even one statue of a snake. But Grisham noticed that only females were represented; there was not one male among them—though he wasn't sure about the snake.

All in all, the cavern felt like a place of worship. A temple of sorts.

Their ogre escort knelt and growled, "Down!"

Grisham knelt, and so did everyone else.

A cracking sound erupted from the white building, and purple flames briefly painted the edges of the doorframe. The doors opened, and chanting drifted from inside the building as a woman appeared in the opening and walked forward gracefully. The woman's movement reminded Grisham of a snake.

Beside him, Nicholas mumbled a prayer.

Grisham was struck by how brightly the woman's aura shone. Brightness correlated with life force, and this woman's aura was like a beacon of light, outshining that of anyone he'd ever seen, with the exception of that cursed wizard Azazel.

He suddenly realized that the other slaves had all bent down with their foreheads pressed to the floor, whereas he'd been on his knees staring at her the entire time. The woman noticed and smiled.

Then her melodious voice broke through the chanting. "Rise. Let me look at all of you."

They stood, and the woman approached. Her hair was so dark that it seemed to shimmer purple where the torchlight reflected off it. Her pale skin, too, shone with an otherworldly radiance. And then he saw the pointed ears, and he recognized her for what she was.

This was a priestess of Lilith.

His father had long ago warned him of the influence that the worshippers of Lilith had on unwary men, and Seder's words came back to him very clearly.

"Avoid the influence of Lilith."

Her silken robes hugged the curves of her body, and those curves weren't lost on some of the other slaves. Attached to her waist was a flail with writhing snakes emerging from its handle. As she approached the line of slaves, the snakes reached out with flickering tongues as if to sniff the objects of the priestess's attention.

She walked slowly down the line of slaves, inspecting each slave she passed. When she reached a teenaged boy, she paused, smiled, and caressed the boy's cheek.

Grisham blinked and rubbed his eyes. He was positive that the teenager's aura had diminished in brightness after she touched him, while hers had gotten slightly brighter. Had she… stolen some of his life force?

The priestess continued down the line, assessing each slave. But when she reached Grisham, to his horror, she stopped and faced him directly.

She cocked her head and looked amused. "Ata Ta'ah?"

She spoke in the old language. *Are you a Ta'ah?*

Grisham bowed his head and responded in kind. "Ken, ani Ta'ah."

Yes, I'm a Ta'ah.

She flashed the fangs he'd known were hiding behind her lips. Then she continued down the line.

This woman immediately recognized me as Ta'ah. How could that be?

When she'd examined all the slaves, she returned to the entrance of the building and nodded to someone behind the slaves.

A human was dragged into the cavern, groaning and screaming. As he was pulled past the line of slaves, they all saw who it was.

The slave who'd tried to escape.

He was bloodied and beaten. Worst of all, he was caught. And now, it was clear, he would be made an example to the rest of them.

The two slavers held the captive in front of the elf priestess. She caressed his bloodstained cheek, and this time Grisham was sure of what he saw: a distinct dimming of the man's aura while hers grew ever brighter. She continued her caress until the man's mouth fell open, a vacant expression on his face, his eyes staring blankly at the priestess.

The priestess leaned in. She tilted her head and exposed her fangs. She sniffed deeply at his neck. And then she clamped down, violently ripping out a chunk of his exposed neck.

Grisham fought to control his nausea. He knew what the others didn't: that that man was dead before she bit into him. The bite was for show. It wasn't the bite that killed him, nor the caress. It was that deep sniff. When she sniffed at his neck, she drained whatever remained of the slave's life essence from him.

If she could do that, what *couldn't* she do?

When the day ended, Nicholas and Grisham lay on their sides and whispered about the earlier events.

The grizzled soldier murmured, "I've never been as scared as I was today, when we knelt in front of that priestess. Her power... and all those female statues... I suspect that if she wanted to, she could simply suck the soul out of any man she wanted."

Grisham nodded. *He doesn't know how true that is.*

"Did you hear what happened to Gregor?"

"Is that the guy who ran away?"

"No. That's the boy the priestess touched. He hasn't spoken a word since."

"What's wrong with him?"

Nicholas shrugged. "Stole his soul?"

Again, Nicholas's guesses were close to truth.

"I was worried we were all going to be fed to the megapedes for what the escapee did," Grisham said.

Nicholas yawned. "Me too. Though I'll tell you this. I think I'd rather face a ravenous megapede than to have that woman lay eyes on me again."

As they lay down to sleep, Grisham decided he agreed. There were fates worse than death.

That night, he dreamt of the megapede pit.

. . .

He floats above the scene, an energy crackling within him. Below him, slavers are feeding what's left of the escapee into the pit. Grisham floats forward so he can see down into its depths, and for the first time in his life, he sees with his own eyes what a real megapede looks like.

It's terrifying.

They are like unimaginably large centipedes, with green-hued interlocking bony armor, six black eyes, and monstrous front mandibles. Against his will, Grisham floats downward, closer, closer, until he can see every detail of the beasts. What they look like. What they sound like. What they smell like.

He is practically on top of them now, and he feels a sharp pain at his neck, and he tries to scream but cannot—

Grisham found his voice as he woke from his slumber with a start.

He screamed.

A shooting pain ran down his back, but as he stretched, still shaking loose the cobwebs, he felt a soothing pop and breathed a sigh of relief.

He looked around and was shocked to see that the rest of the slaves had backed as far away from him as the chains allowed, and were staring at him with wide eyes. They were afraid.

Of me?

He stood, only to realize with a gasp that he was dragging no chain. He looked down and saw his collar at his feet, snapped in half, the chain still attached. Something had happened to his clothes, too. His shirt's seams were stretched almost to bursting, and his pants were torn in strips.

What had happened? Who had severed his collar, and why? What was everyone so afraid of? He'd simply been sleeping, dreaming about the megapedes...

His eyes found Nicholas. He stood closer than the rest, and his expression wasn't one of fear, but of concern.

"Nicholas?" he said. "What's going on? How...?" He gestured down at the broken collar.

Nicholas frowned. "You don't know?"

"Know what? Please, tell me."

Nicholas came forward and touched Grisham's shoulder. "Grisham, I swear on the life of my poor children that what I tell you is true. I was asleep, when I was awoken by a strange sound. I looked over to your spot on the chain, and instead of you lying there, I saw a young megapede making chittering noises. I shouted in alarm, waking the others. We all watched as the megapede bit down on the collar it wore, snapping it easily in two. Then it began to... dissolve... and you were there again."

Grisham stood stunned. *I dreamed of a megapede, and then...*

He did feel different. Like ice was running through his veins. And a crackling feeling, like... like he wanted to explode. He remembered Seder's words.

"I have unlatched powers that were hidden deep within you."

He opened his eyes again and looked at his friend, who was clearly worried for him. "Nicholas, I'm going to escape."

"Yes." Nicholas smiled. "I know you are. And you're going to succeed, my young friend."

"And I want you to escape with me," Grisham said.

The grizzled man shook his head. "Thank you, Grisham, but no. I would only slow you down. A dwarf might have a chance of finding a way through these tunnels. An old man like me..." He shook his head. "And I have no desire to face that priestess again. This is *your* chance. You promised me you would seize it."

Grisham smiled widely. "What if I assure you that I know the way out?"

Nicholas's eyes widened. He narrowed his eyes for a moment, then nodded slowly.

Grisham looked at the others. "What about the rest of you? If I could get all of you freed from your chains, would you leave with me?"

Almost all the slaves nodded.

Grisham took a deep breath. "Okay. I'm going to get us all out of here. But first, I need a promise. That what you've seen me do, and what you *will* see me do... it'll remain a secret between us."

Nicholas turned to the other slaves. "Are we all agreed?"

One of the men laughed. "Of course. Who would ever believe what we just witnessed? I don't even believe it myself, and I saw it with my own eyes."

The other slaves also nodded assent.

"Good," said Grisham. "First, I'm going to break the main slave chain, then you all can slip yourself off. You'll still have the collars around your necks, but you'll be free."

He closed his eyes and reached for the new power that had been unlocked within him. He brought back the image of the megapedes in the pit, recalling every detail, and as he did, a strange sensation surged through him.

His chest cracked. Pain wracked his body. He was changing.

He opened his eyes again, only to be struck by a wave of nausea. Six images assaulted him at once. He had to concentrate on coordinating his six eyes so they could focus on a single object.

The slaves had all scrambled away again. But the main chain lay in front of them.

Grisham crawled toward it on uncoordinated legs. The main chain was thick, thicker than a muscular human's forearm, but it was no match for a megapede's jaws. Grisham bit it cleanly in two.

"We are free," said one of the humans. The voice was familiar, but Grisham couldn't remember the man's name. "Time to go up, Grisham."

Grisham was having trouble thinking clearly, but that cue helped.

He took a tentative bite of the wall nearest him. The rock crumbled away easily. He bit again. His jaws were so powerful, it required almost no effort whatsoever. Soon he found himself tunneling as quickly as his feet could clumsily carry him.

He remembered to angle upwards as he tunneled. Slowly, he began to feel more at ease in this body. His dozens of feet gripped their way up the slope he created, and pebbles tumbled down the newly formed passage behind him. He couldn't remember why he was going up, but he knew it was important. Bite. Tunnel. Move upward. That was all that mattered for now.

He heard creatures scrambling along behind him, struggling

through the cascade of loose scree he left behind. He ignored them. Normally he would have attacked them, but somehow he knew that there was no need. That creating the tunnel, that going up, these things were more important.

The taste of the rock changed after a time. He'd moved from the bedrock he loved to upper rock that tasted bitter and wet. And then he was biting through nothing but disgusting worm-infested soil. He nearly gagged at the taste, and then he broke through the surface and was blinded by the brightest light his eyes had ever seen.

MASTERING MY GIFTS

It seemed like every time Arabelle woke, her joints were stiffer. Sometimes she worried that the poison was getting stronger, that Castien's exercises weren't enough to completely drive it back each time. But once she got her blood flowing, loosened her limbs, and truly built up a sweat, she always felt one hundred percent herself again.

It had been nearly six months since her encounter with the dragon, and Arabelle couldn't wait until the caravan arrived once again at Aubgherle. She wanted to show Castien what she'd achieved, how she'd changed. She was fit, strong, energetic. Tabor was complimenting her reflexes, her speed and agility, and her father even claimed that she was looking happier than he'd ever seen her.

Now, as she lay on the ground, lifting her bare legs into the air and pointing her toes up and down, she studied her muscles.

Her flexing motions no longer showed every fiber like they used to; she'd managed to smooth out some of the ripples.

She was less satisfied with her arms. When she squeezed her fists she could see the new muscles in her arms tense, even though her arms were strong, they still seemed much too thin.

She reached under her mattress and pulled out the mirror she'd hidden there. It was ridiculous that she had to keep her mirror a secret, but her father didn't approve of them—he said they were the tool of vain women and served no useful purpose. Arabelle wasn't vain; she was simply curious about what others saw that she couldn't normally see herself.

And yes, she liked what she saw. Was that so wrong? Her reflection looked back at her with full lips, dark-brown eyes, and rounded cheeks. It was her face, the only one she would ever have, and she liked it. Especially because her father and Tabor said she looked exactly like her mother. She could almost feel a spiritual connection to her mother when she looked at her reflection. For a fleeting moment, she thought she saw a grown woman instead of the young daughter of a Sheikh.

Arabelle tucked the mirror back under the mattress as Maggie entered to prepare her morning bath.

Soon Arabelle was soaking in steaming water, the warmth penetrating her tired muscles. Baths felt so much better after a hard workout.

Maggie brushed Arabelle's hair. "Milady, why don't you like having scents in your bathwater anymore?"

Arabelle stretched her neck and felt a comforting pop. "Because if I need to stalk someone with the intent of spying on them or even killing them, I don't want any unusual scents to give away my presence."

Maggie laughed. "Fine. You needn't tell me. A princess can keep her secrets."

Arabelle kept her eyes closed and smiled. Her life had changed in so many unexpected ways that even her closest companion couldn't believe the truth.

She thought once more of the blue-eyed boy who was still somehow hovering above her tent. Silently she wondered whether he might fly down to meet her.

It was midday, and the caravan had set up near a group of villages on the western edge of the Trimorian valley. A breeze from the northwest carried the sounds of villagers haggling with vendors, and the sounds helped mask the creak of the wooden roof Arabelle rested upon.

Her heart was beating rapidly. Her adversary was dangerous, and she would have to employ all her skills in order to defeat him.

She spotted him, but held her crouching position, preparing herself to leap at just the right moment. When he came within reach, she sprang at him soundlessly.

Tabor merely stepped nimbly to one side and stuck both fingers out in defense.

Arabelle groaned and rolled to her feet. "What did I do wrong this time?"

Tabor smiled at her proudly. "Let's talk about what you did correctly first. It's a much longer list."

She blushed, despite her frustration. "Fine."

They began to walk back toward her tent.

"When you started following me," Tabor began, "I purposely walked through a crowd so that you would lose track of me. For a long while, I couldn't see you. Only minutes ago did I spot you watching me. Do you realize what that means, Princess? It means you managed to make me think you had lost track of me, when in fact it was *I* who had lost track of *you*. That is a very difficult thing."

Arabelle's blush deepened.

"And another thing. Your movement in the shadows was impressive. I'm not sure how you managed it, but you were practically invisible, blending into your surroundings as deftly as an elf."

She laughed out loud. *Thank you, Castien.*

"Now, as to what you did wrong…"

Arabelle braced herself.

"You didn't pay attention to the light, Princess. Whether it's sunlight, moonlight, or a torch, light casts shadows, and shadows can give your position away."

Arabelle smacked herself on the forehead. "How stupid of me. The sun was behind me and you saw my shadow as you passed underneath me."

Tabor winked. "Like I said before, if you weren't our princess, you would make a very fine soldier." He frowned. "No —you are too smart for a common soldier. You would be an officer."

"An officer who will never make that mistake again."

Tabor chuckled. "Of that I'm sure."

They arrived at her tent, and Tabor checked the inside before opening the flap for her to enter.

"Tabor, can you make sure nobody disturbs me until it's time for supper? I would like to rest."

Tabor nodded. "As you wish, Princess. Have a good afternoon's nap."

Arabelle wore the veiled headwrap that Maggie had given her as she ground a large handful of red-threaded *Tishkakh* leaves in her mortar, following the instructions in the book Castien had given her. The dried leaves turned into sand-like particles, and then a fine powder. She poured the powder into a silk bag.

She then moved on to a different kind of leaf, and took the same approach, with slight modifications suggested by Castien's book. She filled another bag with a potent powder and pulled the drawstring to cinch it closed.

Maggie had woven her a belt to which all these bags could be attached. The handmaiden had also modified Arabelle's clothes by adding hidden pockets for small items and inserting invisible slits that would allow the princess to instantly reach her mother's daggers, which were strapped to each thigh. Maggie made it clear that she felt the princess was inviting danger by arming herself so, but at the same time, she did get wrapped up in the excitement of it all. Arabelle knew she would be lost without her friend's help.

When Arabelle had ground the next set of leaves, she took a wooden straw, acquired from Madam Mizmer, and stuffed a tiny piece of cotton into one end. To test the device, she lifted her veil, put the straw to her lips and blew as hard as she could.

The plug of cotton flew out the other end of the straw.

She smiled as she collected another wad of cotton and plugged the end of the straw once more. This time she dribbled her freshly powdered leaves into the open end and sealed it with beeswax.

When she had filled her pouches and straws with potent powders that caused all manner of pleasant and unpleasant effects, she leaned back and surveyed her handiwork with satisfaction.

For the first time, she began to feel like she was nearly prepared to face whatever her destiny placed in her way.

Arabelle was in Madam Mizmer's stall, working on a stew. The princess had asked for permission to try out what she called "my own recipes," and although the look on the motherly cook's face suggested a lack of confidence that any of these recipes would be edible, she had set aside a charcoal grill specifically for Arabelle's use.

At the moment, Arabelle shared the woman's doubt. As she stirred her pot and smelled the steam rising from it, she felt a combination of revulsion and panic.

Alexandra came up behind her. "What, uh... what did you put in it, Princess?" she asked politely.

"Well," said Arabelle, "I like pickled onions and raspberries, so I started with those and then just… added some other things."

Alexandra smiled uncomfortably. "Well, you've certainly created something unique."

"'Unique' is a polite way of saying horrible."

Alexandra shook her head quickly. "Oh, no, sometimes you can't predict such things. When will it be done?"

Arabelle took a whiff of the brewing concoction—and cringed. "I think it needs more time. I'll just continue stirring a while."

At that moment Zoe came running into the stall. "Slavers! Uh, slaves!" She was panting for breath. "They escaped!"

Arabelle knelt in front of her. "Zoe, calm down and take a breath. What are you trying to say?"

Zoe breathed deeply several times, but still she babbled with wide-eyed excitement. "A bunch of slaves escaped from slavers and one of our scouting parties found them and brought them in. One of them is a baby dwarf with a teeny-tiny beard!"

"I would like to see that," said the princess. "Can you take me there?"

Zoe jumped up and down. "Of course, Princess!"

Arabelle looked at Alexandra, then glanced at her stew. "Could you, uh…"

Alexandra nodded. "You know what I think? I think it might get better if we take it off the grill. Perhaps it just needs to cool."

"Yes," said Arabelle. "Thank you, Alexandra, I think that's a wonderful idea."

Secretly she hoped that when she returned, the stew would be nowhere to be found.

The slaves were a ragtag group, emaciated, dressed in torn rags. They were being served soldiers' rations, which they devoured as if they hadn't eaten in years. Tabor was with them, talking with a dwarf and a grizzled old man.

"The tunnel we found led us into the woods," said the man, "and luckily my sense of the seasons and recollection of the caravan's schedule helped us stumble in the right direction."

Tabor scratched his beard. "It's an amazing story. I've rarely heard of a slave escaping, and certainly not in a large group like this. Wasn't the exit to the mines guarded?"

The grizzled man and the dwarf looked at each other for an instant before the man replied. "As I said, our taskmaster left us unsupervised with our tools during rest periods. I suppose they were confident we would never find our way through the maze. Luckily we had Grisham here." The man patted the little dwarf on the shoulder. "He felt air movement and followed it to a ventilation hole—perhaps long-forgotten or even naturally occurring. We knew the ogre couldn't fit into it, and we rarely even saw a human slaver, so I was confident they knew not of it. So we decided to use our pickaxes to break our chain, and we climbed the shaft, and here we are."

Arabelle shivered. How terrifying it must have been to be trapped deep underground for days on end, with almost no hope of escape.

Tabor examined the slave collar still clamped around the man's neck. As he rotated it a bit, the man winced. His skin was raw beneath the metal.

Tabor turned to one of his soldiers. "Get the blacksmith. I want the collars off these men now."

The grizzled slave was suddenly overwhelmed with emotion. "Bless you, sir. Bless you." He actually grabbed Tabor's hand and kissed the back of it—much to Tabor's obvious discomfort.

Tabor knelt down to face the dwarf eye to eye. "And why do you not have a collar?" he asked.

The man opened his mouth to answer, but Tabor raised his hand for silence, insisting on a response from the dwarf.

The dwarf shrugged. "I was lucky. When my slave collar was first clamped on, I heard a crack. I knew that sound from my father's smithy—it's the sound that fatigued iron gives when bent or strained beyond the metal's capacity. I actually feared that the metal might break one day, and that I would be punished for it. But when the time came to escape, I took advantage. A simple tap of a hammer at just the right spot, and the metal shattered."

Arabelle had little experience with dwarfs, but this one seemed very cautious in his words and mannerisms. Perhaps he was simply scared and tired, though she got the impression he wasn't one to feel sorry for himself. Clearly he was a hardened survivor. All these men were.

Tabor stood to address all of the former slaves. "Men, please accept my sympathy for the trials you've unjustly endured. I congratulate you on your fortitude and bravery in escaping these foul slavers. For now you will stay here with us, and we will ensure that you are fed and clothed.

"However, I cannot yet let you walk freely throughout the caravan. I will talk to each one of you individually, and if I am satisfied with your story, I will consult with our leader and make arrangements for you. If I am *not* satisfied with your story, you will be deposited with the Protector of the next town we stop in, and you will be their concern."

The former slaves nodded in appreciation and expressed their gratitude.

"In the meantime," said Tabor with a small smile, "eat up. I've never seen anyone take such pleasure in consuming soldiers' rations."

As Arabelle stirred her next batch of stew, she sniffed it warily. This time Alexandra was teaching her one of Madam Mizmer's recipe, but she was still afraid that somehow she'd produce something less than edible.

"Princess," said Alexandra, "trust me. I know you dislike raw onions, but when they're browned, they change flavors and will enhance the stew."

"What about the celery?" Arabelle asked. "I can't imagine their flavor ever being palatable no matter what you do to them. I hate celery."

Alexandra laughed. "That's why I didn't have you chop it fine. We will take out the chunks after it's done its job. Your stew will be the better for it."

Arabelle frowned at the simmering kettle. "I'd rather eat mealworms than celery."

"Then we will have to try that next time."

Arabelle looked at her friend in shock.

Alexandra laughed. "I'm just teasing you, Princess. Just stick close to my mother's recipe. It will turn out better than your first batch."

Arabelle crinkled her nose. Even mealworm stew would have turned out better than her first batch.

Tabor stepped into the tent and sniffed the air. "Anything available for me to try?"

"Princess, shall we give him some of your first stew?" Alexandra asked mischievously.

Arabelle turned to her aghast. "I thought Zoe took that to feed the sheep."

"She did, but they wouldn't eat it."

Tabor chuckled. "Maybe I'm sorry I asked."

Arabelle gave Tabor her best glare. "*That* remark has just earned you the role of taste-tester. Grab a bowl."

Tabor looked into the kettle nervously. But he picked up a wooden bowl and handed it to her. "I am your willing subject."

She ladled out a bowlful and even garnished it with some slivers of spring onion like she'd seen Madam Mizmer do. As she handed it to Tabor, she watched his reaction closely.

He sniffed the bowl, picked up a spoon, and took a very tentative sample. His stone-like expression betrayed no emotion.

But then he went for a second spoonful.

That means at least he didn't despise it!

After several spoonfuls, Arabelle grew impatient.

"Well? What do you think?"

Tabor gingerly wiped his lips and gave a burp of satisfaction. "It could use more celery."

Alexandra laughed. "Ha! I told you."

Arabelle shot her a sideways look.

Tabor scooped up the last of his bowl and stood. "Don't worry, Princess. I promise that your future husband will grow fat on a stew such as that. Just add celery to it, it would give it some fiber, which is good for everyone."

Arabelle felt herself warm with pride. She was an actual cook, who had made an actual stew... that tasted good? She was suddenly eager to serve this stew to as many people as possible.

A thought struck her, and she looked up at Tabor. "Do you think I could feed this to the escaped slaves?" She remembered how much they'd appreciated cold rations, but men who'd been through such hardships deserved a hot meal.

Tabor smiled, and Arabelle almost thought she saw his eyes glisten with moisture. "My dear princess, that is a very kind gesture. Your mother would be proud." He looked into the pot. "However, you hardly have enough here for more than a serving or two."

Arabelle frowned. That was true. "Perhaps I could bring some to the dwarf child? He seemed so out of place with the rest of the slaves, and we have almost no other dwarfs in the caravan. He's practically all alone."

Tabor nodded his approval. "Yes, he's very different than the rest. I've spoken with him, and he's led a tragic life. I can only pray things improve for him from now on."

Arabelle began ladling her stew into a smaller container. "Then perhaps my stew will be a good start!"

As Arabelle entered the tent where the young dwarf had been put up, she found he wasn't alone. The soldier, Oda, was there.

"Just remember," Oda was saying, "us dwarfs be takin' care of our own. Never let it be said Oda Rockfist didn't lend a hand to a fellow dwarf, even a clanless one. When yer ready, we can talk further."

Arabelle cleared her throat. "Am I interrupting?"

Oda turned, and his eyes widened at the sight of the princess. He bowed quickly and deeply. "Never could you be interruptin', Princess. I was just checkin' in on the lad here, but I'm sure he would prefer your gracious company."

And with that, he hurried out.

"I didn't mean to make him run off."

The young dwarf looked up at her. He was so small. Oda made up for his size with muscles and a blustering personality, but this dwarf was even shorter than Oda, plus he was shy and very underfed.

"It's okay. He was already leaving when you arrived... Princess?"

Arabelle groaned at the use of her title. "I wish you hadn't heard him say that. Please, call me Arabelle. I'm the daughter of the Sheikh, but honestly it would be nice if someone around here didn't know that."

The dwarf smiled. "I'll gladly pretend otherwise if you like, Arabelle. But first let me say how grateful I am to you and your caravan for taking care of us in in our time of need."

Arabelle saw volumes of pain behind his sad brown eyes. She had to resist an intense urge to reach out and hug him. Instead she sat down before him and handed him the small kettle and a spoon.

"I cooked you something. Please eat it. You look hungry."

She was afraid the dwarf would be reluctant to eat in front of her, but he started shoveling the stew into his mouth without even looking to see what it was. She watched with amusement—and no small bit of pride, even though she knew he probably wasn't even bothering to taste anything, he ate so quickly. Her only regret was that she hadn't cooked more.

When the dwarf had scraped the kettle for the last remnants, Arabelle asked, "Did you enjoy it?"

"This is by far the best meal I've ever had, Miss Arabelle."

Arabelle's heart swelled. "Just Arabelle, please. And I'm afraid I don't know your name."

"I'm Grisham. I have no clan, like you heard Oda say. I'm an orphan."

"Some might care about clans, but I don't. So... you really liked the stew? I'm only just now learning to cook, and you're my second test subject."

Grisham laughed. "To tell you the truth, I wouldn't put much value on my opinion. In the mines, we ate nothing but a terrible pasty gruel, and in the orphanage in Cammoria, we mostly ate porridge. It was a treat when we had some rabbit or fowl."

Arabelle felt her heart breaking for this poor little dwarf. Tears came unbidden and she wiped them away.

"I'm sorry if I upset you," Grisham said.

"No, no, it's nothing you've done. Thank you for your honest opinion about my cooking. At least you didn't say it needed celery."

"No, I wouldn't do that. I'm not partial to celery."

She laughed. "Nor am I. So, Grisham, what are your plans now that you're free, if I may ask?"

Grisham held up a leather coin purse. "Tabor kindly gave us each an allowance to buy clothes and supplies. We are allowed to eat with the soldiers each day. Again, the kindness of your people is a blessing. More kindness than I've received since..." He paused, as if revisiting a painful memory, then finished simply, "More kindness than I deserve."

"I'm certain you've received far less than you deserve prior to your arrival here, so I would hope that we do what we can to right the scales."

"Thank you, Miss—Thank you, Arabelle."

"And after you're back on your feet? What then?"

The dwarf shrugged. "Oda offered to have me on as his apprentice."

"Is that what you want?"

"I'm not really sure. In recent years... I suppose I stopped thinking about what I might be when I get older."

Arabelle could see that this young dwarf was at a crossroads in his life. "My father always told me to be open-minded and to consider all your choices. And if you're still unsure, try some things on to see if they fit. This is as true for your vocation as it is for your clothes. You can't know what will suit you until you try."

Grisham nodded. "Your advice sounds like something my father once gave me."

Arabelle knew better than to ask about his father. He'd said he was an orphan, and she didn't want to dredge up painful memories.

"May I ask how old you are, Grisham?"

Grisham stuck out his chest. "I am midway between twelve and thirteen. And you, Arabelle?"

"I'm seventeen."

They were interrupted by Tabor poking his head into the tent. "Princess, it's growing late. You are due to dine with your father." With a fluttering of the tent's flap, he disappeared.

"It would seem I have been summoned," Arabelle said wryly. She stood, and Grisham stood with her. On an impulse, she wrapped him in a hug, and after a moment, he returned it.

She stepped back. "If you get sick of soldiers' rations, I can always bring you more of my stew."

"That would be nice, but don't trouble yourself on my account." He winked and grinned. "And if you do... I'm not against food lacking in celery."

Arabelle was now confident in her abilities to hide in the shadows and to move without noise, and she felt certain that she could travel most places without being noticed. Now she was determined to test that confidence in the midst of a crowd.

It was evening, and she was dressed in her dark-gray outfit with wraparound headdress and veil. As always when she was intent on stealth, she'd abandoned her slippers for bare feet. She stood in the shadows of the marketplace, keeping an eye on her target. She'd selected him randomly, and watched with amusement as he haggled with a toy merchant over a puppet.

Some child is going to be happy soon.

She was pleased with her success at staying perfectly still and blending in with her background. Many had passed by the spot where she crouched, but none had so much as given her a second glance.

And then she felt a tap on her shoulder.

"Why are you hiding here, Princess?"

She jumped and spun, only to find the smiling face of Grisham looking up at her. Fortunately, no one else was paying attention to this shadow-filled corner.

"Grisham! I told you to call me Arabelle."

Grisham shook his head. "Not in public. I made that mistake in the soldiers' mess hall. Someone joked how this was an improvement over what I had eaten as a slave, and I told them about 'Arabelle's stew.' The soldiers got really angry with me before deciding I probably had no idea who you were. I didn't correct them, but I think it's best that you are called Princess by the likes of me. At least anywhere someone can hear."

She grabbed Grisham by the arm and pulled him deeper into the shadows. "How did you see me back here? And how did you know it was me?"

He looked confused. "What do you mean? I noticed the torchlight reflecting off your eyes." He hesitated, seeming uncomfortable.

Is he blushing?

"Your eyes are... well, they're very kind and always darting about, looking for things. And I also saw the whites of your feet. It wasn't hard to spot you from across the market."

"You weren't even close by when you saw me?"

"No, but then again, I do have a unique perspective. At my height, I had a clear line of sight to someone crouching like you were. Do I take it you did not wish to be seen?"

She put a finger to her lips. "Please keep this a secret, but I've been practicing being invisible in public places. You'd be surprised what people say when they don't think anyone is listening."

"Well, you were doing very well, if you want my opinion. You move like a shadow. But your feet and eyes..." He shrugged.

Arabelle looked down at her feet. "Well, I can do something about my feet, but unless I go around with my eyes closed, I'm not sure what I can do about my eyes."

"Maybe squinting would help?"

She laughed. "I'll try that next time."

"And perhaps I will look for you, Princess."

She grinned. "Does that mean you'll be staying with the caravan for a while?"

Grisham nodded. "I decided to do as you suggested. I'll 'try on' being Oda's apprentice and see how the life of a soldier fits me."

"That's great to hear. But that reminds me. There's one particular soldier who's awaiting my return."

"Would that be Tabor?"

"So you've noticed he's my escort. An impatient one, too. I'd better get back to him."

Grisham bowed. "As you wish, Princess Arabelle."

She laughed, hit Grisham playfully on the shoulder, and headed back to the women's clothing tent where she'd left Tabor. But as she snuck away, she noticed a black-armored soldier peer into the alleyway suspiciously.

SEEKING ELVES

Not for the first time, Kirag wished his mother's visions had been more specific. She had said that the elves were trouble, but had not said whether the strangers were elves, were hidden among the elves, were assisted by the elves, or some other possibility altogether. And even finding the elves meant searching many miles of woods. Regardless, he would find them. And then he would question them.

He had selected a Duo of Talons to accompany him on this mission: Vaughn and Zandri. They were good soldiers who did their jobs without asking a lot of questions. Together they hiked the woods, traveling at night and resting during the day. But eventually their curiosity got the best of them. On the third day, the inevitable questions began.

"Sir," said Vaughn, "are we certain that we know what to look for? My ma always told me tales of elves, but nobody I've ever known had seen a hint of one. How do we know they look like what the tales describe?"

Kirag knew what the soldier was truly asking. He was doubting whether elves even existed at all.

He sneered. "I assure you that elves do in fact exist, and that they look just as the tales describe." He recalled the shimmering image of the elf he'd seen appear in his master's throne room. But now he wanted to see one of these creatures face-to-face— and see whether the tales of their preternatural fighting skills held true.

"Why do they hide?" asked Zandri, taking advantage of the opportunity to question their leader. "Why not present them- selves like normal people?"

Kirag grew impatient. "It's said that in the time before the great barrier, elves lived among humans. But Azazel has told me himself that the elves had something to do with the coming of the demons."

"Then it is no wonder they now hide," Zandri growled.

Kirag raised a finger in warning. "Just because one hides doesn't mean they lack claws. And we are in their domain. Keep your wits about you."

He lay on the ground. "No more questions. We depart four hours after midday and continue through dawn. We have a long march ahead of us."

The Talons prepared their camouflage, and Kirag closed his eyes. As he drifted off to sleep, he was wondering if elves' blood ran red.

Kirag knelt at the edge of a cliff overlooking a section of forest that had long been rumored to be the home of ghosts and other mystical creatures. But Azazel had told him that centuries ago, the elves had made this very forest their home.

He breathed in deeply, detecting a scent he couldn't identify. It was of a living creature, but unlike the coppery smell of humans and animals or the brimstone smell of Azazel. It was musky.

Could this be the scent of elves?

Even if it was, the forest below him was expansive. Searching it would take days, even if they split up. And he wasn't sure he trusted his men to—

A tiny wisp of smoke rose from deep in the forest.

Kirag smiled and beckoned his men forward.

"Could that be the location of the elven city?" Vaughn asked once his leader had pointed out the thin streamer of smoke.

"It's likely. I can feel the presence of something unnatural living within these woods."

"But how are we to reach it?" Zandri asked. Elves are said to be clever with the ways of the forest, disguising their paths so naturally that a human could search for hours and only find himself walking in circles."

Kirag studied the trees. The Talon was right: the elves' paths would be well hidden. But from this elevated spot, he was able to spot indentations that hinted at trails he would never have found at ground level. Whether these paths were made by deer or elves did not matter—they were trails that could be followed. Together they formed a maze, and yet every maze could successfully be traversed, especially with a bird's-eye view.

He turned to his Duo. "I will guide your movements from here. Go back down the trail and loop around to the edge of the forest. Keep me in sight, and I will use hand signals to direct you forward. When you lose sight of me, climb up a tree. Do not go far without my guidance, or you will become hopelessly lost."

"How will you follow?" Vaughn asked.

Kirag sneered at the man's idiocy. Had he not need of these men, he might even have killed him on the spot. "You'll be marking the trail as you go along, you fool! Now go!"

The Duo scrambled down the steep path, eager to escape Kirag's anger.

Soon they had circled the precipice and appeared below, looking up at Kirag. He pointed them in the direction they needed to go.

Guiding his men was an arduous process that tested Kirag's patience—especially when they wandered off the paths he had directed them towards, which happened often. But in time, they approached the target he had chosen: a clearing near the location where the wisp of smoke had arisen.

His men had disappeared into the trees and Kirag was awaiting their next appearance when an arrow whooshed past his ear. He threw himself to the ground and scanned his surroundings, but saw nothing. He drew his sword and dagger and sniffed the air. The musky smell had indeed grown stronger.

Then two things happened at once. A commotion arose from the location of his Duo; and two human-sized, yellow-haired men with pointed ears materialized from the trees around Kirag. Kirag cared not for what happened to his men. He'd found the elves he'd been looking for.

Both held bows trained on him, steely looks of concentration on their faces. But they had approached from the steep trail, and with Kirag crouched down, they'd had to come in close in order to line up their shots. Which meant Kirag would have an opportunity.

"Drop your weapons, half-breed," said one.

Kirag's vision turned red.

How many people have I killed for calling me such?

But he had to maintain control. He needed to question these brown-skinned creatures.

He rose to his feet and took a step forward.

One of the elves let loose his arrow. It hit the ground between Kirag's legs. "Last warning."

Kirag took another step forward. "Drop *your* weapons, cowards of the woods."

Both elves fired their arrows, but Kirag was already moving. One arrow caught his left shoulder, yet did nothing to blunt his charge, and he plowed right into the nearest attacker. The elf's bones crunched beneath his weight.

The other elf switched to a glittering sword, which he swung at Kirag's back.

Coward!

Kirag blocked the miserable attack with his dagger and swung his sword at the elf's knees. He intended to disable him, not kill him.

The elf nimbly jumped away and backpedaled to gain some distance.

Kirag growled and ran toward the devious creature. The pain

in his left shoulder reminded him that he would much rather fight with swords than dodge arrows.

The elf drew a second sword and moved both in a blur. One of the swords darted out and nearly skewered Kirag, but he dodged in time and readied himself for an opening.

The elf attacked again, precisely targeting Kirag's injured shoulder. Again Kirag dodged, and this time he countered with his dagger. Spatters of blood appeared within the blur of glittering swords.

So they do *bleed red!*

Kirag again studied the elf's movements. They were impossibly fast, but he was able to follow both swords if he concentrated. Unfortunately, he saw no openings. The elf was skilled with the blades.

His impatience and battle lust overcame his good sense, and his vision flared red with anger. He charged directly at the elf, swinging his own sword with all his might.

The metallic crash of contact jarred Kirag's arms and numbed his sword hand, but he heard the unmistakable crack of a shattering blade—and not his own.

A battle cry escaped from his throat.

Only then did he realize his error. His charge had been too aggressive, his sword not only shattering the enemy's blade but striking deeply into his chest. Red froth bubbled to the elf's lips, and the light in his amber eyes dimmed.

There would be no interrogation of this one.

Kirag returned to the other elf, his anger growing. Kneeling, he felt for a pulse, and found none.

He'd been careless. No—more than careless. He'd been a fool.

Fuming at his own error, he returned to the cliff to see what had become of his Duo.

Both were now visible in the clearing they had been approaching. And yet they too had failed. Zandri now lay dead in a pool of his own blood, and Vaughn was on his knees, an elf standing behind him, holding a sword to the Talon's exposed neck.

The elf looked up at Kirag.

"Kirag, you are intruding where you do not belong. Leave this forest and I will release this man."

How can this creature know my name?

Kirag's shoulder burned as if acid were slowly eating at it, but it was not as troubling as the bile of disgust that rose up within him. His men had allowed themselves to be dispatched by a single enemy.

He shouted down to the elf. "Who are you, to ask this of me?"

"Castien Galonos, sword master of my people, and guardian of these woods."

"We are seeking strangers within Trimoria," Kirag called back. "I would have you release to me such people that you have encountered. And if you find any in the future, relinquish them to the black-armored troops in Aubgherle."

Castien spat on the ground. "Azazel holds no authority in these woods. Our people will never release anyone to his control."

Kirag stepped back from the cliff and retrieved the bow and

quiver of arrows from the nearest elf. Nocking an arrow, he drew, held the tension, and slowly approached the edge of the cliff. "Castien Galonos, know that Azazel, Lord of Trimoria, claims these woods. You are but cowardly trespassers hiding within."

He released the arrow. His aim was true.

The arrow pierced Vaughn's left eye, and the Talon collapsed to the ground, dead.

The look of anger on Castien's face brought a smile to Kirag's.

Wanting blood, Kirag nocked another arrow and sent it at this Castien.

Again his aim was true.

But it did not reach his target.

The elf's sword moved in a blur too quick to follow. He sliced the shaft of the arrow not once, but twice in midair, and the pieces of the arrow fell to the ground harmlessly.

Castien cast a dark gaze upward. "Leave, Kirag... and do not return."

Despite the fire in his shoulder, Kirag dragged the two dead elves to the edge of the cliff and kicked them over the side.

"Something to remember me by."

THE MYSTERIOUS HERB-WOMAN

Father sat back, patted his stomach, and let out a satisfied belch. "This was a very good stew, my dearest. And to think that only a few weeks ago your stew wasn't deemed edible by even the sheep and the goats."

"Hey, that was my first try! I'm allowed to make mistakes when learning, aren't I?"

"Of course you are, my heart." He sighed, and his eyes glistened.

"What's wrong, Father?"

He pulled at his mustache. "I just wish your mother could see you now. She would be just as proud of you as I am. You are growing rapidly into a woman." The cheer returned to his face, and he gave her a conspiratorial look as he whispered, "In truth, your stew is much better than your mother's ever was."

"Really? You aren't just saying that."

He shook his head. "Why do you think your mother hired Janius Mizmer?"

"Mother hired her? Really? Well, it was Madam Mizmer's recipe I followed. I only made a few changes."

"Changing Janius's recipes?" her father said with a chuckle. "You're brave, too."

Arabelle set the dishes aside and pulled out the book she'd brought with her. It was a leather-bound drawing book that had belonged to her mother. Father had given it to her years ago, because Arabelle loved to flip through and see all the sketches her mother had made.

Now she turned to the page she'd been looking at last night. The sketch on that page was of an old crone. Most of her teeth were missing, and she had tufts of hair on her chin. She looked altogether unkempt, and quite a bit frightening. Yet Arabelle's mother had surrounded her with a series of wavy lines like a glowing aura. It gave the old woman a mysterious, almost divine look.

The old woman appeared in a few scattered sketches, but this particular image was so striking that Arabelle had decided to use her inner sight on the old woman—and had found that not only was she a real person, she wasn't that far away. That made her curious.

"Father," she said, holding out the sketch. "Who is this woman in Mother's sketchbook? She appears several times in the book. Is she a relation?"

Her father twirled his mustache as he studied the picture. "It's funny you should ask about her, for I know very little. After we were betrothed, your mother took me to this old woman's home

—a cave not far from here. I asked why, but all your mother would say was that it had to do with one of her visions, and I'd learned by then not to pry when it came to matters involving her visions.

"We walked into the cave, and the old woman was waiting for us. I found her... intimidating, if I'm being honest. She gave off the distinct impression that she could read my inner thoughts. She didn't speak, she simply studied me, and then she nodded to your mother. Your mother smiled and took me by the arm, and we left without any of us ever saying a word. It was very strange. But I felt like I'd passed some sort of test, and for that I was pleased."

"And you never tried to find out who she was?"

"Oh, of course I tried. My curiosity had been piqued, after all. Your mother wouldn't tell me, so I asked around. People had heard of her. Most seemed to think she was a crazy old herb-woman who had left her home years earlier. Some knew her as the Gray Lady. They all claimed she was harmless. Yet now that I think on it, living out there on her own, and yet managing to avoid slavers, wild animals, and other threats, she must not have been as harmless as she appeared. And I certainly didn't get the impression of harmlessness when I was in her presence."

He sighed. "I would like to speak to her again. Perhaps she could tell me tales of your mother than I never knew. But she was ancient even when I met her; I am sure she has passed long before now."

Arabelle knew the woman was still alive; her inner sight had told her so. But she couldn't tell her father that, for she would be unable to explain how she knew.

"There's also something that I wished to speak to you about this evening, my heart. Roselle has informed me about some of the questions you've been pestering her about the past months. Questions she has, understandably, refused to answer."

"Father, I'm sorry. I know certain subjects upset her, but if she won't tell me, how am I to learn?"

He smiled. "I agree completely. But I wasn't able to get her to accept that you weren't wrong to seek knowledge that she felt was... inappropriate. She's rather set in her ways. So, as you rightly asked, how are you to learn?"

He rose to his feet, slid a chest from under his bed, and unlocked it using a black key he extracted from beneath his tunic. Arabelle had long known he wore that key around his neck, but she'd never known what lock it went to, and she'd never seen this chest before. It was bound with black metal bands that strangely reflected hints of red in the lamplight.

Her father removed a tightly wrapped package from the chest, locked the chest once more, and returned it to its place beneath his bed. Then he resumed his seat across from Arabelle and handed her the package.

"Don't open that here," he said. His voice was low, as if he feared listening ears. "I understand Roselle's reluctance to discuss such matters with you, but your questions were fair ones. So, after much searching, I've found for you a very rare and forbidden book that contains the answers you deserve. In it you'll find the only written logs I know of regarding demons, their origin, and the battles of the gods."

Arabelle looked down at the package in her hands. "Thank you."

He kissed her on her forehead. "Keep this knowledge safe, my flower. I have arranged for a chest and key to be delivered to your tent. Keep the book locked up and the key on your person at all times. And whatever you do, never speak of this to anyone. We don't want others like Roselle to attempt to *rescue* you from such knowledge."

"Yes, Father."

Tabor poked his head into the tent. "Sheikh, my apologies. There has been a confrontation with a slaver party. Khalid wants to know what you would like us to do with them."

Father grimaced and stood. "Excuse me, my flower. I need to take care of some devils."

And with a swish of his robes, he exited the tent.

Arabelle snuck away from the caravan, cloaked in darkness. She could only imagine the curses of her escorts as they realized they'd lost her, but her conversation with her father had only heightened her curiosity about the old crone, and the only way she'd learn more was by going to see the woman herself. Her inner sight had told her the woman wasn't far away, which meant this was the perfect opportunity to find her, before the caravan moved on once more.

Arabelle hurried across the grasslands, following the guidance of her inner sight. If she could get to the old woman quickly, and not stay long, perhaps she could come up with a reasonable excuse for her escorts. Maybe—

She let out a yelp and pulled up short as two blink dogs

M.A. ROTHMAN

popped into existence directly in front of her. A dozen or more pops sounded all around her, indicated an entire pack had suddenly surrounded her.

She was startled, and confused, but she wasn't frightened. At least, not exactly. Blink dogs were scavengers, not predators. They shouldn't pose a threat. In fact they were normally quite wary of humans. They followed the caravan in search of offal, but always kept their distance. Which made their current behavior all the more curious.

The two blink dogs in front of her sat back on their haunches and looked at her with yellow eyes. Their tongues lolled out from their dirt-encrusted muzzles.

Arabelle took one tentative step back.

The dogs stood up and—

Ew.

Both animals retched, bringing up piles of partially digested food.

The dogs wagged their tails proudly and sat back on their haunches. A few of their packmates came over and gave a few laughing barks.

What do these animals want?

"I don't have any food with me," Arabelle said. "If I did, I would share it. But now I must get to my destination."

She started forward once more, stepping carefully around the piles of vomit.

The pack moved with her.

She began jogging, and the laughing animals kept pace.

But as they seemed to have no intention of harming her, and since she had no time to waste on them, she continued on. For the next thirty minutes Arabelle ran, surrounded by laughter and frolicking and near-constant pops.

At last, when she approached the looming cliff face where she knew the woman resided, the pack lost interest. They veered away and ran off in another direction.

How strange.

Arabelle closed her eyes and concentrated on the old crone. The woman's heartbeat now thundered in Arabelle's head, indicated that her target was directly ahead. She followed her inner sight forward—directly toward a sheer cliff face. There was no cave here, only rock.

But she trusted her inner sight, and she continued forward, right up to the wall of rock. Only then did she realize that a portion of the wall was actually a well-camouflaged cloth hung over the opening to a cave.

As she stood there, a warm, gravelly, female voice spoke from within.

"Come in, child. I have been waiting for you."

Arabelle hesitated, gathering her courage, then finally pulled aside the cloth and stepped into the cave beyond.

The cave was small and empty, except for three things. The small fire that burned. The stone chair carved into the back wall of the cave. And the woman who sat on that chair.

It was the woman from her mother's sketchbook, and she looked exactly as her mother had portrayed her.

The old crone's eyes studied Arabelle from behind a mass of tangled gray hair, and Arabelle felt stripped bare.

"Sit, child. You are safe here. Nobody will disturb us."

Arabelle looked back at the cloth over the entrance. Even this side was perfectly camouflaged, and had Arabelle not known otherwise, she would have sworn that she was now surrounded by solid rock.

She sat down cross-legged next to the fire. "My mother had drawings of you," she said.

The old woman gave a toothless smile. "I knew your grandmother when she was but half your age, and the die had been cast when she found me."

"You knew my grandmother as a girl? How could you be that old? You don't look like an elf."

The old lady tilted her head back and cackled. "Age is not important, and the threads of destiny form complex knots. You are a child of destiny. Your mother was also one of those children, but she was not *the one*. You, my dear Arabelle, Princess of the Imazighen, bearer of many secrets... *you* are the one I envisioned long ago."

"How do you know my name?" Arabelle asked.

The old woman clucked and shook her head. "Not important. Ask me important questions."

There was a preternatural strength in the woman's words—as if contained in that frail body was a well of power that was ready to explode. And as Arabelle looked closer, she saw a shimmering glow surrounding this woman. Just like in her mother's sketch.

And then Arabelle noticed something else that made no sense. She felt no heat coming from the campfire. Nor did it give off any smoke. She reached a hand toward the fire and felt nothing.

How is that possible?

Arabelle tried to collect her thoughts. "Who are you?"

"Not important. Ask me important questions."

Arabelle was getting frustrated. "You said you envisioned me. Who am I? What am I to do?"

The woman closed her eyes. "Those questions are worthy of consideration." Her jaw moved as if she chewed on her thoughts, then her eyes flew open once more. "You are mistaken in your belief that you carry a curse. A poison. What you carry will serve as a tool. A tool that you will need if you are to successfully walk the path of your destiny."

Arabelle gasped. *How does she know all this?*

"Your success is not certain, my dear. There are many obstacles along your way. There are decisions only you can make. Choose incorrectly, and your people will surely suffer."

Arabelle's heart threatened to beat its way out of her chest. "Can you tell me what I'll face? Can you help me?"

The old woman closed her eyes and made those chewing motions once again. Then her eyes opened and she shook her head.

"I cannot tell you the nature of the dangers ahead. There are too many threads that might change in time." She opened her hand, and a tiny leather satchel appeared out of thin air. "But I can offer you this."

She held it out to Arabelle, who took it. Inside was a scrap of parchment with some sort of recipe written on it.

"What is this?" Arabelle asked.

"Instructions for creating tincture of the new moon. Use it at night when you must travel and wish not to be seen. Apply one drop to each eye."

"What does it do?"

"The tincture will coat your eyes with blackness. The blackness of your eyes will be pure like the new moon. They will neither reflect the lights from the stars, nor any other lights. And while this tincture is active, your superior night vision will be enhanced."

"How—how do you know about my superior night vision? Not a living soul knows about it. I barely understand it."

The old woman smiled mysteriously, then began to fade in front of Arabelle's eyes. The campfire faded too, as did the stone chair on which the woman sat. As the last wisps of woman, chair, and campfire disappeared, a parting whisper sounded in the now-empty cave.

"Not everything is as it seems, young princess. That bird you seek in the sky is bound to land on the ground. Protect the bird, or all you know will suffer."

A NEW APPRENTICESHIP

The three weeks since his escape from the mines had been a whirlwind of activity for Grisham. He'd begun an apprenticeship with a dwarf soldier named Oda. The dwarf was respected by the caravan soldiers, and although he was gruff, Grisham could tell he meant well. But he was very demanding, and Grisham found himself busier than he'd ever been.

Still, in quieter moments, he often thought back to what had happened in the mines. What had happened to him. He had actually *become* a megapede. It was surreal even to think about, but he knew it to be the truth.

And it was more than just a physical transformation; it was mental, too. As he chewed through the rock to get out of the mines, he wasn't very clear on who he was, and he even felt angry that the other slaves were following him. It was as if he had lost contact with the Ta'ah that was inside of him and was actually thinking like a megapede.

Then, when he broke through onto the surface, the bright light confused him. Nicholas later told him that he began lashing out at anything nearby, and only after Nicholas called his name repeatedly did he calm down.

Grisham wondered what would have happened had Nicholas not been there to bring him back to himself. Would he have remained a megapede forever?

Grisham was in the soldier's barracks, repairing one of his master's ripped tunics—Oda was constantly destroying his own clothes—when Nicholas walked in and laughed.

"Grisham! What do they have you doing now? Sewing?"

Grisham grimaced. "Oda says he's all thumbs with a needle and thread, and as I'm his apprentice now…" He shook his head.

"Well you'd better not make your sewing skills too widely known, or every soldier will be coming to you claiming to be all thumbs. The pile of torn clothing will be taller than you, my friend."

In truth, Grisham enjoyed sewing. Or at least, he preferred it to practicing with weapons. Given his size, he didn't think hand-to-hand combat would ever be something he could excel at. Of course, the hadn't told Oda this. He was the dwarf's apprentice, which meant Oda was going to teach him what being a dwarven warrior was all about. And Oda of all people would brook no excuses about being small. He always boasted that anything a human could do, a dwarf could do—but correctly.

"How about you, Nicholas?" Grisham asked. "Are you officially a part of the guard again?"

Nicholas had told Grisham that this caravan was the very one that he had soldiered for at the time of his capture by the slavers.

He'd been worried about whether they would accept him again, seeing as, from their perspective, he'd already abandoned his post once before.

"As a matter of fact, all turned out well. A soldier I knew well, Khalid, is still here—in fact he's the captain now. He remembered me, and I explained what happened—that I didn't abandon my post, but that I did foolishly drink too much in commemorating the anniversary of my wife's passing, and that's what got me captured by slavers. Khalid was very understanding and fair. We're lucky to have him."

"So all is forgiven?"

"Well, yes and no. They've forgiven my actions, but they haven't forgotten about the armor and weapons the slavers took from me. Khalid has assured me that the costs will be taken from my wages." Nicholas shrugged. "Which is as it should be; a soldier is responsible for his own equipment. As I said, he's a fair man."

Tabor walked into the barracks, and Nicholas immediately stood at attention. Grisham, not yet having a soldier's ways drilled into him to the point of reflex, scrambled to follow suit.

Tabor strode directly toward them. "At ease, men." He pulled something from his tunic—a small box wrapped in a silk ribbon. "Grisham, this is a gift from the princess. She wishes you to have it."

Grisham took the wooden box, then looked uncertainly at Tabor.

"Well, go on, open it. I already know what's inside."

Grisham opened the box to find only a note.

Tabor asked hesitantly, "Do you need me to read it for you, apprentice?"

"No, sir, I can read."

He read aloud.

Grisham,

Thank you for your valuable advice. I have arranged for you to enjoy unlimited servings of my stew at Madam Mizmer's food stall in the main marketplace. I hope it helps.

—Arabelle

"You lucky dog," said Nicholas. "Just don't get too fat or you won't be able to do all your master's laundry."

Tabor knelt down in front of Grisham. "Apprentice, it is clear our princess has taken a liking to you. I'm sure you understand that, if I'm to allow this contact between you, you'll be expected to keep yourself entirely out of trouble. It's my responsibility to ensure the safety of everyone in this caravan—but *especially* the princess."

Grisham nodded. "I would never dishonor myself nor abuse my friendship with Arabelle."

Tabor frowned. "You are to address her as Princess. Princess

Arabelle, if you must. Respect is due to the family that carries the heavy burden of responsibility for our people."

Grisham stammered. "Y-yes, sir. Thank you, sir. Also please thank the princess for me. I cannot express how much this gift means to me."

Tabor grunted. "The princess is a very generous young woman, but she's no fool. Apparently you gave her some wisdom that she found valuable, so I'm sure she considers it an even trade."

"Yes, sir."

Tabor stood and turned to go, but then he stopped and looked back at Nicholas. "I expect to hear that there will be no more drinking on your part, soldier."

And as he walked out of the tent, all Nicholas could do was sputter.

It was still hours before daybreak, but Grisham couldn't sleep anymore. He wasn't used to the long nights here in the caravan—back in the mines, their rest periods must have been much shorter. It also didn't help that Oda was snoring like a beast on the cot next to him. The big dwarf's beard covered him like a blanket that fluttered with every exhalation.

Grisham felt his own patchy fringe. It seemed it would never grow in. He hated that he still looked like a child.

Rolling out of bed, he stepped outside for some fresh air. As he walked to the edge of the caravan, one of the soldiers on patrol spoke up mockingly. "Careful, young dwarf. I've heard the prowling of wolves out there. You might look like a tasty snack, if not a very filling one."

Grisham ignored the jab and continued on into the darkness of the night.

One thing he'd learned since mingling with the other races was that they were nearly blind without the light from the sun or a torch. It was a strange defect. There was always natural light around—most rocks, for instance, gave off a small amount of phosphorescence—but apparently those without Ta'ah vision could not see it. They were reliant on the extreme brightness of the aboveground world. The sun, the stars, even the moon was oftentimes so bright that he often wished it would dim a bit so that he could see more of the world's natural glow.

He found a quiet spot in the grasslands about a quarter mile from the caravan's lights, sat down, and breathed in the smell of freedom. It was still a daily revelation to him that he was no longer in the mines. He was free, and could make of this life what he wanted.

If only he knew what he wanted.

And perhaps it didn't matter. He recalled Seder's words.

"Your destiny is to bring your people out of self-imposed isolation. You must find the Thariginian king and, as the representative of your people, strike an agreement with him."

The problem was, Grisham had no idea how to do that. How does one find a king that doesn't exist?

As he sat in the still of the night, he saw the aura of a lone wolf surveying its surroundings. It gave out a yip that translated to, *"Who is there?"*

Grisham didn't mean to do it. He was just watching the wolf, thinking about it, and before he knew it, it just… happened. His arms and legs cracked. His nose elongated. Shooting pains wracked his body. His vision reoriented.

He was a wolf.

He smelled the other wolf, tasted the sweet musk of she-wolf scent. And he sent a yip of his own to announce his presence.

The wolf advanced slowly, sniffing the air. She growled, the hair on her nape standing on end. "You smell of two-legs, stranger. What are you?"

The she-wolf's smell was intoxicating. In fact, the new smells he was experiencing were overwhelming, making his mind reel with all the new sensations.

The howl of a male wolf pierced the grasslands. Grisham stood quickly on all four legs, suddenly afraid.

The she-wolf growled a warning. "Stay away, strange wolf that smells of two-legs. You would not be welcomed by he who leads." She turned and trotted away in the direction of the sound of the howl.

Grisham sat back down on his haunches. It was only when he noticed the motion of torches along the edge of the caravan that he remembered.

I am of the Ta'ah.

I should go back before I am missed.

He released the image of the wolf. Once more he felt the shooting pains as his body changed, and he was Grisham once again.

He was also naked; his clothes had fallen off during the transformation. He made a mental note to plan for this in the future.

As he hastily dressed, he heard the distant sound of horses

approaching from the south. His mind immediately came to one conclusion.

Slavers.

The same sentry met Grisham as he ran back into the perimeter of the caravan.

"The wolves chasing you, little one?"

Grisham panted and shook his head. "I heard horses galloping."

The soldier's joking manner vanished. "Are you sure?"

"I'm sure."

The soldier blew a whistle, and within moments, a dozen soldiers had joined them, including Oda. By now the horses were louder, and some of the soldiers could hear them as well.

"Could it be slavers?" Grisham asked nervously.

Oda's hand fell on his shoulder. "Don't ya be worryin', Grisham. Slavers be dependin' on sneak attacks like the cowardly curs that they are. Horses make too much noise."

More soldiers appeared, these on horseback. The sentry explained what the alert was about, and they rode off to investigate.

As they vanished into the dark, Oda pulled Grisham aside. "Now p'raps you'd like to explain what you be doin' wanderin' about at such an hour."

Grisham's mind raced. He liked the dwarf, but he'd learned his lesson about letting others know about himself.

"I'm sorry, Oda. My sleep is often disturbed by memories of

my father's death, and what occurred in the mines. Sometimes walking alone helps me to flush the images from my mind."

Oda nodded with understanding and pulled his fingers through his thick beard. "I know what you've been through has been difficult. I'll not be insultin' you by saying that those memories will be goin' away. But you'll learn to deal with them." He gave Grisham a rough pat on the shoulder. "I find that the best way to get me mind off troubles is by keepin' too busy to tink about such things. Come. Follow me."

With regret, Grisham realized that somehow his lie had just increased his already heavy workload.

Oda led him to the corral. "These be horses, as I expect you know. They're much too large and stupid lookin', but they be friendly to those who give them treats." He picked up a bag of quizoa fruit and handed it to Grisham. "And as warriors of diminutive stature, it be wise for us to make friends where we can."

Grisham took out one of the green fruits and waved it in front of the nearest horse. The horse leaned down, snuffled at his hand, extended its lips, and grabbed the treat with a wet smacking sound.

The other horses immediately circled around, and when Grisham pulled the next fruit from the bag, three horses pushed their heads forward aggressively.

Grisham hid the fruit under his tunic. "Patience! You beasts are greedy. One at a time."

He waited for the horses to take a half step back before he pulled the quizoa out again. Immediately they all shoved their heads forward again. Grisham laughed and began leading them on a chase around the corral. He barely even noticed when Oda left him alone with his new charges.

Just as Grisham finished playing with the horses, more came clopping toward the corral.

"Oda!" shouted a soldier's voice. "We found some horses tailor-made for you and your apprentice!"

"Bah!" came Oda's reply. "You won't be getting' me on one of dem things, I don't care what you be offerin' me."

Grisham's curiosity was piqued, and he left the corral to see what was going on. A group of soldiers were gathered outside the corral, Oda among them, as a line of horses was led into the caravan, tied into a train by long leather ropes. Some were clearly more wild than others, and they reared up, resisting being herded toward the corral.

Two horses near the front stood out. They were the smallest horses Grisham had ever seen.

Oda spotted them as well. "Ah, now I see what yer talkin' about!"

The dwarf jogged over to meet the first of the two horses, which was brown with a long black mane. As Oda patted its nose, the miniature horse's nostrils flared with uncertainty.

"Now this be a proper mountain pony!" Oda pronounced. "Wherever did these beasts come from?"

The scout leader shrugged. "I don't rightly know. None of them have proper markings of ownership on their hide, yet some, like the little beast you've fallen for, are clearly not afraid of men, and must have been owned in the past."

"Grisham!" Oda called. "Bring me some of those quizoa. I aim to show you how to ride one of these beasties."

Oda untied his chosen horse from the others, and as the remaining horses were led into the corral, he began to teach his young apprentice.

"Step one, Grisham: earn the trust of the beast, and never betray it."

LIFE IS TOUGH

When Maggie didn't arrive to help Arabelle with her training, Arabelle went to Maggie's tent to seek her out. She feared she might find her handmaiden had fallen ill, but what she found instead was a woman who was a complete mess. Maggie's eyes were bloodshot, her nose was running, and she'd clearly been crying.

"Milady! I'm sorry for you to see me like this. Is it already time for your training?"

"Maggie, forget about that! What's wrong?"

Maggie's chin quivered. "Hassan is gone."

Arabelle felt relief at this announcement. Her dreams had recently been very troubled, so her imagination had strayed to things much worse than a broken heart.

"What do you mean he's gone? I saw him leaving on a scouting patrol just last week."

Maggie broke down and sobbed, tears flowing down her face. "He disappeared from the caravan several days ago, and nobody's seen him since."

Arabelle embraced her friend and let Maggie cry on her shoulder. "Are you sure he wasn't on a longer scouting mission? They do that on occasion. I can ask Tabor if you like."

Maggie pulled back and took in a deep, shuddering breath. "I already asked Khalid. He said Hassan left in the middle of the night. Khalid isn't even worried—he says the Nameless aren't to be trusted, so I shouldn't concern myself about him." She looked Arabelle in the eye. "But Khalid is wrong. Hassan was honorable and good. He wouldn't have left without a good reason, and I'm certain he would have said something to me."

Arabelle was at a loss as to how to help. She had no experience with such matters of the heart.

"Maggie," she said, "you may not feel this way right now, but I believe that things usually end up the way they are meant to. I'm afraid that only time will heal your hurt."

Maggie gave a noisy sniff. "Thank you, milady. You're right. I need to get my mind off worrying for him and back to more important things. What can I do for you?"

The poor woman. Even in this state she felt obligated to serve her mistress. Arabelle wasn't having it.

"What you can do for me is take care of yourself today. We'll skip training and duties. Why don't you accompany me to Madam Mizmer's and I can show you my latest recipe? I'm working on a spiced lamb dish, and you can tell me what you really think before I give it to Father."

Maggie smiled and dabbed at her eyes. "Very well, but I hope it isn't like last time. I swear I was tasting garlic for days."

Arabelle grimaced. "Yes, I'm sorry about that. I didn't know that garlic came apart. So when the recipe called for three cloves of garlic, I thought that meant three bulbs. When I told Madam Mizmer what I did, she shrieked with laughter."

Maggie giggled through her sniffs. "Well… it is pretty funny."

"Let's just hope I don't make the same mistake with fire peppers."

Arabelle pulled from beneath her bed the chest her father had given her, and unlocked it with its key. It was a wonderful gift, for she needed a safe place to store her growing collection of secrets: the dagger from Castien; the tincture recipe from the old crone; and the book from her father.

It was the latter that she pulled out now. She hadn't even unwrapped it yet; her father's warnings had made her feel hesitant to read what lay within. But the time had come.

She pulled back the protective cloth wraps to reveal an ancient tome. It smelled of the forest, and its leather binding was engraved with strange symbols.

As Arabelle opened the book, she saw that it was written in two languages. On the left-hand pages was clear dark Trimorian text, and on the right-hand pages was faded writing in a brown ink that was flaking off the parchment. She didn't recognize the faded language, but it employed some of the same characters from the cover of the book. Apparently the Trimorian was a translation of this unknown tongue.

The first page was a note from someone named Bryan Greenwalker.

I am but a humble servant of the elven people. These words you read are not my own, but the words of a depraved dwarf soul who spent time with someone he believed to be Nicnevin, our queen from many thousands of years ago. Despite its title, the story of Nicnevin is not for this book, but suffice it to say that according to the legend, Nicnevin challenged the gods and was forever cast down to live at the end of the world.

Many have searched for this mythical "end of the world," but none have found it, nor has any document or creature possessed even a hint of its whereabouts.

Until now.

Two weeks ago, this book's author stumbled into Eluanethra, naked and alone. How this dwarf managed to wander into the stronghold of our people without our scouts noticing is still a mystery. In his hands he clutched this book, which he had appar-

ently written with his own blood. He shouted crazed warnings about the doom of all of Trimoria and the end of the world. He raved of demons yet to come, and of a savior amongst the humans which we must join. And he demanded that he be presented to the Archmage of Seder.

Since we knew of no such person, most among our people thought the dwarf crazy.

Xinthian is not so certain. He asked that I take the dwarf seriously and talk with him. Unfortunately the dwarf is fevered, and nothing we've been able to do has helped him. I fear that he will perish soon unless something changes.

With the assistance of my apprentice, Eglerion Mithtanion, I have translated the dwarf's blood script into modern Trimorian and included it on these pages. And on the off chance that it is meaningful, I have also placed notes within this book from the fevered ravings of the lunatic. If any of what he says comes to pass, I fear for the survival of our race.

—Bryan Greenwalker

Arabelle spent the next several hours reading with fascination. The entire book was a series of prophecies—and much of the future described had already come to pass. The dwarf had predicted the demon war, a human figure that certainly sounded like the First Protector, and the great isolation between the three races. All of these events were laid out in detail—but in future tense.

Were these actual prophecies? Or were these descriptions of historical events written to look like prophecies?

How old was this book?

Some of the events described were things Arabelle had never heard told. For instance, it said that Sammael's seed was stolen, and that Seder's seed was hidden by the Ta'ah.

The mention of Seder sent a shiver up Arabelle's spine.

She didn't know what to make of this book, but she knew it was important. More important even than her father had realized. There was a reason it had fallen into her hands. Perhaps, like her, this book had its own destiny.

Arabelle's body continued to change. While she'd continued her exercises—Castien's workouts, dagger training, and now stealth training as well—she'd also learned to eat enough to make up for all that energy she was expending. As a result, her muscles now had pleasing curves. Even her arms didn't look like sticks anymore. She was particularly pleased by the little calluses that she'd developed on her thumb and forefinger, formed from gripping a dagger. All of these changes were physical proof of her hard work.

And yet, despite all of her growth, despite all of her new skills, she was still destined to die of the poison that coursed through her veins. Someday she was going to sleep too long, and the poison would settle in her blood and crystallize in her muscles. She would be unable to move. Soon she'd be unable to breathe. And then she would die.

As Arabelle lay in bed thinking of her fate, she suddenly began to sob. There were so many things she had yet to do, and she feared those things would now never come to pass. She'd never even have an opportunity to know a love as fleeting as the love that Maggie had had with Hassan.

When she died, it would be alone in her bed.

Arabelle dreamt, as she often had recently, of the First Protector rescuing their world from the demons five hundred years ago.

The smoke from burning siege engines floats over a battlefield where soldiers desperately fight off demons of all colors, shapes, and sizes, beasts with dagger-like claws and protruding fangs. Even the bony ridges along their joints are knifelike in their sharpness. The soldiers that battle against them are a combination of humans and dwarves, the humans fighting with blades, the bearded dwarves swinging giant sledgehammers.

The soldiers fall back under the demon onslaught, making a last stand on a single hill. From within their midst, a circle of lithe archers looses a never-ending stream of arrows into the demonic horde. And at the center of this last redoubt, at the very peak of the hill, stands a robed man concentrating on a globe in his hands. While those protecting the hill are bloodied and stooping from injury and fatigue, this man's white robe is immaculate.

As the demons tear through the soldiers, the robed man lifts his sphere high into the air. It blazes with power. At the man's command, that power expands, shooting out over the landscape in every direction. When it touches the creatures of the Abyss, they burst into flame and collapse into ashes. Soon the light fills every point on the terrain, from horizon to horizon.

What had been night has now turned to day.

What had been defeat has now turned to victory.

Arabelle knew what she was seeing in her dream: the First Protector's victory. But what happened next was something different. The dream was replaced by a field of white, and she felt a familiar presence she couldn't name. Within the field of white, a scene unfolded...

The night is dark, the only light coming from a guttering camp-fire. Four people lie on the ground around the fire; their black uniforms mark them as Azazel's soldiers. Blood spurts from a wound in one man's throat, yet he doesn't move.

Arabelle looks down at her hand. She holds her mother's dagger, dripping with blood.

The scene flashed white once more.

· · ·

Arabelle walks between the tents in her caravan. A young man in a robe walks alongside her. He is speaking to her, but there are no sounds in this dream.

He turns to her, and it is the face that has haunted Arabelle's thoughts.

It is the blue-eyed boy.

The scene flashed white.

Arabelle looks on, hovering above the scene, watching the blue-eyed boy once more. She does not recognize the location. He is pushing a cart of supplies when he is confronted by four other teens, who block his progress.

They attack.

The blue-eyed boy becomes a blur of motion. He ducks under a punch and kicks the knee of his first assailant, shattering it. He twists the next attacker's arm and gives a swift strike against the elbow, bending the arm unnaturally.

Arabelle knew that such fighting skill could only come from tremendous amounts of training. The boy must be a soldier.

The remaining two assailants circle him, one wielding a dagger, the other a club. They attack at the same time.

The boy spins around and smashed the larger of the two in

the face with a kick. Blood sprays from the attacker's nose and he reels backwards. Yet the other catches the blue-eyed boy with a dagger, and blood flows from the wound…

The scene flashed white.

Arabelle is in her father's tent, sitting next to him. The blue-eyed boy is there, too, seated next to a man who looks like an older version of the boy. His father?

The older man nods, and so does Arabelle's father.

Father waves for the boy to rise. The boy looks uncertain, but does as he is instructed. Father guides him to kneel next to Arabelle.

The boy holds out one arm. Arabelle does the same. And her father loops a white silk ribbon around both of their arms in the ceremony of betrothal.

Arabelle woke with a sudden start, her heart rattling in her chest. She was barely able to catch her breath, and she was a sweaty mess.

She kicked off her covers.

Could these visions be true? Or even some of them? Am I a seer, like my mother?

Oh, please, let me have the opportunity to meet this boy. Could he really be the one I am destined to marry?

As she stretched her muscles and began her exercises,

Arabelle used her inner sight on the older man from her vision, the one she thought was the blue-eyed boy's father.

He, too, was directly above her.

She recalled the words of the old woman. *"That bird you seek in the sky is bound to land on the ground. Protect the bird, or all you know will suffer."*

SPYING ON EVIL

Arabelle's visions had reinvigorated her—especially the vision of the betrothal ceremony. As the weeks passed, she felt certain it was a scene from the future.

And that changed everything for her.

Yes, she was destined to suffer. The poison would never leave her body. But she would also find someone to love— someone who might even give her a feeling of normalcy. And that was all she could hope for.

In the meantime, she worked harder than ever. As the princess—a princess granted a life of privilege—she owed it to her people to be as strong as she could, as skilled as she could, and as knowledgeable as she could. She not only absorbed everything Tabor taught her, and continued to practice Castien's moves, she advanced her studies of various plants and their uses.

Maggie had agreed to be a test subject for her powdered weapons, the poor girl. When she volunteered, she probably didn't realize just how often Arabelle was going to be practicing on her. Of course Arabelle didn't dose her with any of the medicinal mixtures themselves, but she did use her handmaiden to test whether her delivery process was working. She would fill her straws with finely ground crystals of sugar—which she knew were harmless—and then would seize any opportunity she could to sneak up on Maggie with her beeswax-plugged straws. If Maggie tasted the sugar, then Arabelle knew her delivery method had worked.

It did, much to Maggie's chagrin.

Arabelle had also spent plenty of time in Madam Mizmer's supply tent, and she'd mostly completed her arsenal of powdered weaponry. The old cook had by now given up on trying to figure out what the princess was doing amongst her supplies, and simply gave her free rein.

But there was one last item Arabelle needed to prepare, and to do so, she needed one elusive ingredient: the powdered ash of damantite slag. It wasn't a food ingredient, but was used by some herbalists to treat exotic illnesses. Madam Mizmer said she possessed some of the rare substance, but as she almost never used it, it could be buried anywhere within her supplies. The woman was organized when it came to her primary vegetables and spices, but the back of her supply tent was a jumble of random ingredients.

Arabelle had already searched the tent for the damantite several times, and was beginning to worry that she wouldn't find it. Naturally, it was the last place she looked—the very last dust-covered box on Madam Mizmer's shelves. She let out a squeal of excitement when she found the yellowed packet with "damantite" scrawled on the outside. Inside was a finely ground black powder. She put it in her bag, then restored Madam Mizmer's storeroom to a semblance of order before returning to her tent.

She now had all the ingredients to create the recipe that the old crone had given her: *Tincture of the New Moon.*

She gathered all of the ingredients on her table and arranged them neatly. She double-checked the instructions one last time, then got started.

My most complicated recipe yet.

One by one, Arabelle put the dried ingredients into her stone mortar, grinding them as instructed with one hand as she dripped in the pure oil of quizoa leaves with her other. When all the ingredients but one had been added, her concoction was a fine, emulsified liquid.

She set aside the oil, took a pinch of the powdered damantite between her fingertips, and sprinkled it into the mixture. As the powder contacted the tincture, it flashed with tiny red sparks. She stirred everything thoroughly for exactly one more minute—and she almost shrieked with glee when the gray stone mortar and pestle suddenly turned a black so deep that it almost sucked the light out of her tent.

This was proof of her success, for the recipe had clearly stated:

If properly mixed with utensils of non-porous stone, the final tincture of the new moon will signify its completion by permanently discoloring the implements used in its creation.

. . .

She poured her creation into a glass vial and stoppered it. Then she turned to her bed, where she had laid out the darkest outfit Maggie had made her.

Time to test this out.

Arabelle tied off the end of her headwrap and tucked her mother's daggers into their sheaths. Her belt was loaded with color-coded straws containing all of the different powders she'd created. Some were weapons, such as the powdered leaf Castien said would cause short-term memory loss, whereas others were mere medicines—simple pain relievers and stimulants. All of these accouterments—daggers and concoctions—were disguised beneath her outfit.

The last item on her table was the tincture. She dipped an empty straw into her unstoppered bottle, put her finger on the end of the straw, and lifted a wobbling drop of the potion. Taking a deep breath, she tilted her head back, raised the straw above her right eye, and removed her finger from the end of the straw. The tincture hit her eye with a cool sensation, but no discomfort. She repeated the process with her left eye.

She kept her eyes closed for a minute, to make sure the tincture would not dribble out. She felt nothing out of the ordinary. But when she opened her eyes again, she felt an instant wave of dizziness. Her depth perception was completely thrown askew. Everything seemed to be closer than it really was. And the brightness of her lamp overwhelmed her.

She retrieved her hand mirror and looked at herself. The face that looked back at her was… frightening. Her eyes had turned completely black. There was no pupil, no brown, no white. Just solid black from eyelid to eyelid.

It was just about the creepiest thing she'd ever seen.

I just hope it wears off—or I'll have a lot of explaining to do.

Now came the real test. The herb-woman had said her already enhanced night vision would be further improved. She peeked through the slit at the entrance to her tent, looking into the darkness outside.

The effect was amazing. Arabelle focused in on a guard who stood at least fifty feet away, and she could see every detail of the man, right down to the beads of sweat on his forehead. Excitement coursed through her as she realized how useful this would be.

She'd already discovered that with her dark outfits and new stealth abilities, she was able to sneak out without her guards seeing her—if she waited for the right moment. Now that would be even easier.

She watched and waited. Soon the distraction she was hoping for came: another guard stopped to talk with the men watching her tent. She seized the momentary distraction and slipped away into the shadows of the caravan.

The darker her surroundings, the more her vision improved. It turned out that she could spy on someone from nearly a hundred yards away and still see their face well enough to read what they were saying.

As she snuck about the caravan, she heard a conversation that interested her.

"Any information from the captives?" said a voice.

"None. The boy remains stubbornly silent, but we'll get something from him. I know he's hiding something."

Captives? Boy?

The voices came from a nearby tent. Arabelle watched and waited to see who emerged.

The tent flap opened, and a black-armored soldier stepped out. He marched off in the direction of the marketplace.

Arabelle's heart beat faster. *That was one of Azazel's enforcers.*

She'd also caught a glimpse inside the tent, and had seen the other speaker. This, too, was one of Azazel's men, and he had been writing something on an easel.

She knew what she *should* do. She should leave this alone. Tabor had always taught her to avoid Azazel's soldiers, and everyone she knew was afraid of them. But her curiosity was piqued. Against her better judgment, she approached the tent and listened carefully through the wall.

All she could hear was the scratching of a writing instrument. If only she could see what he was writing...

She looked around. This section of the caravan was empty. Perhaps if she was quiet enough...

She tiptoed silently to tent's entrance and used one of her straws to pull aside the tent flap ever so slightly. Then she put her eye up against the sliver of an opening.

The black-armored soldier had his back to her. His body blocked her view of what he was writing on the easel. But off to his right, another parchment was attached to the wall. The writing was small, but she was able to make it out.

Seeking Strangers to Trimoria.
    Send a Quad to patrol the border of the cursed swamp.
    Maintain three Duos scouting the path of the caravan.
    Await Kirag's orders regarding the forest.
    Extract from captives—

Before she could make out the rest of the last line of text, the flap of the tent was ripped aside, sending Arabelle falling backward in shock. The soldier stood over her, his face a thunderstorm of anger.

Arabelle backpedaled quickly, but to no avail. The brute grabbed her tunic in one mighty hand and lifted her in the air. With his other hand he reached to his belt and brought his dagger to bear.

Without thinking, Arabelle brought the straw to her lips and blew the powder into the soldier's face. She didn't even know which powder that was.

The soldier cursed and dropped her.

Arabelle pulled out the entire wad of red-colored straws she'd tucked into her belt, blew them all at once into the man's face, and ran.

SLAVERS

Grisham never would have predicted it, but he'd grown to like riding a mountain pony. He was also proud that this same pony had refused to take a saddle from Oda, yet had allowed Grisham to ride him—after much care and attention, of course. As Oda had advised, Grisham had gained the animal's trust.

Oda was not so sanguine about the pony making its preferences known. He'd taken to calling Grisham's pony a sway-backed nag in retaliation. Fortunately the other mountain pony was less particular and would let anyone ride—even a boisterous dwarf. Today he had even set out on the pony with a group of other soldiers on an all-day scouting trip, leaving Grisham behind.

Grisham didn't mind. He enjoyed his quiet work—polishing weapons, grooming horses. In fact, Oda had suggested that perhaps Grisham's true calling was groomsman rather than soldier. Apparently even the grizzled dwarf was beginning to realize that Grisham would never be a warrior.

Grisham was rubbing down some of the horses when another group of soldiers entered the corral, with Nicholas among them.

"Grisham! It's good to see you've moved on to more suitable duties." He chuckled amiably. "As long as you're here, would you like to go with us on a short trip?"

"Where are you going?"

Nicholas cinched up the saddle on his favorite bay. "Some sheep have broken through their pens and wandered away. The shepherd needs help retrieving them. They can't have gone too far."

Grisham decided he wouldn't mind going for a ride. "Sure. I'll help out."

He laid a horse blanket on his pony and grabbed some tack, and soon he was trotting with Nicholas and two other soldiers toward the broken pens.

Nicholas pointed east. "I see their tracks heading down to the valley."

He spurred his horse into a gallop, and Grisham followed his example, holding on to his mount for all that he was worth.

Since joining the caravan, Grisham had learned that fog was frequently found in low-lying areas, especially in the mornings. Today was no exception. The fog was so thick in the valley that Grisham could barely see the rump of the soldier's horse in front of him.

"How can we possibly find the sheep in this weather?" he asked.

Beside him, Nicholas put his fingers to his lips and reined his horse to a stop.

Grisham did the same, listening for anything that might be out there. He heard the whuff of a horse on the other side of Nicholas. And then, after almost a minute of total silence, he heard what sounded like the bleat of a sheep in the distance.

"Did you hear that?" he asked Nicholas.

His friend shook his head. "I didn't, but if you heard a sheep, then lead on."

Grisham strained his ears again. When he heard another bleat, he nudged his pony in that direction. The others followed him. But he couldn't see a thing in the gray mists, and he hadn't gone far before he pulled on his reins so he could listen once more.

One of the other soldiers groused, "Can't even see my own horse's hooves, much less tracks."

Grisham heard another bleat. Except… it wasn't right. He heard a similar sound from another direction, and then again from yet a third direction.

It must have been loud enough for the others to hear as well, because Nicholas laughed. "I guess we're surrounded. That makes finding them easier."

Grisham's heart thumped in his chest. "Those aren't real sheep, Nicholas," he whispered. "Those are people imitating sheep."

Nicholas pulled his sword. "Are you sure?"

"Positive."

Nicholas turned his horse toward the other soldiers. "Be careful, boys. Let's get out of here."

At that moment, the hiss of blades being drawn echoed in the fog, and gray silhouettes coalesced out of the mist. They were not only surrounded, they were vastly outnumbered.

"Halt!" shouted the soldier nearest Nicholas. "Or suffer the consequences!"

A half dozen nets dropped from the fog and landed on top of their group.

Grisham's pony panicked, immediately getting tangled with the nets. Grisham was thrown to the ground in a jumble of flailing legs, and a sharp blow struck him on the head.

The murky gray of the fog dimmed to black.

The pain in Grisham's head was excruciating. He was emerging from a cloud of unconsciousness, only to realize he was on the hard bed of a wagon bouncing over a rocky trail. Every bounce was agony.

He cracked open one eye to assess his situation. It was even worse than he feared.

He was bundled within a cage, chained to it by a collar around his neck. After a few brief months of freedom, he was once again a prisoner, chained up like an animal.

His cage was on a large flatbed wagon along with two others. The cage nearest him housed an immense swamp cat with amber eyes. It smelled of infection, and indeed, pus oozed from a gash on its right haunch. The cat gave a low rolling growl—a cry of pain and frustration.

The third cage contained one of the other soldiers who had accompanied Nicholas. Grisham didn't even know the man's name. He, too, was wearing a collar, and Grisham groaned when he saw the construction. It was identical to the collars he and the slaves had worn in the mines.

Perhaps he was going back there again. To the very same mines he'd once escaped. Perhaps he would even be brought before the priestess.

He shuddered at the thought.

But now he knew what to do about it.

He closed his eyes and imagined a megapede. He reached within himself for the inner power he knew was there. He groped for the pool of energy, found it, grasped at it—

A blinding pain in his head took his breath away, and he felt nothing more.

A WARNING FROM KIRAG

rabelle watched as her Father tore a piece of bread and scooped up another bite of her spiced lamb in brown sauce with raisins and nuts. He chewed slowly, expressionless, and she waited expectantly.

But instead of giving a pronouncement, he took another piece of flatbread and reached for yet another sample—now his fourth.

Arabelle could wait no longer. "Father! Can't you tell me what you think? It's driving me crazy."

The tips of his mustache shook up and down as he exploded with laughter. "I've never tasted better, my dear."

She swelled with pride. She knew he wasn't simply saying so to please her. Father took his lamb very seriously, and didn't hesitate to be critical of poorly executed meals that involved his favorite meat.

"What about the bread?" she asked. "You seem to prefer Madam Mizmer's flatbread."

He handed her the loaf she'd prepared. "Have you tried it?"

"No, but it looks good. It was perfectly browned, and I think I used all the right ingredients."

Father smiled gently. "Taste it."

As she took the loaf, she noticed right away that the weight was oddly distributed. And when she ripped it open, she found that it was soggy on the inside—a dense, bready clay within a nicely browned crust. She took a nibble of the crust, and her lips puckered. Way too much salt.

"Eww." She grabbed a glass of goat milk and washed the salty taste out of her mouth. "I'm sorry, Father. I didn't mean to almost poison you."

He chuckled. "My heart, I love that you're learning new skills. Keep it up. You're well on your way to being a fantastic cook."

A commotion erupted outside the tent. Soldiers yelled profanities until Tabor yelled for silence. Father had just stood to see what was going on when Tabor stuck his head into the tent.

"One thousand pardons, Sheikh, but Azazel's lead enforcer insists on talking with you. Are you willing to see him?"

Father grunted his acquiescence and motioned for Arabelle to stand behind him. She had barely moved into place before Azazel's man pushed his way into the tent. Tabor and two of his men flanked the brute.

He was truly a giant, so tall that his head scraped the top of the tent, and his menacing yellow eyes scanned the area like a predator. He took in the remnants of their meal, then faced the Sheikh.

"What a pity," he said, his booming voice dripping with sarcasm. "Have I interrupted your meal?"

Father was gracious enough to greet the intruder with a smile. "Nothing that cannot be restarted. Would you care for some?"

Kirag snarled. "I didn't come to exchange pleasantries. I have an issue with how you are administering your agreement with Azazel."

Father paled. "Whatever do you mean? Have I not fed your soldiers from my supplies? Have we not been circling through the Trimorian wastes on the prescribed path and schedule?"

"Bah! There has been treachery. One of my soldiers was attacked by someone whose tracks led back into the tents of your people."

Arabelle's stomach knotted when she realized what the giant soldier was referring to. He was talking about *her*. *She* was the one who had attacked one of Azazel's men.

Her instinct was to run, but she willed herself to remain still.

Father shook his head. "I know of no such attack. Are there witnesses? Have you presented the soldier to Tabor to file a complaint?"

The enforcer's fist tightened, and his knuckles made popping sounds. "The soldier is unable to remember what happened. In fact, he cannot even recall his own name. But the tracks of the attacker do not lie. They lead back to your tents, which means the attacker is one of yours."

The man didn't even recall his own name? Arabelle felt a pang of guilt. In her panic, she'd blown not just one, but all four of her straws of the ground *Tishkakh* leaf that was supposed to cause short-term memory loss. That was far too much—and she might have caused permanent harm to the soldier.

Then again, *he* had intended to *kill* her. Had she not acted, his dagger surely would have been buried deep within her.

Her father shrugged impassively. "I will have Tabor ask among my people to determine if anyone has seen anything. I see nothing else I can do to help."

"*Honfrion…*" the enforcer spat.

That was Father's name, and to use it to his face showed an egregious lack of respect. One of the soldiers hissed, and Tabor had to place his hand on the soldier's weapon arm to remind him to stay calm.

"Any other unfortunate incidents will be reported *directly* to Azazel," the enforcer continued. His yellow eyes alighted on Arabelle, and his mouth curved into a wicked smile. "You will recall that the last time Azazel's attention turned toward your family, it didn't end well."

Arabelle involuntarily took a step backward.

With a malicious grin, Kirag reached into his armor.

Tabor and the soldiers immediately launched themselves between Kirag and the Sheikh and princess. But the enforcer did not remove a weapon from his armor.

He retrieved a bloody hand.

A hand with six fingers. *Hassan!*

With a sneer, Kirag tossed the hand on the ground. "You know, Honfrion, that Azazel is seeking strangers that have arrived in Trimoria. I am sure your man has told you this. Azazel expects full cooperation from your people—and that cooperation includes notifying us of any so-called 'Nameless,' or any others who cannot be vouched for. It's truly a pity that my soldiers had to find such strangers hiding among your people themselves. I expect better. And I assure you, Azazel expects *much* better."

With that, Kirag turned and walked out of the tent.

Arabelle couldn't tear her eyes away from the severed hand. She was relieved when Tabor instructed one of his soldiers to remove it from the tent.

Her father put his hands on her shoulders. "My heart, are you okay?"

She nodded silently. She couldn't form words.

He pulled her into an embrace. "Don't be frightened. Nothing will happen to you, my flower. I will make sure of it."

She tilted her head back to look up at her father. "What did he mean about Azazel? What has Azazel done to our family?"

Father gave Tabor a meaningful look, and Tabor and his man departed the tent, leaving Arabelle and her father alone.

He cupped her cheek with one hand. "Come. Sit." He took a seat away from the now-trampled dinner dishes, and motioned for Arabelle to follow suit. He then poured her a cup of steaming tea, which she held in trembling hands.

"Arabelle," he began, clearly struggling to find the right words. "You've grown up knowing me as a merchant, and a very good one. Ours is a family of merchants. We have long been known for our ability to eke out a profit when nobody else could.

"But we have also been known for another ability. The ability to foretell the future. Before the tragedy of the demon war, we prided ourselves on counting at least one wizard or seer in each generation. It was because of this latter ability that we drew the attention of Azazel."

He took a deep breath.

"My grandfather told me this tale when I was but a child. A tale that occurred when he was but a child.

"Azazel visited our people—specifically, my grandfather's father. Our family gathered together for Azazel's arrival, as it was believed that he was coming to negotiate an agreement.

"Azazel came with no escort. He needed none. He simply appeared within our family's midst from a ball of black sparkling magic. He demanded that our people assist him in seeking out those who had magical skills, even if those people were our own, and to bring them to his tower near Cammoria.

"Naturally, my grandfather's father refused. As you know, the Imazighen are not ones to assume the yoke of obligation or slavery to anyone. And my grandfather's father certainly wouldn't betray his own people.

"Azazel's response was immediate—and merciless. With a wave of his hand, he incinerated our entire family, all except for the youngest among them. My grandfather."

Arabelle gasped and covered her mouth.

"Grandfather was only a boy. Ten years old. What was he to do in the face of such power? So for the sake of our people's survival, he did the only thing he could do. He swore that we would assist Azazel. He agreed that we would provide escort for his agents through the Trimorian wastes, and that anyone we encountered who showed even a hint of magic would be reported to these agents."

Father looked away, as if he could not bear to face his own daughter.

"And now, I continue that contract which Grandfather agreed to. I serve Azazel. For the sake of our people."

Arabelle didn't know how to respond. Shame and anger warred within her. Their people had been subjugated by this horrible wizard for two generations. And they had allowed it. She herself had benefited from this arrangement, living in privilege at the cost of those who had been betrayed.

Men like Hassan.

Fury washed over her, and she pointed at the spot where the bloody hand had lain. "How dare we let them do that to one of our people? Even a Nameless. That man was under our protection, Father!"

He nodded. "My heart, sometimes we must tolerate things that are... intolerable. Try to put this behind you. We will persevere."

The look on his face was one Arabelle had never seen before. Her father, the greatest man she had ever known, the Sheikh of her people... was haunted by shame at what he had done. At what he continued to do.

He was, Arabelle saw for the first time, only a man.

As Arabelle stomped back to her tent, furious and frustrated, she heard the gruff voice of Oda.

"What you mean they be long past due? Where did you send Grisham?"

Arabelle turned at the mention of her friend's name. She

scanned the area and saw the fiery dwarf speaking with a soldier. A few other men had gathered around them, including Khalid.

The soldier pointed to the west. "The party was tracking some escaped sheep. But they haven't been seen since this morning."

Oda stomped his feet. "What's wrong with you? It don't be takin' a full day to find lost mutton."

Khalid held out a calming hand. "Take it easy, Oda." He turned to the other soldiers. "We need a scouting party. No less than a dozen soldiers. Let's find our lost men."

"And dwarf!" Oda added.

"Oda," said Khalid, "I assume you'll join us for the search?"

Oda raced away on his short legs. "I'll get my pony and meet ya at the west gate!"

Arabelle felt Tabor's hand on her shoulder. "They'll find him, Princess."

Perhaps. But they could use my help.

Arabelle closed her eyes and brought to mind an image of the little dwarf, complete with sad brown eyes and scraggly beard. Her inner sight responded immediately, and she turned to face the direction it pointed her.

She opened her eyes. She was facing north of the caravan, not west.

"Princess," said Tabor, "have faith in our people. With Khalid leading the search party, they will find him."

No. They won't. Because they're going the wrong way.

But Arabelle couldn't explain that to Tabor, or to anyone else. She couldn't tell anyone *how* she knew that Grisham had gone north.

Besides, she had no interest in talking to anyone at the moment. She was still tense with the emotions churned up in her father's tent, and now those emotions had blended with the fear she had for her friend.

She could do nothing for the situation her people were in. She could not end their subservience to Azazel. But she could do something for Grisham.

"You're right, Tabor," she said. "Khalid will find him."

She walked back to her tent, trying to appear unconcerned. She gave a large yawn and told her escorts goodnight as she entered.

But she had no intention of sleeping.

Tonight, she was going to find her friend.

Arabelle ran north of the caravan, crossing the dusty plain in complete silence, following her inner sight to Grisham. When she sensed that she was getting close to his location, she slowed and crept cautiously forward.

She came upon a small camp set up in the wilderness, centered around a wagon. There was no fire burning, but with her gifts of vision and the enhancements from the tincture, she could easily take in the scene.

One man stood guard. Several others were asleep on the ground. And three more were on the wagon itself. She couldn't see the directly over the sides, but she could see their outlines. One of them was Grisham.

Underneath her headwrap, she smiled.

She knelt in the grass and picked up a small rock. She flung it high and far, so it landed on the opposite side of the tiny camp.

When the guard moved to investigate, she crept toward the wagon and peeked over its side.

Her heart broke at the sight of her friend. Grisham sported a bloody gash on his forehead and a collar around his neck chained to the inside of his cage. There were two more cages lined up beside his. The next one over contained the largest swamp cat she'd ever seen in her life, and the third contained a caravan soldier, asleep or unconscious, also chained with a slave collar.

Arabelle poked the bottom of Grisham's foot.

The dwarf moaned loudly.

Arabelle cringed and looked over her shoulder, but the guard was apparently out of earshot.

She nudged Grisham's foot again, but he wouldn't budge. That's when she remembered her straws. She pulled out the one loaded with powdered stimulant, leaned forward, and blew the powder as close to Grisham's face as she could.

The dwarf gave a shuddering breath. His eyes fluttered open and he reached for the gash on his head with another groan—this one even louder than before.

Arabelle once again ducked and turned. The guard had settled back into his watch. Surely he'd heard that; he just didn't care.

Arabelle gave Grisham another poke on the bottom of his foot. This time he blinked his eyes open to look. His eyes widened when he saw her, but she put a finger to her lips and climbed softly, nimbly up onto the bed of the wagon beside him.

Grisham spoke in the barest whisper. "Not worth risking yourself. Please go."

Arabelle shook her head. "I plan to get you out," she replied just as softly.

The question was how.

If only I'd thought to ask for lockpicking lessons.

Not only was the cage locked, so was the collar around Grisham's neck, and there was no sign of a key anywhere on the wagon. She turned to the lone guard and sighed.

He has the keys.

Grisham must have read her mind because he hissed, "Don't do it. He's a trained soldier, and vicious. He'll think nothing of dragging a princess to the mines."

"Are there other guards?" she whispered back.

"No, they departed to retrieve additional slaves. But Arabelle—"

"Why are you in a cage and not with the others?"

"We're in the wagon because we're injured and unable to keep pace. The others are chained together and were drugged for the night. Arabelle, don't get any ideas. The other slavers will be back at dawn."

Then I'd better act now.

As she slid from the lip of the wagon bed, Grisham breathed, "Don't…"

Arabelle slipped into the darkness, pulling her mother's daggers from their sheaths, and stalked toward her target. She concentrated on all of the things she'd practiced. She kept the tension in her legs so she could spring in any direction. She crept on the balls of her feet to minimize the sounds she made on the hard, dry surface. She approached the guard from downwind so he wouldn't detect any scents. Though she certainly detected his. He stunk.

One of the drugged slaves grunted in his sleep, and the guard turned his head toward the noise. She saw a glaring malevolence in the man's eyes and knew that this was a person who cared nothing for others. As no slaver ever really could.

Before she attacked, she watched the guard's movements. He shifted his weight back and forth, favoring his right leg and putting more weight on his left.

Left leg it is.

She lunged forward and used both daggers at once. With one, she slashed a deep cut across the back of his left knee. With the other, she stabbed at the base of the man's back.

The slash across the knee felt almost like slicing through several ropes. The stab in the man's back felt like skewering a piece of meat, with two bony plates guiding her strike.

The guard's leg collapsed beneath him, and he screamed in agony, flailing his arms about, though his legs moved not at all.

Arabelle stepped back and looked at her handiwork with growing nausea.

She'd expected a lot of bleeding from the wound to the back, but saw none; instead a clear liquid oozed out of the knife wound. When the liquid's flow slowed and then stopped, so did the man's spasms and screams.

A moment later, his breathing stopped.

For a moment, Arabelle just stood there, stunned and horrified by the realization.

I killed a man.

She ripped off her headwrap and heaved uncontrollably all over the ground.

What have I done?

But then she remembered her mission. What she'd done, she'd done for a reason. If she didn't free these slaves, she wouldn't even have that small justification. She had only an hour or two left before dawn. There wasn't enough time to return to the caravan and bring back help before the other slavers returned. It was up to her alone to free these poor souls.

None of the captives around her had so much as stirred; clearly they were heavily drugged. She looked back at the wagon and saw the swamp cat pacing about, but the soldier still lay motionless. Unconscious, then.

There were no other sounds out here in the darkness.

She held her breath and searched the body of the slaver. She carefully patted and explored every inch, much to her disgust, looking for the keys that she knew had to be in his possession.

She found none.

Arabelle shivered uncontrollably, took a deep shuddering breath, and sobbed.

Behind her, Grisham cried out in pain. Arabelle shook off her tears and ran to her friend.

"What is it?"

"It's… it's nothing," said the little dwarf. "I suffered a blow to my head, and the pain… it comes and it goes."

Even as he spoke, he continued to clutch at his forehead. Clearly the pain was much worse than he was willing to let on.

"I can help," said Arabelle.

She put her headwrap back on, then found the straw filled with powdered willow bark. "I will blow this powder in your face. Inhale it. It should lessen your pain."

Grisham stretched as far as the chain of his collar allowed and presented his face. Arabelle lifted her headwrap slightly with the straw, placed her lips tightly around the end, and blew as hard as she could.

The cotton plug flew from the end of the straw along with a cloud of billowing powder. Grisham inhaled deeply, then coughed.

"That tastes horrible."

Despite the seriousness of the situation, Arabelle laughed. "I didn't promise it would be tasty."

"How quickly does it work?"

"I don't actually know. Soon, I hope. Now rest. I'm going to try to break you out of there."

Lacking a key, there was only one alternative she could think of: breaking the lock on the cage. It was a faint hope, but she had to pursue it. She began searching the area for a large rock with a sharp end. If she could find something heavy enough, and connect with just the right spot on the lock, then maybe...

"It worked, Arabelle. The pain has lessened. I can reach my power now."

She returned to the side of the wagon. "Your power?"

"Arabelle, please don't be angry with me for keeping this from you. And don't be frightened, either. I'm going to get out of this cage now. Please step back from the wagon just in case. And if I don't come back to myself… say my name."

"Say your name?"

But Grisham was already doing whatever he was about to do. He closed his eyes, and a glow formed around him. As it brightened, Arabelle stepped back, watching with ever-widening eyes.

When Grisham's body was glowing a bright white, Arabelle heard the cracking and popping of bones.

And Grisham *changed*.

His body elongated. His face grew ferocious claw-like jaws. A hundred insectile legs burst from his torso. Grisham the tiny dwarf had become Grisham the half-beetle, half-centipede.

For a moment he was smaller, and wriggled easily out of his collar. And then he *grew*. His body became too large for the cage, and his head was pressed between the bars. His jaws snapped madly—and bit down on the bars of the adjoining cage, tearing them apart as if he'd taken a bite of crusty bread.

As Grisham thrashed, trying to use his jaws on his own cage, the giant swamp cat took advantage of the new opening in its prison. It stepped out of the cage, launched itself off the wagon—landing with a noticeable limp—and glared at Arabelle with fevered eyes. She backed away slowly, unsheathing her daggers.

Up on the wagon, the Grisham beast finally managed to bite his way out of his cage. The bright glow returned as he changed shape once more, the sounds of cracking and popping bones returning.

But he didn't turn back into a dwarf.

As the bright light faded, a second swamp cat stood upon the wagon. Grisham, in cat form, leaped between Arabelle and the injured cat.

The injured swamp cat sniffed at Grisham and let out a growl that Arabelle felt reverberating deep within her chest. Grisham returned the growl, and then the injured cat swished its tail and limped away.

"Grisham?" Arabelle said hesitantly.

Grisham Cat sat back on his haunches and the glow surrounded him once again. Moments later, he was a naked young dwarf.

Arabelle blinked with surprise. She tried to stifle an inappropriate laugh, but succeeded only in making an obscene-sounding snort.

Grisham looked down at himself, gasped, and ran back to the wagon to collect what was left of his shredded clothing.

When he was mostly decent, they tried to wake the other captives, but with no success. The soldier in the third cage was still unconscious. And neither Arabelle nor Grisham was strong enough to carry even one man.

They needed to get help, and quickly, or all that Arabelle had done here tonight would have been wasted. Dawn was rapidly approaching.

"How fast can you run?" Arabelle asked.

"As fast as I have to," Grisham replied.

"How long have you been able to change into different animals?" Arabelle asked as they ran.

He looked her up and down. "How long have you been secretly stalking the nights, rescuing dwarves and killing slavers?"

Killing.

The word stirred an unexpected emotional response, and tears blurred Arabelle's vision. "I couldn't leave my friend in a moment of need."

He kept pace with her, his bare feet plodding through the grassland. "Thank you, Arabelle. I'll never be able to repay you."

"Just continue to be my taste-tester," Arabelle joked.

The dwarf laughed. "Gladly. But Arabelle... about my ability. Can we keep that knowledge just between us?"

"You keep my secrets, and I'll keep yours."

"Your secrets are safe with me. But what are we going to say to the guards when we arrive at the caravan? We can't possibly tell the truth."

Arabelle saw the first lights of the caravan on the horizon. "I don't know, but we have about thirty minutes to come up with something."

TALKING WITH A SWAMP CAT

G risham couldn't believe his fortune in having escaped a lifetime of enslavement not once, but twice. He gazed at the wondrous girl who ran effortlessly ahead of him. He'd have to find some way to repay her for the unbelievable kindness she'd shown him.

The eastern horizon was just beginning to lighten when he heard a warning growl in the tall grass behind them.

"Arabelle," he said, "stop!"

She halted, daggers appearing in her hands.

"It's okay," Grisham said. "It's not a threat. Just a swamp cat growling an alert, as if to say, 'I am here.'"

"The injured one you freed?"

"No. This one is a female. I can see her aura in the grass."

"Aura?"

Grisham shrugged. *If I can't tell Arabelle everything, then who can I ever tell?*

"Yes, I can see an aura around all living creatures. They convey moods and attitudes."

"You can read minds?"

He chuckled. "No, I can't read minds. I can just see the kinds of things you might read from body language. Like if someone is angry, or being deceitful."

"And what does this cat's aura tell you?"

"That she's curious."

A giant cat's whiskered face broke through the grasses. She sniffed deeply, sneezed, then made a rapid coughing noise followed by deep growling vocalizations.

Grisham translated for Arabelle's benefit. "Well, that's interesting. This cat thinks I'm a cat in a dwarf's disguise."

"You understand her? Did the other cat talk to you too?"

"Yes, but the other cat was fevered, probably dying, and didn't make much sense. I think his infection had affected him so much that he was acting purely on instinct."

"So..." Arabelle said, nodding toward the she-cat. "Are you going to talk to her?"

Grisham grinned. "How do you propose I make those sounds?"

"Well... you *could* change shape again."

Grisham knew they didn't have a lot of time, but he was curious how this creature had identified him as a swamp cat. When he changed shapes, did some... essence of the forms he took remain with him?

He dug within himself and found that pool of power that he now knew well. He felt the familiar pain of transformation, the disorientation of changing senses, and then the process was complete. He was the fevered cat from the slaver wagon.

The female cat eyed him curiously. "Your scent is... confusing. You smell like a swamp cat... *and* a no-tail. You look like Midnight... but you are not Midnight."

"Midnight?"

"He is my mate."

"I'm able to look how I choose." It was all the explanation Grisham could come up with. And it was, mostly, the truth.

"Why would you choose to disguise yourself as a no-tail?"

Grisham was amused, and decided to humor the cat. "There is much to learn from the no-tails. I have been studying with them."

"How do you do this thing? Can I do it as well?"

"No, only those of my kind can."

Grisham wondered if that was even true. Was this a Ta'ah ability? But he'd never heard of such a skill before. Maybe he had this ability only due to Seder's intervention.

"Your kind?" asked the cat. "Do you mean your family?"

Grisham's tail swished nervously. "Actually... I have no family. They are all dead."

The female swamp cat made a noise that sounded almost like chirping, and her aura filled with sadness. "I feel such pain. No-tails captured my mate and killed all my cubs. I found their broken bodies. I have not seen Midnight again."

"I have seen him. He lives."

The cat's aura brightened with hope. "You must tell me where to find him."

"He is heading north. I was captured by the same no-tails

who captured Midnight, but with the help of this female no-tail, we released your mate. He is injured, however. The wound smells bad. I would go to him quickly."

The giant cat gave a quiet purr. "Thank you, strange one. When you are done with the no-tails, come to the swamp. My mate and I would welcome one such as you in our family."

She stood, turned, and sprinted away.

Grisham and Arabelle had decided there was no way to explain the princess's involvement in the night's events, but that one dwarf alone could present a plausible story. So they split up. Arabelle ran ahead, sneaking back into the caravan unseen, and Grisham lagged behind, doing his best to look injured and bedraggled—an easy thing to do in his condition.

As soon as he staggered into sight of the caravan's guards, their whistles blew an alert. A cloud of dust rose from the caravan gate, and horses galloped forward. The eyes of the riders widened when they slowed at took in his appearance.

His clothes were covered with blood, mostly from his head wound, and the clothes themselves were so tattered he thought more of him was showing than was hidden. He had no idea where his shoes had gone.

The last set of hooves to pound the dusty plain belonged to Oda's pony.

"By Seder's long white beard, boy, we thought you be captured or dead!"

Arabelle's powder was wearing off, and Grisham's head

throbbed. Now that he was back to the safety of the caravan, the exhaustion of the night's events suddenly caught up to him all at once.

"I escaped," he said.

"I don't remember anything after that," Grisham explained to Nicholas.

The two of them lay on adjoining cots in the soldiers' infirmary. Nicholas had splints on one arm and one leg, but was in good spirits. Khalid had taken a party to the slaver camp to rescue the injured soldier and free the other slaves.

"Now it's your turn," Grisham said. "How did you avoid capture? What happened to your arm and leg?"

Nicholas shrugged. "Lucky I guess. I got thrown by my horse when the nets fell, and he broke my leg when he landed on it. I must have passed out when that happened. Apparently I suffered a bleeding head wound too. Evidently the slavers thought I was dead, or soon would be. When I awoke, I was right where I had fallen, the horse still on my leg."

"What about your arm?"

"Not sure about that. I feel like I remember being run over by a wagon. The slavers, I guess. They have no more respect for the presumed dead than they do for the living. Anyway, a search party found me and poor Robert. He didn't make it. He broke his neck when he fell from his horse."

"I'm sorry."

"I am too. He was a good man."

They were both silent for a long moment, then Grisham said. "So… did anyone ever find the sheep?"

Nicholas chuckled wryly. "You know, I asked the same question. Wouldn't you know it, those damned sheep found their own way back at feeding time."

Grisham groaned. "Figures."

VISIONS OF THE PAST

Arabelle had long ago gotten her sleeping routine down pat, and her internal clock reliably woke her every two hours, without fail. But sometimes that didn't seem to be enough. She would wake, and her limbs would feel sluggish, as if the poison were already taking hold.

This morning when she awoke, her condition was even worse. Her limbs wouldn't respond at all.

She panicked.

Did I oversleep?

She was sure she hadn't. She tried again, concentrating, struggling to move her arms and legs.

Finally she felt the cracking of muscle fibers. Overcoming the stiffness of her limbs, she slowly lifted herself to a sitting position. Her breathing was coming in short pulls of air, and she had to strain to take in deeper breaths.

She was still alive. But these symptoms grew worse with each incident.

She began her stretching exercises. Her muscles screamed in protest at first, but soon they loosened, and by the time she was done and soaking in the bath that Maggie had already prepared, the morning's panic was behind her.

The prior night's events, however, were still on her mind.

I killed a man.

A snake of guilt coiled tightly around her stomach. She knew she'd never forget the moment when, at her hand, the light in a man's eyes faded to darkness.

She tried to push the image away and focus on the positive instead. She had rescued her friend from slavers. After returning to camp, she'd kept watch to make sure he made it back safely, and she saw the rescue party go out after the others. Hopefully they could be freed too. No one should be subjected to a life like that. No one.

Maggie poked her head in at the tent flap. "Milady, are you finished soaking?"

"I suppose I should be."

Arabelle stood, stretching her arms and legs until they popped. The sound reminded her of the Grisham's shape-changing ability. Maggie handed her a towel, and Arabelle rubbed herself from head to toe.

She noticed Maggie looking at her strangely. "What?"

Maggie smiled fondly. "You aren't a little girl anymore, Princess."

"Of course I'm not! I'm now eighteen."

"I know. But I still remember when your arms and legs

looked like sticks and you kept tripping over your own feet. Now you move gracefully like a cat, and your curves... well, they're going to be catching everyone's attention."

Arabelle blushed at that last remark. She, too, had noticed that her hips were wider than they used to be, and her waist tapered nicely inward. But she wasn't sure how comfortable she was at the idea of drawing that kind of attention.

"Well, Maggie, it's either have curves or lose weight, and you already yelled at me for being too skinny."

Maggie gasped. "I never yelled." Her face reddened. "I might have hinted you needed to eat more."

The princess winked. "From you, that's yelling."

She expected her handmaiden to giggle, but she didn't. In fact she seemed rather melancholy.

"Maggie? Is something wrong?"

Tears welled in her friend's eyes. When she spoke, her voice cracked with emotion. "Hassan is dead."

She knows! Oh, my poor dear. But... how much does she know?

"I am *so* sorry, Maggie." Arabelle sat on the bed and patted the spot beside her. "Sit with me. Tell me what happened."

Maggie sat on the edge of the bed and took a deep breath. "Tabor was kind enough to come to my tent last night when he found out. He said Hassan died valiantly on a long-distance scouting expedition to fight slavers." She sniffed and gave a small smile. "But he was given a proper burial—just like an Imazighen. I always knew he would prove himself worthy of our people."

Arabelle gave her friend a heartfelt hug. Tabor was indeed

kind. That story was much better than the truth. Still, it changed little. Maggie was still brokenhearted.

Arabelle kissed Maggie on the cheek. "He was worthy, Maggie. Stay strong. And remember, time heals all wounds."

All wounds except mine.

———

Almost as soon as Maggie had left, Tabor arrived. "Princess? Can we talk?"

Arabelle waved him in. To her surprise, he had brought her a tray of breakfast, which he set before her.

"Why, thank you, Tabor," Arabelle said, sitting down to eat. "I would be delighted if you would break your fast with me."

"No thank you, Princess, I have eaten already. But I figured you would be hungry after last night's activities."

She froze in the middle of ripping off a hunk of bread. *Did he see me sneak out?*

"Activities?" she said innocently.

His bearded face revealed no hint of what he was thinking, but his brown eyes studied her carefully. Finally he said, "It's nothing. I might have thought you would sneak out to console Maggie regarding what happened to the Nameless soldier."

Arabelle scooped food into her bowl nonchalantly. "No, I didn't sneak out to talk to Maggie. Though this morning she did tell me of your talk with her. It was kind… what you told her."

To her surprise, Tabor looked sheepish. "Given her fondness for the Nameless soldier…"

"Hassan. His name was Hassan."

Tabor nodded. "Yes. I felt it was best that her memory of him remained a pleasant one. I apologize for not talking with you first, Princess, but you had already retired to your tent and I didn't want to disturb you."

Arabelle gulped at the thought of what Tabor might have found had he come to her tent to speak to her. "I would have agreed with your actions. As I said, it was a kindness. I would want Hassan to be remembered not as a Nameless, but as one of the Imazighen."

Tabor grunted his assent. "Thank you, Princess. It's within your right to declare such. I know I overstepped my authority."

It is within my right?

Arabelle had never given it much thought, but she'd seen her father expel lawbreakers from the Imazighen and declare them Nameless. Why not the opposite?

"I will tell my father you secured my assent beforehand. You deserve credit, not criticism."

Tabor shook his head vehemently. "No, Princess. I have already told your father what I have done. I cannot keep anything from him."

"And?"

"Your father replied as you have. He declares no fault in my actions. He cleared my honor, for which I am grateful."

Arabelle stood and wrapped him in a hug. "You're the most honorable man I know, and I love you for it." She took a step back. "Can I ask a favor?"

Tabor's face seemed to mask warring emotions just beneath the surface. "Anything you ask is my will, Princess."

"I'd like to learn some things about combat, and I need you to answer me truthfully, without asking why I'm asking."

Tabor frowned and eyed her curiously for a long moment. Finally he spoke. "Finish your food, Princess. You will need to keep up your strength." He turned toward the exit. "I'll return in fifteen minutes with some supplies to start our conversation."

As the flap closed behind him, Arabelle said aloud to an empty tent, "Supplies?"

Tabor sat across from her with various pieces of armor and weapons arrayed between them. "I've brought with me a number of items involved in combat. Many of these are items you will likely never use—such as heavy plate. But you should know about such things and how to combat foes who do wear it."

Arabelle suppressed a smile. This was more than she had intended to ask about, but she welcomed the opportunity to learn.

"Can I start by asking a few specific questions?"

He nodded. "Of course, Princess. Anything you want to know, I will try to enlighten you."

Arabelle rubbed her chin. "I've been thinking about the use of my daggers. All this time, we've trained on fighting tactics, improving my reaction times as well as gaining muscle memory for all of my attacks and defenses. I'll be honest, I had a dream in which I needed to strike out, but couldn't see how to achieve a quick kill. It frightens me that we've never talked about the natural use of these things you've taught me. If the moment ever arises, I would hope to kill instantly or not attack at all. What are the most lethal approaches for striking an enemy with only a dagger?"

Tabor nodded. "Princess, that is a very important question. I'm happy that you've brought this up. Lesson one in combat, you don't unsheathe your dagger unless your intent is to kill, and kill quickly." He pointed a finger at her to emphasize. "No bluffing either. If your intent isn't to kill, you shouldn't bear a weapon."

Tabor picked up an iron dagger and pointed to its cutting edge. "Notice the straight edge of this dagger. It's good for a slashing motion to open someone up, and slicing attacks with a blade are most effective against the soft tissues of your enemy." He illustrated by placing the dagger against his neck. "Either side of the neck will cut the blood supply to the enemy's head. This is almost always a fatal strike."

"What if you want a silent kill?"

Tabor gave her a devious smile. "Good question. Especially useful if your others are nearby who might come to assist." He illustrated the dagger traveling from one side of the neck to the other. "A similar but stronger slash is required to cut through both the side and front of the neck. Breathing and speech travels through the middle of the neck, so to limit the sounds, your knife will need to cut through the sinew and cartilage that protects the throat. But understand, this will require both a well-placed slash and a good amount of power."

"Like trying to slash through a steak?"

His eyes twinkled with amusement. "More like a steak with lots of gristle and cartilage. Such an attack is also very messy. Blood will spray in all directions."

"Any other locations for a quick kill?"

Tabor touched the back of his neck. "A dagger plunged into the base of the skull is sure to cause an instant death, but be aware, there is a significant risk of your blade being deflected by the bones of the shoulder or spine." He then touched two spots on his chest. "Your heart lies behind a bone in the center of your chest. If you stab off-center, at an angle, you should be able to cause a near-instant death as well. Just beware of getting your dagger stuck. Your blade can get wedged in between the ribs, making it difficult to retrieve."

"Do the tactics change depending on the dagger used?"

"Another good question. They can. Each dagger has its own weight, heft, and shape, and this—"

"What about this one?" Arabelle interrupted. She had made ready her own "supplies" before Tabor returned with his, and now she pulled one of her mother's daggers from behind her back.

Tabor's eyes widened. "May I see that, Princess?"

She handed the dagger to him and smiled as he passed his fingers gingerly along the flat of the blade. "I haven't seen this weapon in many years. I am pleased to see it has found its proper home. I assume you also have its mate?"

Arabelle nodded.

"Good. These daggers were specially crafted by dwarven smiths many hundreds of years ago, and are the ultimate in assassin's weaponry. They are made of the rarest of metals, damantite. It's said to be unbreakable, and once set true by the smith, its edges never need honing. And you see this slight wave along the edge? That causes more damage, and wounds from such a dagger often cause heavy bleeding. This is a most lethal weapon, my princess." He handed it back to her.

Arabelle approached her next topic cautiously. "What if I am attacking from behind? Would a stab to the back be sufficient?"

Tabor pointed to the right and left of his lower back. "Strikes here are mortal, but the victim will not die quickly, and would retaliate. I would again recommend a stab to the base of the skull."

"What about a stab in the middle of the back?"

Tabor shook his head. "Even with your fine weapons, such a strike is risky. If successful, it can be instantly fatal, but there is a lot of bone along the spine to protect the vulnerable parts."

Arabelle looked down and sucked on her lower lip dramatically.

"What troubles you, Princess?"

"I had another vision, Tabor. In this one, I wondered if my enemy was a demon."

Tabor's eyes widened with concern. "Why do you say this? What did you see?"

"After I attacked my enemy from behind, he flailed about. There was almost no blood, but a clear liquid oozed out from the wound in his back."

Tabor breathed a sigh of relief. "No, Princess, even if your vision was a premonition of a real event, this wasn't a demon. A lucky strike into the back could sever the spine, which contains a clear fluid. Even mild injuries to the spine can result in paralysis, leaving soldiers unable to move their legs or even their arms."

He picked up a piece of chain mail. "Now, let's cover attacks on armored enemies…"

Arabelle turned in her saddle and watched the long procession of wagons trailing behind. They were now east of Cammoria, on the move again after having finished trading with a cluster of villages that specialized in leather goods and high-quality farming supplies. The caravan's next stop, to the north, would allow them to trade with those who grew the best grapes and produced the best wines in all of Trimoria.

Father enjoyed his wine, and Arabelle smiled as she thought of the enjoyment he got not only from sampling a new year's vintage, but from talking with the people who made it. He was a committed friend to his people. He'd often explained to her that his respect wasn't given to him by virtue of his being Honfrion, Sheikh of the Imazighen, but that his respect was earned by virtue of him looking after the welfare of those who depended on him.

"Always treat people the way you hope for them to treat you," he would say. "My heart, this is the way of our family and our people."

They crested a hill, and Arabelle appreciated the view behind them. The vast forest south of Cammoria was as beautiful from afar as it was disturbing up close. Frightful rumors spread about the place.

"It's haunted, I say..."

"The witch of the woods will capture your soul..."

"Many a soldier has entered that misty forest, never to return."

When she was a young girl, she ignored those rumors and ran

as free in the Cammorian forest as she did in the one near Aubgherle. Until the day she heard the song—a song that, for a reason she knew not, chilled her from head to toe. She sprinted back to Tabor, who was always nearby, and cried on his shoulder.

Her father later forbade her from ever going near that forest again, and uncharacteristically she obeyed. She didn't want to go back there.

It was strange how something so frightening up close could seem so harmless, even glorious, from a distance. Still, Arabelle was happy to turn and put her back to the supposedly haunted place. It was time to move forward.

There was wine in her future.

A regal-looking elf with brown skin and pale hair walks through the woods at the edge of an empty, uncultivated land. She pauses —waiting for something?—and a look of concentration appears on her face. She closes her almond-shaped eyes, and from her fingers blooms a ball of sparking energy.

The ball fades, and now a dark line appears in the air. Ribbons of energy flow from it, forming a purple maelstrom of light.

A second elf steps out of this maelstrom. Her hair is raven-black, and her complexion is almost entirely white. The sparks cease behind her, the line vanishes, and the two elves greet each other, each holding up one open hand with splayed fingers.

"Avud," says the regal elf.

The pale elf shakes her head. "I will not own that name,

Queen of Seder. We were never lost. It is the women within Eluanethra who remain in ignorance of what true power is. My people simply seek fulfillment of our true power through our Lady and mistress, Lilith."

The regal elf shrinks back at the mention of this name.

Her opposite laughs, flashing serpent-like fangs.

"What can I do for you, lost one?" asks the regal elf.

The pale-skinned elf leans forward. "I seek a discovery of the Ta'ah, Ellisandrea. Those dwarven wizards will not speak to us, but I know that you maintained a relationship with their cousins. They hide an artifact that Lilith would cherish."

Ellisandrea shakes her head. "The dwarves of this time barely recognize the existence of their brethren. Besides, anything your mistress would cherish is no concern of mine. I will never help you find what you seek."

The pale elf gives a guttural snarl and shows her fangs once more. "Fine. But know that I will find the object for my queen. Your refusal changes nothing—other than to force me to dig up all of Trimoria."

With a wave of her arm, those same purple flashes appear around her, and the pale elf vanishes.

Ellisandrea shakes her head. "What has your evil mistress done to you, lost one?"

The scene flashed white.

.   .   .

Ellisandrea defends the entrance to a large underground chamber, holding a magical shield against the onslaught of a demon that towers over her. The demon's skin has been torn from the elf's attacks, and their battle has damaged the very walls around them. The demon spies a crack in the wall and dives through it.

The floor begins to shake. The elf reels back as clouds of dust burst from the fissure. And then the demon reemerges, crackling with a mystical energy. It now wields an orb of glowing white, which throbs as if in time with a heartbeat. The look on the demon's face is triumphant.

But that expression changes to one of surprise—and then of pain. Its body cracks. Its skin bursts. Steam pours from within it.

Black streams of power erupt from the orb and spear the demon. A black nimbus of power grows around its head, and licks of flame flash in an expanding torrent of power.

A cloud of steam obscures the demon, but the sounds of tearing flesh and shattering scales are clear, as is the unearthly scream of pain.

The orb drops and rolls toward Ellisandrea. She grabs the orb and runs for the exit. Behind her, the chamber collapses, and laughter rolls after her.

The scene flashed white.

The vision flies through mist-covered woods, slowing and circling as it reaches a clearing. In that clearing is a small wooden building... and a dark black altar.

The altar emits a slow throbbing pulse.

The vision moves closer, and closer still. The throbbing increases. Soon the dark stone structure is everything and the booming heartbeat is deafening.

The altar shakes with the reverberations, and a geyser of noxious fumes erupts, filling the scene completely.

Arabelle screamed as she jumped out of her bed, her nightclothes soaked with sweat.

A guard's voice called from outside. "Princess! Are you well?"

She looked around her tent, trying to slow her heart. "Yes, I'm fine. I... had a nightmare. Sorry."

"Nothing to apologize for, Princess. If you need anything, simply ask." His footsteps receded.

If I need anything, simply ask.

She definitely needed something. She needed to understand these visions. Were they real? If so, were they premonitions of the future, or scenes from the past? And why was she having them at all?

She had so many questions, and no one to ask. There were no seers in the caravan, had not been since... since her own mother.

As she began her exercises, she wished, and not for the first time, that her mother were here with her.

As they traveled the next day, Arabelle asked her father how her mother had come to make sense of her own visions.

He laughed. "I don't think she did. Your mother spent a lot of time contemplating her visions, but she was almost always left utterly perplexed. But the answers almost always revealed themselves when the moment was right."

"But how could she use her visions if she didn't understand them until much later?"

Father turned in his saddle and eased his horse closer to hers. He leaned in and whispered in her ear. "Are you having visions, my flower?"

She shrugged. "I'm having something. But it's hard to be sure what's a vision of truth and what's... just a dream."

Father nodded. "That was how it was with your mother. She was always frustrated by just that question. Perhaps you have the gift. If you do, time will reveal it. Be patient. When you need to know the truth, it will come to you."

That night, Arabelle's dreams were again troubled—and yet each time she awoke, holding on to them was like grabbing mist. It was not until her final sleep session of the night that she was struck by a vision that she could not forget.

The blue-eyed boy is in a boat floating on a river. He rides with what is probably his mother, and in her lap is a very tiny swamp cat. They are racing another boat that carries the boy's father and brother.

The boy and his mother win, and they hit their palms together in celebration.

All four of them guide their boats into a cave and climb out. They are laughing with one another as they retrieve their supplies.

And then the earth begins to shake violently. The family members look panicked and afraid, and grasp at one another desperately—

Arabelle jolted awake, a scream caught in her throat.

Say it isn't so. Please don't let it be…

She accessed her inner sight, praying to find the boy floating overhead as she always had before.

She found him. He was alive. But he wasn't overhead.

Her inner sight pointed north.

A MAJOR DECISION

The gray mare nudged past the other horses, trying to grab at the quizoa in Grisham's hand. She was always a pushy one.

"Wait your turn, you greedy beast."

He pushed her nose gently away and fed the quizoa to a white mare that had been waiting patiently.

"Grisham!"

Nicholas was hobbling toward the corral, heavily favoring his splinted leg.

Grisham pushed through the horses and met his friend at the edge of the corral. "Good to see you walking about! How are you doing?"

Nicholas smiled. "As well as can be expected." He nodded toward the horses. "I see you've made some friends."

Grisham absentmindedly patted a nose that had placed itself

on his shoulder. "They enjoy their treats, and they especially seem to appreciate the person who grooms them."

"Many of us are the same way." Nicholas winked. "Well, I just thought I'd say hello as I'm passing by. I promised to report to Khalid as soon as I was walking. If you can call this walking."

"You're doing great, Nicholas."

"Thanks. I feel even older than I am." He grinned and hobbled off.

Grisham was still entertaining the horses when he heard a commotion. He turned to find a group of harried soldiers chasing after Arabelle, who ran toward the corral with her hair and robes flapping wildly behind her. She leaped over the corral gate and nearly collided with him as she came to a stop.

"What in the…?" Grisham said.

Arabelle laughed hysterically, then whispered in his ear, "He's here."

Arabelle's smile was so infectious, he couldn't help but smile in response. "Who's here?"

"The boy in my visions. He's north of here. Not far at all."

The guards had stopped at the corral gate, but it was Tabor himself who pushed through and entered the corral. "Princess, we've talked about this. For your own safety, you must stay within sight of your escorts. Your father asked me to notify him the next time you escaped them. I pray you don't force my hand in this."

"I'm sorry, Tabor," Arabelle said, though she didn't look sorry at all. "I was just excited to talk to my friend. I wasn't trying to avoid your men."

Tabor was clearly exasperated. "Regardless of what you were

trying to do, please understand that your guardians have a job to do. And that they are not as... fleet-footed as you. If not for your own sake, please do it for them. Or for me."

"Yes, of course. I'm sorry, Tabor."

With a shake of his head, the soldier left the corral.

Arabelle immediately turned back to Grisham. "Can you believe it? He's here!"

Grisham only vaguely recalled the story she'd told him about the blue-eyed teenager in a dream, and didn't understand why this was such thrilling news. "I mean... that's great. But why did you come running at me like a demon was chasing you?"

She glanced back at the soldiers and spoke in a low voice. "Because I need your help. I'm going to take two horses north, find him, and bring him back here. I need you to create a distraction that will allow me and the horses to slip out of the caravan unnoticed. Can you do that?"

"Princess, are you sure? Why not take an escort? Certainly your father would allow that."

Arabelle shook her head. "Father is gone with a scouting party this morning, and Tabor would never allow me to leave the caravan without my father's explicit permission. This is a case of me having to ask forgiveness instead of permission."

"You seem to do that a lot lately." Grisham scratched at his thin beard, then sighed. "Fine. When do you need this... distraction?"

Arabelle grinned. "Give me ten minutes. I'm going to meet Maggie at the clothing tents. I'll lose my escorts there, then return here. Thank you, Grisham. Thank you so much!" She leaned in, kissed him on the cheek, and abruptly ran off once more, her escorts hurrying to keep up.

Before the princess returned, Grisham cleared the corral of anything that might cause injury to the horses. Then he patted the nose of his mountain pony. "I hope you'll forgive me, but I owe her much. I cannot deny her this."

He was just finishing up when he felt a tap on his shoulder. He spun around to find Arabelle standing right behind him, in the same outfit she'd worn on the night she rescued him.

"Impressive. I didn't even hear you enter the corral." He nodded toward the horses. "Go ahead and take your choice; they're all good beasts. Except my mountain pony. I'm somewhat partial to him."

Arabelle placed her fingers to her lips and touched his forehead with them. "Thanks."

She selected two stallions, both nearly sixteen hands tall. She readied them quickly, cinched their saddles tight, and then with a quick wave to Grisham she hurried them through the corral gate and turned toward the residential quarter.

A princess, cook, master horsewoman, and assassin. I hope this blue-eyed boy is worthy of her.

Now it was time for Grisham's distraction. He unlatched the corral's gate and let it remain ajar, but just barely. Then he walked to the back of the corral, reached into his pool of energy, and pictured the black swamp cat, Midnight.

The familiar painful sensations tore through his body as joints popped out of place, bones elongated, and fur grew.

As expected, the horses panicked when they saw the swamp cat in their corral. Grisham had to leap out of the way to avoid being kicked or trampled. The horses tore toward the gate, and one well-placed hoof broke it open. The herd raced out of the corral and scattered throughout the caravan.

That would keep the soldiers busy for a while, though it would do little for Grisham's reputation for taking good care of his four-legged charges.

He was about to transform back into himself when his cat eyes caught sight of a very large man standing some fifty feet away. He was the only person around who wasn't watching the escaping horses; instead he stared intently at the residential quarter.

The hair on Grisham's nape stood on end. He *knew* this man. Knew him… and *hated* him. Though he wracked his memory to recall why.

And then it hit him. This was the man who had accompanied Azazel on the fateful day his father was murdered. This was the man who had smelled young Grisham's fear as he hid in the cave behind the spell his father had cast.

And now he was here, in the middle of the caravan that Grisham called home.

Grisham roared in anger and defiance.

The man turned to him, snarled, and drew his sword.

Grisham extended his claws. *I am no longer defenseless, no-tail.*

His cat mind wanted desperately to fight, to seek his revenge.

But his Ta'ah mind was still faintly present, and uttered a warning.

If this creature is here, Azazel might be present too. And I will die.

Grisham's heart beat rapidly in his great chest, and every beat told him the same thing.

I must escape.

And not just escape this one no-tail. He had to escape all of them. No-tails were dangerous in numbers.

As the snarling no-tail tightened his grip on his weapon and advanced, Grisham sprang to the side and ran. Racing heedlessly through crowds of panicked onlookers, he headed for the only place he knew of where he would feel safe.

The swamps.

———

Grisham's shoulders ached with fatigue. He'd managed to leave the no-tails far behind, and his nose picked up the musty smells of the swamp ahead.

He sniffed for marked trees and detected the scent of another cat, but it wasn't recent.

Abandoned territory?

He didn't want to cause trouble and assert himself without knowing more about this place. And he was too tired to fight. So he roared a query, sat back on his haunches, and waited.

Soon a dark shape appeared from within the swamp.

It's her.

The familiar female slinked closer and snarled a greeting. "It is good to see you. Have you finished walking with the no-tails?"

She had sleek lines and a healthy build, and he felt a purr rumbling deep within his chest.

"I wanted to see if the swamp was a good place for me. Also, I remembered what you said, and I want to talk to you and the family leader."

The female bumped her shoulder against his. "You cannot. After I left you, I found my mate as you described. He died before reaching the swamp. He was our leader, and when he died, what remained of his family dispersed. But... if you are willing, you and I could form a new family. I'm ready for cubs."

Instinctively, he nudged her, nipped at her neck, and rubbed his cheek against hers. She purred.

"We must make our territory out of reach of the no-tails," he said, growling.

She rubbed against him. "Follow me. I know a place we can go."

As they jumped across patches of water, she asked, "What should I call you?"

He paused. For some reason, he couldn't recall his no-tail name. But he did remember the name of the prior leader.

"Call me Midnight."

BLUE-EYED BOY

Arabelle had taken the two largest horses she could find; they would need long strides to handle the pace she had planned for them. She was walking them through the residential quarter when she heard a commotion behind her. Whinnying horses, the splintering of wood, and the yowl of a swamp cat.

She suppressed a laugh as she realized the ploy Grisham had used for his distraction.

As soldiers raced past her to investigate, she patted at herself to make sure she had everything she needed—only to realize that she did not. In her excitement and hurry, she'd left behind her eye drops and powders.

She would have to go back for them.

She tied up her horses and snuck back to her tent. Only one guard was watching her quarters, and he was distracted by some crumbly morsel he was enjoying, picking bits of it out of his beard.

Arabelle slipped past him, and inside her tent she found Maggie sitting at her desk, reading a book of poetry. Arabelle put a finger to her lips and whispered. "I forgot something. Don't worry, I wasn't seen. I'll see you in the morning. I love you for doing this."

She snatched up her things, slipped back out, and returned to the horses.

Soon she was taking advantage of the turmoil in the camp to slip out a side gate. And then she was off in the grasslands, following her inner sight to the blue-eyed boy.

Arabelle's path led her through the grasslands of Trimoria. Her only companions, apart from the two horses, were the occasional pack of scavenging blink dogs. She steered wide of villages, since they often hid bandits and unsavory characters, and she didn't want to chance anyone following her.

She rode throughout the day, switching mounts periodically. The land was beautiful, and the ground level, but the heat of summer was oppressive, even as the sun began to meet the horizon. She pulled on the reins, allowing the horses to slow to a walk, and steered them to a stream where they could drink and cool off.

She needed to cool off, too. She was sweating profusely, and the tight mesh of her outfit grabbed at her sweaty limbs. It was not only uncomfortable, it might slow her movements. She made up her mind. Drawing out her dagger, she carefully cut the sleeves off her outfit, then did the same with her pant legs. A cool breeze blew across her exposed skin, and her relief was immediate.

But now she had a new problem: her pale skin would be far too visible at night. That, too, could be solved. Dipping her hand into the stream, she came back with a finger full of fine clay, which she rubbed on her leg. Yes, this would work perfectly. She continued coating her exposed skin until both arms and both legs were covered in a thin layer of clay.

Cool and camouflaged.

She remounted and continued on her journey. She was nearing the swamps to the north, but her inner sight told her she was also drawing closer to her target—*much* closer. She'd practiced such tracking for months now, and was getting skilled at gauging the distances indicated by her inner sight. She continued forward until she estimated she was a mere half mile away. Then she dismounted and tied her horses to a tree.

She took a deep breath. She was actually about to see the blue-eyed boy from her visions. Her hands shook with nervousness and excitement. She had to will herself to slow her breathing and calm down.

By now, darkness had fallen, and her night vision allowed her to see the outlines of many creatures. But in addition, there was one bright dot of light that would have been visible to anyone.

A campfire.

That was where the blue-eyed boy was.

Why did they create a campfire so near the swamps and wastelands? Don't they realize the dangers?

Arabelle applied her eye drops, and the world brightened.

Now the campfire appeared much closer, and she could make out than one dark dot sitting around the campfire.

Arabelle crept forward silently, making sure not to betray her location. She didn't how the boy had gotten here or who had brought him. Would there be enemies? Resistance?

And then another thought dawned on her.

What am I going to say?

"Hello, I saw you in my dreams, and I think we're destined to be together."

He'd probably run away screaming.

Arabelle continued forward and saw more detail. There were four distinct shapes huddled around the fire. Three were lying down, and one was sitting up. Was this the boy's family?

It was easy enough to find out.

She concentrated on the four images from her visions, picturing, one by one, the mother, the brother, and the father. Her inner sight unfailingly pointed straight to the campfire each time. And of course, the blue-eyed boy was there as well.

Movement in the darkness caught her eye. A group of figures quietly approaching the campfire from off to her right. She focused her vision, and gasped.

They wore the black armor of Azazel's enforcers. All were armed with glistening black daggers, and two had crossbows strapped to their backs.

Arabelle remembered what she'd seen written in the tent of the man she'd attacked.

Seeking Strangers To Trimoria.

Send a Quad to patrol the border of the cursed swamp.

She had to stop them. But how? Killing a single slaver from behind was one thing. Now she was facing four of Azazel's trained assassins. She had the element of surprise... but not much else.

She silently prayed. But no hidden wisdom appeared in the sky, and no visions flashed in her mind.

She was on her own.

As the wind picked up, she caught snatches of conversation among the men and saw their heads huddled together. They were debating their next move.

An idea dawned on her.

She withdrew one of her pouches of powders, loosened the drawstrings, and hefted it in her hand.

Yes. This will do nicely.

With practiced steps she crept toward the men, silent as the night, the opened pouch in one hand, one of her mother's daggers in the other. She adjusted her approach slightly to make sure the wind wouldn't betray her position.

Soon she heard their argument clearly.

"We already know them to be fools. Who creates a campfire so close to the swamp? They deserve to be skewered."

"Kirag said we are to try to extract information."

"I don't care what Kirag said. It's too much trouble capturing people and interrogating them."

Arabelle lobbed the bag of memory-loss powder right into

the middle of their huddled conversation. It struck the ground, sending a cloud of powder right up into their faces.

The men staggered back—and one of them spotted her. Arabelle acted quickly before he could alert the others.

She launched herself forward, dagger extended, and sliced deeply across the front of his throat. She felt a slight resistance as skin and muscle parted, then the scraping of her blade as it ripped through cartilage, and a plume of hot, sticky blood erupted from the wound.

Arabelle didn't pause; she kept running. In fact she sprinted for her life, expecting a crossbow bolt in her back at any moment. But there was none, and when she looked back over her shoulder, a hundred yards later, all four men lay on the ground, motionless.

She returned to the scene. The man she'd attacked was clearly dead, and lying in an unbelievably large pool of blood. The others still breathed, their chests rising and falling. If the powder worked as intended, they'd remember nothing of this when they awoke.

If it worked as intended.

She paused for a long moment.

I can't risk it.

The dagger still in her hand, Arabelle used the technique Tabor had taught her. She sliced each man's neck open and watched as their lifeblood drained from their bodies.

When she was done, she stood. Her hands were covered in gore. Four men lay dead before her—three had never even had a chance to fight back. She looked down at what she'd wrought, and was overwhelmed. She collapsed to her knees and cried silently for the men she'd just murdered in cold blood.

Arabelle couldn't approach the campfire with black eyes, torn clothing, and covered in blood. She would have to clean herself off. But there was no clean water nearby, and after one encounter with enforcers, she was afraid to leave the campfire unguarded. So for now she stayed where she was, standing watch from a distance, ensuring no harm came to these people.

At dawn, the family rose, snuffed out the fire, and began walking south. Arabelle followed. She would find a chance to clean herself up. And then she would approach them.

But someone else approached them first. A man on a horse galloped forth from the north, and for a moment she feared it was another assassin. But with relief, she saw it was not. It was a man she recognized, the Protector from Aubgherle, which lay not far off.

For the first time since she'd encountered the enforcers, Arabelle relaxed. This Protector was a good man, a giant of a man, and skilled in combat. As he dismounted before the family, she knew he would keep them safe, and would take them with him to Aubgherle.

Which meant Arabelle had missed her opportunity to meet the boy. For now.

But she would meet him. She was sure of it.

As for right now… she desperately needed a bath.

SUSPICIONS

The day had started simply enough. Kirag walked the length of the caravan as he always did, looking for anyone who seemed out of place. Normally these walks resulted in nothing, but on this occasion his eye had been drawn to the dark-clothed person slinking from shadow to shadow with a practiced stride. *This* was a person of interest.

The figure led him to the corrals, then took a pair of horses toward the residential quarter. But before Kirag could follow, the horses in the corral went mad, smashed the gate open, and went racing away in all directions. Somehow a swamp cat had gotten into the corral. Where had that creature been a moment before, and how on earth had it gotten in there?

The cat's eyes were riveted on him. Kirag pulled his sword from its sheath, ready for the challenge, and advanced on it slowly. The cat gathered itself for a leap, and he braced himself. But instead of attacking, the damned cat raced away.

Still itching for a fight, Kirag ran in the direction of the mysterious shadow. He caught a glimpse of the person, minus the horses, and followed. The shadow entered a tent and departed seconds later.

Again Kirag followed. The fluid movements of the shadow reminded him of an elf—which made him burn with anger.

And then the next thing he knew the shadow was mounted again, heading out a side gate, and riding off toward the north. Kirag snarled in frustration, knowing he'd never catch the elf without a mount of his own.

Why north? he wondered. If this was an elf, why not east toward their forest? The only thing north of their current location was the swamp.

Why was an elf even here?

He turned on his heel and strode back toward the tent he'd seen the elf enter. A guard was assigned to watch the tent, but he was slovenly and incompetent. He was so preoccupied with his pastry that even the giant Kirag had no trouble slipping past him and into the tent.

It was opulently appointed. A large bed with a rich mattress. A wooden storage box inlaid with colored stones. An ornate tub for bathing. An actual writing desk. And sitting at that desk was a girl, her mouth agape. She seemed unable to utter a word, and the color drained from her face.

Kirag showed her his empty hands, palms up, and closed the distance. "I simply want to ask you one question. Give me that answer, and I'll leave as quickly as I entered."

The girl nodded shakily.

"Who was the dark-clothed person who recently visited this tent?"

The girl's eyes widened, and he could see that he'd struck a nerve. She knew something.

The girl shrugged and whispered hoarsely, "I don't know. She entered the wrong tent... sir."

"*She*? That was a she?"

The girl gasped, and a look of panic crossed her face. "No, I meant he. He was lost and entered the wrong tent."

Anger boiled in Kirag's gut. The girl was obviously lying.

"Your choice is simple, young wench. Tell me the truth, or you won't live to regret your error."

Her reaction wasn't unexpected. She took a deep breath, readying herself to scream.

Kirag lunged and placed his huge hand over her mouth, muffling her. She flailed about, then stuck a hand into a partially open desk drawer and yanked out a dagger. She slashed at him with ferocity, but a complete lack of skill.

Kirag laughed as he caught her wrist. He pulled her over the desk by the arm while his other hand still covered her face.

And then he got a good look at the glittering, rune-covered dagger. He'd seen its kind before.

Elven make.

His vision went red with fury. He lost control, and he squeezed. The girl's bones snapped like branches, a most satisfying sound, and he dropped her lifeless body at his feet.

She wouldn't lie to anyone again.

The next morning, word raced throughout the caravan about a murder. Kirag couldn't hide his smile as he listened to the anguish of the women and the outrage of the men. They had hidden an elf in their midst; there was a price to be paid for such treachery against Azazel's enforcers.

And yet there was one element of the rumor that took Kirag by surprise. It was being said that the victim of this murder was the princess herself.

That was interesting.

Kirag made his way back to the tent where he'd crushed the foolish girl. Of course it was a buzz of activity. Dozens of soldiers had gathered, and at their periphery at least a hundred citizens were looking on with despair, sharing ever more wild rumors of the fate of their beloved princess.

Kirag pushed through the crowd. An area around the tent had been cordoned off, and in that cleared area stood Tabor and the Sheikh. At their feet was the slovenly guard who'd been watching over the tent so incompetently. The guard was kneeling with his neck stretched across a log. His arms were tied to the bottom of the log, and a large bruise was forming on the side of his head.

Kirag shoved his way to the nearest Talon. "What's going on?"

The Talon was watching the scene with obvious pleasure, but when he heard Kirag's voice he straightened obediently. "S-sir! I —I'm told the guard on the log was tasked with watching the princess's tent, and she was murdered."

A nosy bystander overheard this and cut in. "Not what I

heard. I heard it was the princess's handmaiden who was killed, and the princess is missing."

"What is planned for the guard?" Kirag asked the bystander.

The man spat on the ground. "That buffoon failed at the most important job he could ever have the honor of being assigned— guarding the princess, the light of our people. The Sheikh will surely sentence him to death."

Kirag nodded. *Death for incompetence. Maybe I misjudged this mustachioed fool.*

As it turned out, the Sheikh did not bother with sentencing or pronouncements. He simply nodded to Tabor, who drew his saber and, with one swift stroke, separated the guard from his head. The onlookers fell silent as the head tumbled onto the ground.

With a smile, Kirag pushed his way back toward his tent, putting the puzzle together.

That was the princess's tent. But it was not the princess I killed.

How did an elven-made dagger end up in the princess's tent? Was it possible the princess herself was the dark-clothed "elf"?

For that matter, what were the powders and straws he'd found hidden in the princess's tent after murdering the girl? Kirag now wished desperately that he'd been able to open the second chest he'd found, the locked one beneath the bed. Given different circumstances, he would have taken it, or simply demanded it be handed over to him. But given the murder, he had felt it best to slip away. Now he wondered what answers it contained.

There are too many unanswered questions. I need to look into this princess. Something about her isn't right.

CONSEQUENCES

Arabelle knew she was going to have to do a lot of sweet talking with her father and Tabor when she got back to camp. But at least she was no longer a bloody, muddy mess. After dunking herself repeatedly in that cool river, the flakes of brown and clouds of red washing away downstream, she felt like herself again. She had definitely made the right decision not to approach the boy and his family in that state. They would probably have fled screaming into the darkness.

But now the time had come for another form of coming clean. It was midday, and she and the horses had made it back to the village that the caravan had stationed itself next to. She decided to dismount here and tie up the horses to a hitching post —she would retrieve them once she'd dealt with her father. But she immediately realized she had ridden right into a serious commotion. It seemed everyone was out and about, clustered in small groups, talking and crying.

A boy ran past her, and Arabelle grabbed his arm. "Excuse me. What's going on?"

The boy yanked his arm back and kept running. Over his shoulder he shouted, "The princess is dead!"

Arabelle repeated the words. "The princess... is... dead." She screeched. "What?"

She feared sweet-talking would not be enough. Not nearly enough. If her father thought she was dead... and Tabor... the entire camp...

She couldn't imagine what she'd put them through.

No, there was no talking her way out of this one. She'd have to clear things up. Honestly.

She spotted some soldiers not far off, and strode directly toward them. But before she could take more than a few steps, a teenage boy stepped directly in her path, blocking her. "You don't want to go there," he said. "They're hurting people. I'll take care of you."

He grabbed her by the arm and started to pull her away.

She looked down at the dirty hand on her arm. Judging by the smell of manure, it wasn't dirt. And the boy was covered with it. But he was muscular, and she couldn't pull free of his grip; his hand was like an iron manacle.

He sneered at her resistance and pulled out a small rusty dagger. "This can be done the easy way, or it can be done the hard way."

Arabelle screamed at the top of her lungs.

The boy cursed and thrust the dagger at her face.

She'd managed to draw one of her daggers, and she just barely deflected the attack in time. Panicking, she then slashed at the arm holding him, and though she had only intended it to be a shallow wound, the skin parted and bled profusely.

The boy released her so suddenly that she lost her footing in the mud and fell to her knees. That was lucky, as it helped her dodge his next dagger thrust. But he followed up that thrust with a knee to her cheek, and that strike connected. Arabelle's head snapped back and her vision dimmed.

She heard the sound of metal against metal, followed by a cry of pain.

Was that me?

She felt herself being lifted into the air.

"Princess? Wake up. Please wake up."

The voice was familiar, but Arabelle was still stunned and disoriented, and couldn't respond.

"She's hurt," said the voice. "Run ahead and get another tent ready for her. I'll take her to her father. And you! Drag the pieces of that scum outside the village. Let it be eaten by the blink dogs and vultures. If he has family, promise them that I will personally see them get the same treatment if they think to bury him."

The light began to return to Arabelle's eyes. She managed to mutter, "I want to be in my own tent, please."

She heard Tabor near her ear. "Princess, thank goodness you are waking. Everything will be fine now." She heard a catch in his throat as he added, "I thought you were dead."

She opened her eyes. The light caused spears of pain in her head, so she settled for a squint. Tabor was carrying her like a baby, and as he walked, he hummed a lullaby that she remembered from childhood.

Her heart nearly broke when she managed to focus on his

face. This strong, honorable man, a man who always disguised his emotions, was now an emotional wreck. His eyes were blood-shot, his beard soaked with tears.

"I'm sorry, Tabor. You were right. I should never have left my tent last night. I would never have intended to worry you like this."

Tabor shook his head. "No, my dearest princess. Thank Seder that you *weren't* in your tent last night."

She didn't know what that meant, and she didn't care. She just couldn't bear to see Tabor like this.

She raised her head to look around, and was shocked to see at least twenty soldiers escorting them. But her neck hurt, so she once more rested her head against Tabor's chest. She was so sleepy and confused. But there something. Something...

The poison.

In a moment of crystal clarity, she understood precisely the trouble she was in. If she were to fall asleep in her current state...

"Tabor, promise me something."

"Anything, Princess."

"A vision has told me what I must do now. I have some of my mother's abilities. You understand?"

He paused only a moment before whispering, "Yes. Perfectly."

"Don't let me sleep. I absolutely must be awake. Get me a mortar, pestle, and the bark of the willow and the leaves of the khat bush. I must make a tea from that to get better. If I don't, I may die. Please tell me you understand."

"Princess, rest assured, it will be as you ask."

Tabor raised his voice. "Khalid."

"Yes, Tabor."

"I have a request I need you to take care of personally. Find Janius Mizmer and get a supply of willow bark and khat leaves. We need it immediately. If she doesn't have any, find it. I don't care what you have to do."

"Of course." Khalid's footsteps raced away.

Arabelle tried to concentrate on staying awake, but her mind wandered. *Did I lose my mother's daggers? What happened to that boy who attacked me? Poor Maggie must be frantic.* A thousand thoughts ran through her head, and her consciousness slowly drifted…

Arabelle cupped another steaming mug of tea and sipped at it. The pain in her neck had diminished, thanks to the willow bark, and she was wide awake, thanks to the khat leaves. Thankfully Tabor had insisted that Madam Mizmer mix the tea herself, and they woke Arabelle long enough to force it down her throat. In the days since then, she'd been drinking it constantly.

But no tea, no medicine, no painkiller could treat the grief and horror and guilt she now felt.

Her father had told her about Maggie.

Arabelle wanted to crawl inside her own wretched shell and die. She deserved to. Maggie didn't. Maggie was a good person, a trusted friend.

Arabelle was neither. She hadn't even told her father the truth.

When she was feeling better, her father and Tabor had met with her to understand what had happened that night. And she lied. She told them that she'd had a vision telling her to secretly travel north, though she knew not why, and that the journey had taken longer than expected.

Of course, her father assumed that this vision had been sent to her to keep her from danger. "It's a miracle, my precious daughter. I will forever be thankful for the guiding spirits that saved you that night."

But Arabelle knew there were no guiding spirits behind her actions. There was only her. She had chosen to depart that night. And Maggie, a girl she'd loved like a sister, had paid the price.

She barely ate. She moved only enough to keep the poison at bay. She hadn't even given thought to a bath. No bath could wash away her guilt.

The caravan's healers had told her that she would be fine. The swelling on her cheek had already diminished greatly. But those around her still treated her like a piece of glass, extremely fragile—and emotionally, she was. When the caravan moved on to a new location, rather than riding, she was placed in a covered supply wagon. Normally that wagon carried supplies; now it carried only a bed, Arabelle, and Tabor standing guard.

She didn't object.

Her guilt had only grown when she asked Tabor if Grisham could visit her. The young dwarf was the only person in this world to whom Arabelle could have told the full truth. And Grisham would have listened, would have cared.

Would have, but didn't. Because Tabor informed her that Grisham had disappeared on the same day she had. Somehow the horses had escaped that day, Tabor explained, frightened by a swamp cat that had gotten into the corrals when Grisham was supposed to be watching them. No one was blaming Grisham for the event—not exactly—but for him to disappear immediately afterward was considered highly suspicious.

Arabelle wondered what exactly had happened. The dwarf had caused a distraction, just as she'd asked, and then… somehow… had not been seen since. She feared he, too, was dead, for when she sought him out with her inner sight, she could find no sign of him. No response.

She might *never* know what had happened. All she knew for certain was that it was somehow her fault.

———

"Where is our next stop?" she asked Tabor one morning as they bounced along in the covered wagon.

Tabor paused in honing the edge of his sword. "Aubgherle."

"Already? But we have several villages between here and there."

"Yes, and your father insisted we bypass them. He sent patrols to let the residents know we'll be staying at Aubgherle for two months and to seek us out there."

"But why?"

"After that boy attacked you in the village, your father fears for your safety. In these smaller villages, there are only more of those pigs like the one who assaulted you. In the larger cities, there are Protectors, and people must follow the laws. Throll, Aubgherle's Protector, is a dutiful keeper of order."

"What about Kirag?" Arabelle asked in a low voice. "Aren't we required to follow the same path we always take?"

Tabor beamed with pride. "Your father stood his ground and gave Kirag an ultimatum. Either we skip the wasteland villages and go to Aubgherle, or we ride directly to Cammoria and settle this with Azazel himself. We are the Imazighen!"

Arabelle felt a flush of pride. "My father did that?"

Tabor nodded. "It was glorious."

Arabelle wished she had seen it herself.

"What happened to the boy who attacked me?" she asked.

Tabor's voice dripped with bitter hatred. "That vermin will never bother anyone ever again."

"What… what exactly happened? After I got hit in the face, everything was foggy and unclear. Next thing I knew you were carrying me."

Tabor gave her a serious look. "Truth?"

"Yes. I'd like to know everything."

"Very well. As you know, we believed you missing, probably dead. All of our men were searching for you—in the caravan, the village, the surrounding lands. I happened to be near the other side of the village when I heard your yell. I knew immediately two things. You lived, and you were in trouble."

His eyes moistened with tears.

"I sprinted toward the sound, and got to you just in time to see that beast kick you in the head. I already had my sword drawn. The boy saw me coming and took a step back. Let's just say that he fell to the ground in more than one piece."

She understood that what Tabor had done was a horrible thing, yet under the circumstances Arabelle found herself unable to feel any sympathy for the boy. "I imagine he soiled his pants when he saw you bearing down on him like an unleashed demon."

Tabor chuckled darkly. "Who could tell? He already smelled like an outhouse."

A hollow laugh escaped her chest as she realized Tabor was probably right.

It was three weeks after their arrival at Aubgherle by the time Arabelle finally felt ready to wander the caravan again. Physically, she knew she would be safe—instead of one or two guards, Tabor had told her she was now to have nothing less than a six-guard escort anywhere she went. But emotionally, she still felt unsure.

Her father must have understood that a soldier could not provide all the support a young woman needed, so he took the bold step of arranging for a new handmaiden to tend to her, to talk to her. Arabelle was uncomfortable with the idea—nobody could ever replace Maggie—but she couldn't form a good argument against it.

So it was that the next morning as she stretched under her covers, a brown-haired head poked her face into Arabelle's new tent.

"Princess?" she said nervously.

The poor girl looked terrified. And somehow, that made Arabelle like her right away. *This is harder for her than it is for me.*

She sat up in bed and waved the girl in with her best attempt at a smile.

The girl entered. She was petite and young—probably a few years younger than Arabelle. A rosy blush filled her cheeks as she looked at her feet and mumbled, "Princess, my name is Miriam. I'm here to help you with anything you need."

Arabelle tried to put herself in Miriam's shoes. The girl was so young, and she'd been told to go work for the princess. To not upset the princess. That the princess was emotionally fragile. She was probably told all those things and more.

And of course everyone knew that the last person to do this job had died brutally.

Arabelle reached out a hand. "Miriam, I'm Arabelle. Would you be so kind as to break your fast with me?"

Miriam bit her lower lip uncertainly. "I don't cook very well. Are you sure?"

Arabelle couldn't help but laugh. This poor girl knew nothing of what her role entailed. "Come," she said. "Sit beside me. Let's get to know each other."

She patted the bed beside her, and though Miriam looked like she'd rather do anything else in the world, she sat down beside the princess.

For the next half hour, they talked. Arabelle learned what Miriam liked to do and what she was skilled at. She learned about her family—it even turned out that Miriam and Arabelle were distant relations, on Arabelle's mother's side. Miriam's father was a scrivener, and her mother was a painter, and both lived in Cammoria where books and art were highly prized.

Miriam had joined the caravan to apprentice with a merchant and learn basic trading skills.

Miriam smiled, seeming much more at ease. "I'm really good with numbers, Princess. I also like to play music."

"I adore music."

Miriam grinned.

"Miriam, will you do me a very big favor?"

Her eyes widened. "I will do anything you ask, Princess."

"When you and I are alone, can you please just call me Arabelle?"

Miriam's eyes darted toward the tent's entrance. "Are you—are you sure, Princess? It's improper."

"Is it? I am the Sheikh's daughter. If I say a friend can privately call me by my given name, why would that be improper?"

At the word "friend," Miriam's eyes widened with surprise. "Arabelle," she said, seeming to like the sound. "I would be honored to call you by your name. And I would be honored to be your friend. You would be my first friend since leaving Cammoria."

Arabelle gave the girl a hug. "Thank you, Miriam. We're going to get along just fine, I promise you."

———

Arabelle and Miriam spent the day together, and Arabelle was surprised to find herself laughing often. Miriam took in with great astonishment many things that Arabelle took for granted, and it allowed her to see the world with new eyes. Arabelle soon saw that her father had made a good decision in pairing the two of them. She didn't necessarily require a handmaiden... but she needed a friend.

That same day, Arabelle began exercising again in earnest. She had been passively going through the motions for weeks now, staving off the poison but not maintaining her strength and flexibility. It was time to get back in shape. And to her delight, Miriam asked if she could join in.

Not surprisingly, the young girl didn't have the stamina to keep up, but if she stuck with it, she would. For now, she stopped midway, wiping her sweaty dark-brown hair from her face, and merely watched Arabelle for the rest of the routine.

It was invigorating to really be moving again, and Arabelle realized she longed for weapons practice, too. She unlocked her chest and retrieved her mother's daggers.

Castien's dagger, of course, had gone missing. She had foolishly left it in a desk drawer instead of locking it up in her chest, and it was lost or stolen on the night of Maggie's death. The loss of the dagger paled in comparison to the loss of her friend, but she had treasured the gift from the sword master, and this was just one more source of sadness on top of all the others. And she couldn't even tell anyone to look for it, as they didn't know it existed.

Arabelle stood with her mother's daggers and performed a series of lunges and blocks, along with the more complicated moves that Tabor had taught her, and finally she did the weaving attack that Castien had shown her. As her hands blurred, the blades became extensions of her body. She could feel them more than see them as they sliced rapidly through the air, serving both as shields and weapons. Arabelle maintained the blurring weave for as long as she could, then lunged with both daggers at an imaginary target.

Miriam gasped with surprise. "Arabelle, you are your own wall of iron. I've never seen the like."

Arabelle liked that. *A wall of iron.* She remembered the feeling of dragging her blades roughly across the cartilage of the enforcers' throats—and for the briefest of moments, she found herself wanting to relive the scene.

Perhaps to make up for the awful thought, she decided to be honest and truthful with her new friend. "I was taught this by the sword master of the elven people."

Arabelle fully expected Miriam to laugh at her, like her father did anytime she brought up the men of the woods. But Miriam was awed.

"That's amazing," she said. "Do you think I could meet one someday? I've read that they study the positions of the stars and make instruments to observe them. I have so many ideas and thoughts about the stars, but nobody believes that I could make something to see things far away."

Arabelle continued her weave for a few more seconds, then threw both daggers at a log set up in the corner of the tent. She stretched her arms and felt the comforting tautness of muscles, and when she went over to retrieve her daggers and put them away, her thighs and calves flexed and relaxed comfortably.

"I promise that I will try to arrange that meeting for you someday," she said, grabbing the bowl of fruit from her nightstand.

Miriam's eyes lit up, and Arabelle held up a hand.

"Just remain silent about what I've said and what you've seen in this tent. Many people think the elves are fairy tale creatures."

"I won't say anything, Arabelle."

The princess popped a gooseberry in her mouth and placed the bowl between them. "Now, let's replenish our energy. You too. I want you to work out with me again later."

Miriam smiled wanly.

That night, as she did every night, Arabelle used her inner sight to find the boy. He was tantalizingly close.

Could I possibly find a way to see him? Maybe it's time to visit the Aubgherle market.

She smiled with anticipation as she snuggled under her sheets, and as she closed her eyes, she hoped for visions of that blue-eyed boy.

Sometime during the night, a vision did flash into her mind.

Gathered in a field is a vast army that includes all manner of soldiers—humans, dwarves, even elven races—and through their midst rides a young general on horseback, barking directions to the various platoon leaders. He is handsome, with defined cheekbones and sparkling blue eyes, and his armor and sword glow with a fiery-red glint.

The general unsheathes his sword, waves it above his head, and points to the ridge just ahead. Beyond that ridge a black cloud has formed, radiating despair, and beneath that cloud is another army—this one borne of nightmare.

The armies begin to advance on one another.

The scene flashed white.

A giant ogre walks on a natural stone bridge across a chasm, whipped by wind that threatens to pull him into the abyss below. The ogre is equipped in plate armor that glows a pristine white and emits sparks with every movement. His sword, sheathed at his side, is the largest greatsword Arabelle has ever seen, with a pommel of red.

Following behind the ogre is a blue-eyed wizard, a look of concern on his bearded face. In one hand he carries a sparking metal staff, and in the other, a brilliant diamond the size of a melon. It pulses with radiant power.

On the opposite side of the chasm stands a fiend of blackness and fire, reeking of brimstone and emanating waves of heat. The fiend matches the ogre in size, and it, too, wields a giant sword.

As the two great beasts, ogre and fiend, meet at the middle of the bridge, another presence is felt. Behind the fiend, at the edge of the chasm, stands a deeper, darker presence, palpably evil, so enormous that it dwarfs both fiend and ogre.

The ogre clashes with the fiend, and the wizard raises the diamond above his head.

. . .

Arabelle lay in bed while she replayed the visions in her mind. The blue-eyed characters… they looked something like the boy. Was she seeing his future?

Miriam poked her head in. "Princess, it's time to wake. I've brought your morning meal."

Arabelle waved Miriam in. She was glad to see her hand-maiden had brought enough food for the both of them.

As Miriam set down the tray, Arabelle scrambled out of her sheets and took a seat. They both proceeded to fill themselves on stewed vegetables, yellow rice with raisins and nuts, roasted eggs, and a fruit salad drizzled with cream and honey.

As Arabelle patted her stomach at the end of the meal, Miriam laughed. "Arabelle, I've never seen anyone your size eat so much. If I did that on a regular basis I think I'd be rolling around here instead of walking."

"Well, let's just say that when I exercise as much as I do, I have to eat a lot. When I first started exercising, I didn't eat so much, and I ended up losing so much weight that Mag—um, Tabor actually commented on my being too thin."

Miriam self-consciously looked at her own body. "I don't think I could do all that you do. Maybe I'll just exercise less and eat less."

"It's okay, Miriam. I won't force you to exercise with me. But you're always welcome to."

Miriam looked relieved. Then her eyes widened. "Oh! Arabelle, did you have the vision last night?"

"What vision? You mean the First Protector's vision?"

Miriam shook her head. "No, everyone in Trimoria has that one. This one *felt* like the First Protector's vision, but it was a different battle. Or two battles. One battle was between armies, and another was between an ogre and a wizard and gigantic demons. I don't usually remember my nightmares, but I remember everything about this one. That's why I thought maybe it was a vision, like the First Protector's vision."

Arabelle sat silently, eyes wide.

"Arabelle? Are you all right?"

Arabelle shook her head. "I'm fine. But—that *was* a vision, Miriam. I saw it too. Everything exactly as you said…"

Suddenly Arabelle swayed, and everything went white.

Arabelle is lying on the ground, unconscious. The location is unknown, its features blurry. Father stands over her, distraught, and is being consoled by Gwen, the wife of the Protector of Aubgherle. Next to her is a brown-haired woman who glows with a white nimbus of light. The woman's hands flash with a bright shimmering rainbow of color, and she leans over and touches Arabelle.

The scene shimmers and is replaced by another. The marketplace in Aubgherle. A blonde girl is walking with two brown-haired teen boys. The younger of the two boys leads a swamp cat on a rope. The boys have sparkling blue eyes, and Arabelle feels a twinge of jealousy as they leave the market.

Arabelle hears a clicking sound. The vision turns, revealing one of Azazel's enforcers taking aim with a crossbow. She realizes he is aiming directly at the girl and two boys.

· · ·

Arabelle heard the click again and smelled something terrible. She woke, her eyes flying open, screamed a warning, and scrambled backward—bumping right into Tabor's knee.

Her father was leaning over her, holding a device before her face. It clicked, and a cloud of acrid smoke emerged.

"Stop it, Father! I'm awake!"

She was still in her tent. Tabor was at her back, her father was in front of her, and Miriam was looking on with worry from the side.

Arabelle turned to her. "It's all right, Miriam. I'm sorry if I frightened you."

"My flower, you can thank Miriam for calling for help. She said you were talking about last night's new vision and you stopped mid-sentence. Your eyes turned pure white and you fell forward into her arms."

Arabelle turned to Miriam. "My eyes turned white?"

Miriam nodded. "Like two glowing pearls."

Arabelle's latest vision suddenly came back to her. "Yes—because I had a new vision. Tabor, I need to get to the market, *now*, and I need a full escort. It's a matter of life or death!"

Her father held up a hand. "You are still recovering. There is no need to rush off."

Arabelle shook her head. "Dad, I'm fine! If you ever believed in Mom's visions, believe me now. I have the same visions. I'm sorry I've been hiding it from you. It started a year ago... when I visited with the elves."

His eyes widened. "The elves?"

"I don't have time to explain right now. Just humor me,

Father. What harm can come of it? Send double the escort if that makes you feel better."

To her surprise, he cupped her chin with his hands. "I believe that you had a vision, my daughter. When Miriam told us about your eyes turning white, I had no doubt."

"Mom's eyes turned white when she had a vision?"

He nodded. "Usually her visions were in our private bedchambers, so I'm the only one who ever knew that detail. You have the gift, my heart. I just hope you're interpreting your visions correctly."

"So can I go?"

Father turned to Tabor. "I want you to triple Arabelle's guard. I need you here to oversee the shipment, so make sure Khalid oversees her escort. I will take no chances."

Tabor banged his fist to his chest. "I'll arrange it immediately. Princess, I will have your escort ready in ten minutes." He turned and left the tent.

"Princess," said Miriam in a quiet voice. "Can I come with you?"

Arabelle smiled. "No, my friend. Not today. Some elements of my vision are dangerous. I would not risk you."

Miriam started to protest, but Father cut in. "Miriam, would you mind spending the day with me? I'll show you how this caravan really runs." He winked. "Maybe you'll learn enough to help your parents understand the merits of joining us and widening the market for their goods."

Miriam smiled and bowed. "Yes, Sheikh. That would be very educational. Thank you."

Father kissed Arabelle on the forehead. "Do what you must,

my dear, and no more. And please don't drag your guards into those damned woods you so enjoy. You know how our people feel about tightly enclosed places."

She hugged him tightly. "Thank you for believing in me."

"I pray Seder is truly leading your steps."

I really think he might be.

CONFRONTATION

E ver since the events surrounding the princess's temporary disappearance, Kirag had sought a way to talk with her. But she was now guarded by at least a half dozen soldiers at any time, and these men were nothing like the lazy slob who'd been on duty before. They had a fanatical look in their eyes, nothing was beneath their attention, and no one came near the princess's tent without undergoing their scrutiny.

At least the girl had started to leave her tent again, along with another wisp of a girl. Still, six armored men surrounded them whenever they went out. It was going to take some effort to talk alone with this girl about her nighttime journeys and that elven-made dagger, which he still carried with him.

One of the Talons poked his head into Kirag's tent. "Unusual activity at the princess's tent."

Maybe this is my opportunity.

Kirag jumped up from his cot. "Good job. Have a Duo within

sight of the tent in case I have need of additional eyes or ears." The man withdrew.

Kirag strapped on his sword, pulled on his boots, and stepped out into the bright morning sun.

He found a much larger than usual group of soldiers gathered around the princess's tent. Tabor's second, Khalid, was giving assignments and arranging the soldiers in formation.

Kirag had watched Khalid and knew him to be a deadly swordsman, as good as some of Azazel's best Talons. Kirag would so love to have an excuse to fight the man. There was no question who would win that fight, but he would relish the humiliation Khalid would endure as he was defeated without Kirag so much as getting winded.

Long, dark hair appeared between the soldiers as the princess exited her tent. Then the protective circle slammed shut around her, blocking her from view.

Princess, where are you going that requires so many guards?

The princess and her escort walked the short distance to Aubgherle on foot, which made it easy for Kirag to follow. In fact, as far as anyone watching was concerned, he wasn't following at all; he was merely walking along the main trail.

He had, of course, sent a Duo ahead, into the city as well. They would help keep an eye on things from there.

Apparently their destination was the Aubgherle marketplace, and the princess's escort was soon jostling their way through crowds of citizens and merchants. Kirag had no such trouble.

Between his black armor and imposing size, people tended to get out of his way. The downside of this was that stealth was difficult, so he had to hang back for his pursuit to not be obvious.

Perhaps their destination was not the market after all, for they veered right, passed through a less-busy part of the market, and then passed right out the other side. As the yelling of the merchants selling their goods began to fade, Kirag wondered what this trip was all about.

Where are you leading me, Princess?

They headed south, back out of the city once more, and onto a trail that the southern farming communities used to bring their wares to market. Here the crowds thinned greatly and the farmlands opened up. Kirag was going to be even more conspicuous, and it would be harder to explain away his presence out in the open. Why would he be traveling south of Aubgherle? He increased the distance between him and his quarry.

Suddenly the princess's escort drew their weapons, ran forward, and grabbed a man in black who'd been hiding in the bushes. They threw him down on the ground and someone gave him a swift kick to the jaw. The man stopped moving.

A snarl crossed Kirag's lips. This man was one of his troops! He'd stationed them all around the city to watch for strangers. How dare the Sheikh's men assault an enforcer of Azazel?

He spotted a flicker of movement from deep within the grass beside the trail. One of his Talons was hiding in the grass with a crossbow. At that moment the bolt shot forward and landed squarely in the back of one of the caravan soldiers. Instantly two more bolts shot forth from nearby rooftops and sprouted from other caravan soldiers. The Duo he sent ahead must be hiding there.

Kirag growled in frustration. These caravan fools deserved their deaths for what they had done, but who in their right mind attacks with four to one numbers against them?

I am surrounded by idiots.

In the commotion, Kirag caught a glimpse of a dress and the flash of a drawn dagger. The princess had parted company with her protectors, ducking past them as they scrambled to help their fallen or chase after the idiotic Duo scurrying across the rooftops. Only Khalid had enough of a working brain to run after his charge.

Kirag too gave chase. He was shocked to realize that the princess wasn't fleeing—she was *pursuing* the Talon who had been hidden in the grass. She was quick, too, in addition to being brave. And foolish.

He picked up his pace and came up behind Khalid, who seemed entirely unaware that he was being followed. Kirag already had his sword drawn, and with one swift motion he slashed across the back of the guard's thighs and kicked him. Khalid fell, struck his head on a rock, and was knocked unconscious.

Kirag smiled.

He'd never expected such an opportunity so soon.

But his quarry was the princess, and he left the soldier behind. The Talon was leading her toward the forest that bordered the farmlands. The home of the elves.

The princess threw a dagger at the Talon. It buried itself in his back. She ran past him with yet another dagger and slashed across his neck. A plume of crimson erupted from the wound.

This princess has claws. Fascinating.

Kirag ducked into the grass to watch her next move.

She paused to confirm the Talon was dead, then ran into the woods.

Why? Why not head back to your guards?

Yet he was glad that she had not, for this presented a perfect opportunity.

Kirag's best approach was to try to intercept her before she got too deep into the woods. He took a parallel course into the forest, and with his long strides he was easily able to easily outpace her.

When he'd taken his position in front of hers, he ducked behind a large tree and pulled out one of the marked straws that he'd taken from the princess's tent. Now that Kirag had had the time to examine the contents—and even test them on a Talon—he knew what the powder inside did: it put a target to sleep almost instantly. It also seemed to have effects on memory.

The girl was fleetfooted, but her heavy breathing gave her away. He heard her approach, one of the straws to his mouth, and blew just as she passed in front of him.

She was enveloped in the cloud of powder. After several coughing steps, she fell face forward into a pile of leaves.

He laughed as he walked toward her. "Hello at last, Princess. I think it's time we take you to a place where we can talk. I have some unpleasant, but very entertaining, questions for you, my princess."

Before Kirag could take another step, an elf materialized from the nearest trees, a glittering sword in his hands.

"Kirag," he said, with murderous rage in his eyes. "I told you once before to stay away from here. Now you will pay for all that you've done."

Kirag drew his sword. "Castien Galonos," he snarled. "Welcome to your death."

The elf wove his blade through the air, moving it so rapidly that the air hummed.

But Kirag was unfazed. Grinning, he retrieved the elven dagger from his belt and held it up. "Recognize this, elf?"

That caught the elf's attention. And just as Castien's gaze flicked to the dagger, Kirag threw it—directly at the unconscious princess.

With impressive speed, Castien launched himself at the dagger and slashed it out of midair. But Kirag had been expecting this—or at least the attempt—and was already sending a powerful thrust of his sword at the off-balance sword master.

The elf dodged, but came out worse for the encounter. A few droplets of blood seeped from the arm of his tunic.

Kirag chuckled. "First blood, mine."

The elf resumed weaving his sword in a dizzying pattern. The annoying buzzing sound grew louder.

Kirag jabbed with his sword, testing his opponent. The elf lunged with blinding speed; had Kirag not already planned to step backwards, he might have found a sword in his lung. Instead the tip of the sword master's blade sank into Kirag's shoulder before whipping back out.

Castien smirked. "Both of us are now blooded."

The elf resumed the irritating pattern of sword motions, but this time he drew a second sword from his back and added it to the blur. The buzz grew to a high-pitched wail, and the elf gave Kirag a wicked smile.

The thought crossed Kirag's mind that, for the first time in his life, he might have encountered a combatant who was as dangerous as he was.

But his rage overrode his caution, and his vision clouded with red. Kirag kicked dirt in the elf's face and sent a vicious strike into that buzzing maelstrom. His blade connected with one of the two swords, shattering the elf's blade with the impact.

Kirag laughed.

And time seemed to slow.

The broken shards of the elven blade drifted to the ground... followed by the sword that had been in Kirag's hand.

How odd, Kirag thought distantly.

He looked down. The pommel of a sword protruded from his chest.

The elf's hand grabbed it and ripped it out. Rhythmic gushes of blood spurted from the wound. And as Kirag watched, the ground seemed to rush up toward him.

As he lay with his cheek in the dirt, he wondered why he felt so cold on a warm summer day.

He heard that buzzing sound again.

And then nothing more.

POISON

A rabelle hovered over her own body in the forest. Her mind was... cloudy. She couldn't remember how she'd gotten here—or why her body lay on the ground before her, asleep.

And then she remembered the vision that had sent her on this visit to Aubgherle.

Yes. The vision. Details started to come back to her.

The vision had shown only the single assassin, and she'd been shocked when the chaos erupted around her. But she'd spotted the man in black armor, the one from her vision, running away with an empty crossbow strapped across his back, and she knew she couldn't let him escape. Only after she'd chased him down and finished him off with a running slash at the neck did she realize that her guards had not followed her.

It then dawned on her that this was her opportunity to slip away and speak to Castien. She needed to tell him about the blue-eyed boy and his family, new to Trimoria, so Castien could help watch over them. And she needed to warn him that there were assassins crawling all over Aubgherle.

Her inner sight told him he was close.

She ran into the woods, following her inner sight. And then…

And then?

She couldn't remember anymore.

And now she was looking down at herself, awake but not really awake, and she heard Castien's melodious voice, and the clashing of steel, but saw nothing.

She willed her body to move, but nothing happened.

I can't control my body if I'm not in it. Can I?

After a while—how long she wasn't certain—Castien was there, visible now, kneeling over her body, gingerly turning it over. He felt at her neck and exhaled loudly in relief.

"I'm sorry I arrived too late to prevent this, poor girl." He swiped his finger across the bridge of her nose, touched his tongue to his finger, and spit. "You've inhaled *Tishkakh*, the leaf of forgetfulness. I am not sure if you can hear me, but I need to check you to ensure you haven't suffered any additional injuries."

He began patting her carefully from head to toe. Strangely, though Arabelle was not in her body, she could feel his touches. Faintly.

He talked as he examined her. "My dreams were visited by Seder this morning. I thought I was going as crazy as old Xinthian, but now…" He shook his head. "Seder told me I would find you this day, and that when I did, I was to bring you to your father. He said you would die if he did not find you. I presume that means he is going to come looking for you."

Apparently satisfied with his examination, Castien picked up her body and carried her through the forest. Arabelle drifted along behind.

"I would prefer to watch over you myself. I don't know how much *Tishkakh* you inhaled, nor do I know if your father is aware of the poison that courses through your body. If he allows you to sleep…" Castien grimaced. "I will trust my dreams, but I will also keep watch from afar. I will not allow you to succumb, even if it means exposing myself to the human world."

In the distance, Arabelle heard her father yelling her name.

Castien whispered, "Seder was right again. It is time, my pupil. I am leaving you in an open space. I will make sure your father finds you here."

He placed her body under a tree, straightened her dress, and wiped away the leaves that had fallen in her hair. Then he vanished among the trees.

Her father's shouts came closer. Arabelle wanted to call out to him, but couldn't. How would he find her here if she could not tell him where she was?

A rock struck a nearby tree.

"Arabelle, is that you?"

Another rock struck the tree. Castien. He's drawing Father closer, while staying hidden.

"Arabelle?"

Moments later, her father appeared. He ran to her body, knelt beside her, and lifted his head in praise. "Thank you, holy spirits, I've found her, just like you said I would."

He put his hand on her forehead. "Don't worry, my heart, I'll get you some help. I even brought Logan to take us back."

Arabelle drifted along behind as her father cradled her limp body in his arms and walked back to the edge of the forest, where the horse waited. Father balanced her across Logan's back while he mounted. Logan began trotting across someone's cultivated fields, Father holding her body in place with one hand and the reins with the other.

Arabelle had no trouble keeping up, but she wondered how she would ever get back into her body.

"Arabelle," her father said, "I have a confession. When I was a child, I too used to have visions, like your mother." He took a deep breath. "But then my mother died in an accident, and I cursed those powers for not giving me enough information to warn her. And with that curse, the visions left me. Until now.

"Soon after you left, I had a horrible feeling something would go wrong. I prayed for your safety. And I was struck by my first vision in thirty years. It told me to find you in the forest, where secrets would be unveiled. I can't tell you how relieved I am to have you with me again, just as my vision predicted."

They passed the fields and Logan stepped onto a path.

"There's a farmhouse up ahead!" Father said. "I'll find out where the nearest surgeon is. You'll be looked at immediately."

He urged the horse forward, but in his anxious state he must have kicked the horse with too much intensity, and poor Logan reared up on his hind legs, sending both Father and Arabelle's body onto the ground with a thump. The startled horse galloped away.

Two women hurried down from the farmhouse. One with

brown hair, the other blonde and clearly pregnant. Arabelle recognized the pregnant woman—this was Gwen, the wife of Aubgherle's Protector. Though it appeared Father didn't know her, nor she him, for no look of recognition passed between them.

"What is wrong with you, sir?" snapped Gwen, wagging her finger. "You shouldn't ride so recklessly—look what has happened!"

"I had no choice," Father said. "It's my daughter... she was lost in the woods. I went looking for her, and found her unconscious. She will not wake. She needs help immediately."

"Why did you bring her here?" asked the brown-haired woman suspiciously.

"Your home is the first I saw upon exiting the forest. I had hoped you could direct me to a surgeon or physician. But that infernal horse—"

Gwen shook her head. "You're one lucky man to have called upon this of all houses."

The brown-haired woman knelt beside Arabelle's body. "Tell me... in what position did you find her? Was anything lying on her, maybe a fallen limb?"

Father shook his head as he rose. "Nothing like that. She was leaning back against a tree, as if she'd sat back and fell asleep. Nothing had fallen on her. Not even a leaf."

"I'll need to look her over carefully before we do anything," the brown-haired woman said. "If she were conscious, I could offer her a tonic, but as long as she remains like this..."

"Are you a physician, woman? Please, do whatever you feel is necessary."

The woman began removing Arabelle's dress. She stopped when she found the discolorations she carried on her ribs from her encounter with the dragon. "It seems she's been bitten by something poisonous. Are there snakes in the woods?"

Gwen answered. "There is only one poisonous snake known to live in those woods. A death adder. A single strike is said to kill within hours."

Still hovering over the scene, Arabelle was impressed at how quickly they diagnosed her poison. Even if they had no idea that the poison had nothing to do with a snake.

The physician whispered something to Gwen, who nodded. "Do what you must. You cannot avoid using your gift, if it's for a good cause."

Gwen helped Father to his feet. "Come with me. Your daughter is in good hands, but Aubrey needs room to work."

"But—"

"We are not leaving her. We are merely giving her a little space."

Father allowed himself to be pulled back several feet.

Aubrey placed her hands on Arabelle's body and closed her eyes. At first, she just sat there perfectly still. Then a breeze blew, and Arabelle felt her vantage point *shift* in an inexplicable way. And now she could see.

The woman's hands glowed with a shimmering energy that crackled and spit with some preternatural force. The glow crept up her arms, and soon streams of energy erupted from the woman's every pore. Those streams coalesced, coming together into a mass of sparkling white that hovered over her. The longer she concentrated, the larger the cloud grew.

Her father and Gwen were watching all this, Gwen patting Father's hand in a comforting manner, but neither showed any reaction to the pyrotechnics taking place before them. Father gazed at his daughter with the same distraught look as before.

Can they not see what is going on? This woman is a wizard. She's practicing magic on my body!

Aubrey shifted her posture slightly, and the sparkling cloud above her head stopped growing. Instead, it began to drain. Ribbons of scintillating white energy flowed out of the cloud, through the woman's hands, and into Arabelle's body.

The breeze blew again, shifting Arabelle's vantage point once more. The cloud vanished. The energy vanished. And yet this Aubrey still had her hands on Arabelle's body, a look of intense concentration on her face. She was tiring, that much was clear— the toll of her work was beginning to show.

Arabelle looked down at her own body and saw it changing. Her bruised wounds changed color, and a sickly yellow fluid erupted from the spots where she'd been infected by the dragon.

The scene flashed white.

"Young Arabelle, Princess of the Imazighen, bearer of many secrets, you can rest assured that your ordeal with the poisoned dragon is over."

"Seder?"

"Yes. I want you to know that, although your body is rid of the substance that was a piece of Sammael's essence, your role is not yet over. My plans are only now beginning to unfold.

"Your body is now trained. Given time, your mind will follow.

You are key to many things. Just remember that your value rests not in who you are, but how you treat others. Now—rest well, Princess of the Imazighen. You have earned it."

Arabelle's eyes fluttered open. She was no longer hovering over the scene, she was looking at it from below.

From her own eyes.

Above her was the exhausted face of the physician, Aubrey. The woman gave Arabelle a tired smile.

"Arabelle!" her father cried. She turned her head and saw tears streaming down his face. "Arabelle, you're awake! Oh, my poor baby, you have come back to me!"

Arabelle tried to sit up, but the world spun around her, so she lay back down. Aubrey tipped some liquid from a flask into Arabelle's mouth. She drank a few sips, and a warmth spread through her body.

"Drink it all," Aubrey urged. "It will help your body restore itself after its ordeal with the poison."

Arabelle had never cared much for cow's milk, but she felt the effects of the draught as she drank the warming potion.

Finally Arabelle felt well enough to stand. She waved everyone away—only to realize that most of her dress had been pulled up. With a gasp, she rapidly covered herself before rising to her feet.

Father wrapped her in an embrace, and she welcomed the feel of his strong arms around her.

Then he stepped back and turned to Aubrey. "How is this possible? She was bitten by an adder! None live through such a bite. You gave her no medicine, no incision, and yet here she looks as healthy as she did before she left home."

Aubrey's expression was blank, innocent. "I saw no bite. Perhaps you were mistaken."

"But... but..."

"Instead of questioning what happened, why not simply be thankful that your Arabelle has recovered from an ordeal we should all forget?"

Father stared open-mouthed. Finally, he nodded. "You're right. I... must have been mistaken. And I owe you a tremendous debt—a debt I am honor-bound to repay. My name is Honfrion, and I represent the interests of this season's caravan. Anything you need, you must simply ask."

Gwen's eyes widened. "Do you mean to tell us that you are Honfrion, the Merchant King?"

Father smiled. "Some have called me that, yes."

"Well, Merchant King," Gwen said drily, "it would appear that your horse has abandoned you. Come. We will send the boys to look for it. In the meantime, please join us in the house for food and drink."

While Father and the women talked, Arabelle ate a snack and relaxed, letting her body recover. She was surprised at how loose she felt now that the poison was gone from her body. All of her motions felt much smoother. It was as though her joints had all been lubricated. She wondered how this would affect her exercises.

Then it dawned on her. *I don't have to exercise anymore. I don't have to wake each night to prevent my muscles from being paralyzed.*

But even as the thought struck her, another took its place.

I don't want to lose these muscles, these skills. I can't let myself lose them.

At that moment the main farmhouse door was thrown open and Tabor charged in, his eyes frantic.

"Tabor!" Father exclaimed. "Calm down, my friend. Everything is all right."

"Sheikh, my apologies, but your disappearance, and the disappearance of the princess..."

Father raised his hand. "I'm sorry to have worried you. Today has been a very... unusual day." He turned to Gwen. "Please forgive my guard for entering like that. He's worried for us, that's all."

Gwen nodded. "I understand. Tabor, is it? Would you care for a refreshment?"

Tabor shook his head solemnly. "Thank you, Lady of the Protector..."

"Call me Gwen."

"Thank you, but I cannot partake."

Tabor withdrew a cloth-wrapped package from his tunic and handed it to Arabelle. "Princess, as I tracked the whereabouts of my lost Sheikh and his daughter, a very unusual man walked out of the forest and handed this to me. He gave his name as Castien. If I didn't know better, I would say he was an elf."

Arabelle unwrapped the package and gasped.

My mother's daggers!

With all that had happened, she hadn't even realized they were missing. But they were still coated in dirt and gore, so she quickly rewrapped them before anyone else could see. "Thank you, Tabor."

She was afraid there would be questions from both Tabor and her father. *What is in the cloth? What do you know of this mysterious elf? Why is he sending you packages?* But Tabor mercifully forestalled any such questions by turning to the Sheikh.

"Sheikh, this Castien had a message for you as well."

Father raised an eyebrow. "Go on."

"First, it seems that the injury given to Khalid was done by a giant enforcer with yellow eyes."

"Kirag."

"I can only presume so. Castien reports him dead. In his words, 'The forest has claimed him as its own. This minion of Azazel no longer lives.'"

"I cannot say I mourn his loss, though the consequences of this may be dire."

"I share your concerns, Sheikh. There is one other thing. Castien made a point of mentioning that our princess is welcome to visit his people in the woods at any time she wishes. Especially since, again in his own words," he looked meaningfully at Arabelle, "'she already knows the way.'"

Arabelle looked down at her lap, but felt the stares of everyone in the room. Oh, yes. There would be questions.

"Sheikh," Tabor continued, "one more thing. Khalid was injured in pursuit of our princess. My men have taken him back to our people to address a slash across his legs and a bump on the head. With your permission…"

Father clamped his hand on Tabor's shoulder. "Of course, go. Make certain that he's well. I know how much your only son means to you."

As Tabor banged his fist against his chest in salute and departed, Arabelle felt her mouth drop open, and had to forcefully shut it. *Khalid is Tabor's son? How did I not know that?*

While Father talked further with Aubrey, Gwen escorted Arabelle to the kitchen to clean up. The truth was, Arabelle was far cleaner than she had any reason to be. She had managed to avoid the blood spray from the enforcer she had killed; she was merely a bit muddy from having fallen in the woods.

But it seemed that wasn't Gwen's real reason for leading her to a washbasin. She smiled and whispered, "I thought you might want to wash those daggers."

Arabelle's eyes widened. "You saw?"

"Fear not, I believe I am the only one who did. I saw no reaction from your father, if that is your concern. A princess with daggers… now I've seen it all."

If she only knew how un-princesslike I've been.

Gwen left her alone to her ablutions. When her daggers were clean and dry and re-sheathed, and she had tidied her face and hands and was feeling like herself once more, she returned to the other room.

Father was ready to go; it seemed Logan had been found. Arabelle hugged both Gwen and Aubrey, and it was only then

297

that it struck her—she recognized the brown-haired woman too. How had she not realized from the start?

This is the blue-eyed boy's mother!

She wanted to say something, but she was so stunned that her words got stuck in her throat, and the next thing she knew, her father had led her out the door… to an even bigger surprise.

A tall, lanky teenaged boy was leading Logan toward the house.

It's him.

Arabelle felt the heat rushing to her cheeks as her father took the reins from the boy and handed him a coin for his troubles. She'd dreamed of this boy for what seemed like forever, and now she was actually looking into his brilliant blue eyes and he was gazing back into hers. She could lose herself in that gaze.

A smaller boy stood next to him—the younger brother. He tugged on his older brother's sleeve, but the blue-eyed boy didn't tear his eyes away from Arabelle.

"Well," Father said to Arabelle, clearing his throat. "Shall we?"

Arabelle realized she'd been staring, and her blush only grew. "Of course, Father."

They both mounted Logan, and Arabelle turned away to hide her burning cheeks.

Father nodded to the boy. "I appreciate your help in finding my horse. Give your mother my thanks again. And remind them that Honfrion owes them a great debt that he intends to repay. They just have to name it."

And with that, they began trotting back toward the caravan.

Arabelle twisted in the saddle to take one last look at the boy. He, too, had turned to watch them depart.

Arabelle sighed and leaned back against her father's chest. "Father… that boy who found our horse. The older one you gave the coin to?"

"Yes, dearest?"

She breathed in deeply, gathering her courage.

"I had a vision about him."

"Oh?"

"He's the boy I'm going to marry."

AUTHOR'S NOTE

Well, that's the end of *Agent of Prophecy*, and I sincerely hope you enjoyed it.

I should note that when I wrote this story, years ago, I never intended for it to really be published. You see, I'm a stuffy science researcher type and I don't go around talking about dwarves, elves, dragons, magic, and such. I just don't. The origins of this story really began because as a relatively younger father of two boys, I would come up with bedtime stories for them.

After a while, the details of the story began getting jumbled in my head, so I began writing things down. And the stories grew in complexity. It became a saga to entertain what at the time were seven and eight-year-old boys. And when I was done, those stories remained in my desk drawer for a long time.

But along the way, something had happened to me. I'd gotten the writing bug.

I learned that I enjoyed the process of creating stories, and because I can't leave well enough alone, I began thinking about maybe writing something for myself.

Don't get me wrong, I enjoy epic fantasy, and grew up on Tolkien, Eddings, and various other authors who set me on the path, but I equally enjoyed Crichton, Asimov, Grisham, and many others in genres that dealt more with action and adventure.

I'd made friends with some rather well-known authors, and when I talked about maybe getting more serious about this writing thing, several of them gave me the same advice, "Write what you know."

Write what I know? I began to think about Michael Crichton. He was a non-practicing MD, and started off with a medical thriller. John Grisham was an attorney for a decade before writing a series of legal thrillers. Maybe there's something to that advice.

I began to ponder, "What do I know?" And then it hit me.

I know science. It's what I do for a living and what I enjoy reading nowadays. In fact, one of my hobbies is reading formal papers spanning many scientific disciplines. My interests range from particle physics, computers, the military sciences (you know, the science behind what makes stuff go boom), and medicine. I'm admittedly a bit of a nerd in that way. I've also traveled extensively during my life, and am an informal student of foreign languages and cultures.

With the advice of some New York Times bestselling authors, I started my foray into writing novels.

And then the unexpected happened.

People began reading them!

And then I hit a national bestseller list or two.

This hobby had suddenly become something a bit more than I'd expected.

And even though I'm not, strictly-speaking, a full-time author, by the end of this year, I should have over twenty books out in a relatively short period of time.

Those bedtime stories had turned into something much more than I'd ever imagined.

And then I opened that drawer where everything started.

The musty and yellowed sheets of printed paper I'd set aside long ago, I began reading those stories and cringing.

I am so much better than I was back then. Somehow or another, I'd picked up some skills and instincts that hadn't been there a decade earlier.

I thought to myself, "Maybe it's time for me to see if I can make something of those old stories?"

After reading the work I'd done long ago, I realized the stories were still quite solid. It was the prose I was uncomfortable with, and the ages of the main characters needing to be tweaked, but it probably wouldn't be too bad to revamp the old stories and bring them to the public.

Decent book covers, proper editing, audio books, the whole shebang.

And here we are, dear reader.

I'm assuming if you're reading these words, that you hopefully enjoyed the story. If this is the first book of mine you've read, then let me explain a few things about what you'll always see in my books.

There is always an author's note to the reader. That's the section you're currently reading, and this is where I talk to you directly about what I do, who I am, and why I do it.

I did want to talk a bit about my contract with you, the reader.

I write to entertain.

That truly is my first and primary goal. Because, for most people, that's what readers typically want out of a novel.

That's certainly what I always wanted. Story first, always.

In this particular story, I dive deeply into a fantasy world that doesn't necessarily have a strong correlation to the science of our world, but this is a four-book series, and trust me, there is some science coming in the upcoming books that is real and does apply.

You'll find that in this series I do what everyone says I shouldn't: I cross the streams between science fiction and fantasy.

Some have called my past writing choices eclectic, unexpected, but the vast majority of feedback I've received to date has thankfully been positive. So, thank you to those who have been readers of my other books. Posting reviews is, of course, the easiest way to let me and others know what you thought of this novel or any of my work. Word of mouth is precious to us poor authors.

However, even though I enjoy writing about events, history, science, and now dipping my toe into fantasy, my primary goal always circles back to entertaining.

As always, at the end of this book, I have an addendum where I cover certain details regarding the creation of this novel, the research that went into it, and of course, I go into the science and technology—mostly because I can't help myself.

I do hope you enjoyed this story, and I hope you'll continue to join me in the future stories yet to come.

Mike Rothman
April 2, 2020

I should note that if you're interested in getting updates about my latest work, join my mailing list at:

https://mailinglist.michaelarothman.com/new-reader

If you enjoyed this story, I should let you know there is more where this came from. Book two, *Heirs of Prophecy*, picks up where this story leaves off. If you wanted to know about that blue-eyed boy, his family, and how they come into this new world to finally meet and interact with a whole new cast of characters, including Arabelle, this should hopefully be a treat.

I include a preview of the first chapter of the next book, but before I do that, if you're a fan of the fantasy genre, and have enjoyed this story, I should also point out that, aside from this series, I do have one other book (as of now) in the fantasy genre. It also features a seventeen-year-old girl who…

Well, if you'll indulge me, below is a brief description of *Dispocalypse*:

In a post-apocalyptic world ruled by a governor who is both feared and worshipped, Willow is a seventeen-year-old girl who is trying to get through her last year of studies. But when her father dies, she experiences strange dreams that change everything about how she looks at the world and at herself.

Haunted by the tragedy, Willow pushes herself beyond anything she could have imagined she was capable of. It's only when she catches the attention of some of the governor's informants that her world is turned upside-down

PREVIEW OF HEIRS OF PROPHECY

Ryan's heart raced as the radiating arcs of white energy crackled between his fingertips. He felt the heat on his face as the prickling energy bloomed even brighter.

None of this made sense. There had been an earthquake, and a bright flash of light. An explosion? Then he and his family had found themselves on the edge of a swamp in an unknown land—not at all where they'd been moments before.

And now this. His fingers…

He looked to his father, whose blue eyes matched his own, and saw only fear there. Dad was as lost as the rest of them. But one thing was clear.

This was definitely not the vacation Dad had planned when they left home just twelve hours earlier…

As Ryan Riverton shoved the last of his clothes into his suitcase, he couldn't remember the last time he'd felt so excited. Today his family would be leaving for their first summer vacation in years. And a long one, too—two whole months. Dad was an engineer for a major manufacturing company, and had been saving up his vacation time for years.

"Come on, everyone!" Dad yelled from downstairs. "We have a plane to catch!"

Ryan just barely managed to pull the suitcase's zipper shut. He dragged the heavy bag from the bed and staggered down the hall with it.

Dad met him halfway down the stairs. "Goodness, Ryan, how much did you pack? Give it here—I'll help you with that." He took the suitcase from Ryan and lifted it with ease. "Would you find your brother and see that he gets his stuff to the car?"

"Sure, Dad."

Ryan went to look for his little brother. Aaron wasn't in his room, though his suitcase was sitting there, already packed. He grabbed it and set it by the front door.

"Aaron!" he shouted.

His mom called from the kitchen. "I think I saw him heading for the garage. He'd better not have run off, we're going to be late as it is!"

Mom was less enthusiastic about the vacation than Ryan was, probably because their last family vacation, four years ago, hadn't been her cup of tea. They'd spent the whole time exploring Japanese ruins and learning about making samurai swords. Ryan and Aaron had been in heaven; both of them were heavily involved in martial arts, so they thought it was amazing.

Mom, however, would have much preferred to remain in the United States, soaking up the sun at a lazy resort.

And perhaps this time she would get her wish. Or not. Ryan didn't know where they were going, and neither did his mom. Only Dad knew.

His father had always loved surprises. They'd all been pestering him for months about their destination, but all he would do was wink and say, "Sorry, that's top secret." All they knew was that it would be "warm and wet," they wouldn't need passports, and that they were bringing Silver, the family cat—which meant they couldn't be going too far, Ryan reasoned.

Ryan found his brother rummaging through the shelves in the garage.

"I brought your suitcase down for you, you lazy bum."

Aaron was fifteen, two years Ryan's junior. He rolled his eyes. "I would have gotten it."

"What are you doing in here anyway?" Ryan asked.

"Trying to find clues."

"Clues to what?"

Aaron scoffed as if this should be obvious. "To where we're going. Dad has to have left clues around here somewhere."

"Well, you won't find anything in here."

"How can you be so sure?"

"Because I already looked."

Aaron put his hands on his hips. "You could have told me that earlier."

At that moment, Dad walked in with Aaron's suitcase. "There you boys are. Don't go anywhere, I'm just finished loading up.

Aaron, use the bathroom if you need it. Ryan, come help me shut down the smith."

Ryan followed his father to the shed that had become Dad's workshop—or "smithy" as he'd started calling it ever since he'd installed a blast furnace. Dad could get a little nutty when he latched on to a new hobby, and he always dragged the boys into it—for good or bad. Ryan had enjoyed learning about the history of metalsmithing, but after countless hours of banging away on the anvil and working with red-hot metal, he'd decided it wasn't for him. Not only was it hard, sweaty work, it was a challenge to get the metal to just the right temperature and all too easy to accidentally ruin something he'd spent hours working on.

It also bugged him that his little brother was so much better at it than him. Everything Aaron made turned out well, while Ryan usually ended up with a pile of malformed junk.

He helped his dad make sure everything was shut down and locked up—not that his dad needed his help—and then headed back to the garage, where Mom was running through one of her typical last-minute checklists.

"Well?" Dad asked her.

"We've got everything," she said.

"Including Silver?" Dad asked.

Mom pointed to a cat carrier in the back seat. "He wasn't happy about it, but yes."

Dad grinned. "Then let's get going. Vacation awaits!"

Their destination proved to be Tucson, Arizona. Or at least, that's where their plane landed. They then loaded their things into a rented SUV and Dad took the wheel, driving them southeast through scenic landscapes. They were surrounded by the vast Sonoran Desert, dotted with towering saguaro cacti and prickly plants that resembled creosote bushes.

"Arizona in the summer," said Mom, checking the weather forecast on her phone. "What were you thinking, Jared? It's supposed to be over a hundred and ten degrees today. We're going to melt!"

Ryan was silently in agreement. He was used to the cool of the Pacific Northwest; he couldn't even imagine what one hundred and ten degrees would feel like.

Dad's face fell. "It won't be too bad," he said, unconvincingly.

Mom forced a smile, perhaps sensing his change in mood. "You're right. We'll have a good time as long as we're together."

"Um... Dad?" Aaron said. "Is there going to be shampoo where we're going?"

Dad perked up again. "No, there won't be any shampoo." He turned to Mom, smiling. "There won't be any room service or electricity, either. We're going camping."

Mom's smile vanished, and she sighed. "We'll have a good time as long as we're together," she repeated, as if by saying the mantra enough times it would be true.

At the entrance to the campgrounds, a ramshackle lodge stood next to a river, with a large sign out front that read "Canoes for Rent." As Dad went inside to check in, Ryan and Aaron hopped out of the car and made straight for the river.

"Maybe we'll be able to go fishing," Ryan said.

"Do you think Silver will freak out about the water?" Aaron asked. He'd brought the gray-and-black-striped cat from the car, insisting he needed the fresh air.

"Let's find out."

Ryan took the cat from his brother's arms and set him down on the bank. Silver sniffed at the water, then pounced on a tiny grasshopper near the river's edge.

"There's your answer," Ryan said. "Silver will be fine. He'll have lots to distract him out here."

At that moment the grasshopper leapt from shore to a large stick floating in the water. The cat jumped after it—and got dunked. The boys cracked up as the cat came back to shore yowling and wet.

Dad exited the lodge with backpacks and life jackets for everyone.

"Aw, do we have to wear those?" Aaron groaned.

"Yes, Aaron, we all have to." He gestured back toward the lodge. "I've rented lockers for most of our stuff, so let's start unloading the car."

"What do you mean, you rented lockers?" Mom asked. "Aren't we taking our stuff with us?"

"Of course not! All that stuff would never fit in a canoe. I've rented two canoes; we'll take them downriver where I have a plan for a camping spot for tonight. Take no more than what you can fit in a backpack; we'll leave the rest here at the lodge."

"Only what you can fit in a backpack," Mom repeated, grumbling. "You might have told us that before we left home, Jared."

Ryan and Mom took one canoe, and Dad and Aaron took the other. As they pushed away from the pier, Mom looked back at Ryan uncertainly, a paddle in her hand. "What am I supposed to do with this thing?" she asked.

Dad and Aaron were having no such trouble. "Race you guys to the turn in the river up ahead!" Dad shouted, and he and Aaron shot into the lead.

Ryan leaned forward and showed his mom how to hold the paddle. "It's easy, Mom. When I say 'stroke,' put the flat side of the paddle in the water so its facing you, pull it toward you as hard as you can, and then lift the paddle out of the water. That way we can keep the same pace and stay on a straight line."

"Okay…" Mom nodded and gripped her paddle.

"Stroke… stroke… stroke…," Ryan chanted.

They kept a steady pace, carving a straight line downriver. Up ahead, Dad and Aaron were paddling madly, but their strokes weren't coordinated, and their canoe swayed left and right. Soon Ryan and Mom went right past them—much to Mom's delight and Dad's chagrin—and by the time they reached the next bend in the river, they had such a lead that they stopped paddling and waited for the others to catch up.

"Come on, slowpokes!" Ryan shouted.

Mom laughed, and they high-fived.

They'd been riding the current, paddling on and off for about an hour, when Dad called for the two boats to pull up side by side. They were traveling between cliffs, one of which was covered with greenery near the waterline.

"Okay, guys," Dad said. "This is our destination—for now. There's a cave system in these cliffs, and I brought headlamps for everyone. We're going to explore a bit of history."

Mom looked dubious, but Aaron and Ryan craned their necks to look up at the cliff. This was going to be cool, Ryan could tell.

"The natives of this area," Dad said as he passed out headlamps, "natives who lived here for thousands of years, mind you—came to these caves to commune with the spirits. According to their stories, the veil between worlds is thinnest right here at this very spot. I expect we'll find lots of very interesting petroglyphs, and maybe even a spirit or two if we're lucky."

"What's a petroglyph?" Aaron asked as they guided their canoes toward the cliff.

"It's a carving or painting on the stone," Dad replied. "Kind of like an Egyptian hieroglyph. The natives used them to tell stories and communicate ideas. I'm hoping to find some that are *really* old."

"How old is really old?" Aaron asked.

"Well, Native Americans have been on this continent since the last ice age at least, so… pretty old. If we find a carving that depicts an extinct animal—say, a mammoth—then you know you're looking at something special."

Dad was steering them directly for the base of the cliff, and as they got closer, Ryan understood why. Through the canopy of greenery, a cave opened directly into the cliff from the water. The tips of their canoes parted the hanging vines, and they paddled right on through.

Mom swatted at a plant that grazed her face. "Jared! You just led us through a bunch of poison ivy! Kids, don't touch your eyes, mouth, or anything."

"My feet are itching," Aaron whined.

"You have shoes on, Aaron," Mom said, shaking her head.

"My arm itches," Aaron whined.

"Then dunk it in the water," Mom said. "In fact, it might be a good idea to find a place to park our canoes so we can all take a dip in the water. A swim would be nice anyway. I've never sweated so much in my life."

Ryan pointed to a wide shelf of sand up ahead. "How about there?"

"That looks perfect," Dad said. "In fact, since there's plenty of driftwood scattered around here, I'll see if I can make a fire for us."

"I don't think we need a fire," Mom said. "I want to cool off, not warm up."

"It's pretty cool in this cave," Dad said. "And you'll need the fire to dry off your clothes after you swim in them."

"I brought my suit."

"Yes, but we did just push through poison ivy. It's all over your clothes now, so… what better way to wash it off, right?"

Ryan grinned.

Mom groaned.

As the fire crackled merrily, Ryan lay next to the flames and tried to dry off, along with his clothes. They were all soaking wet—all except their hiking boots, which they'd removed before swimming, and Silver, who had no interest in getting wet again—but they were cool, and it was fun being in this dark cave lit only by a flickering fire.

"Boys, put your hiking boots back on, the rocks around here are kind of uneven and have sharp edges."

Ryan grabbed his socks that stuff in his boots and began putting them back as he looked over to where Dad was studying something on the cave wall. "You find a petroglyph?"

"No, just noticing there's a thick seam of mica in this rock wall. You never know, we might even find some gemstones in this cave, like the old miners used to."

"How far back do these caves go?" Mom asked.

"They go on for miles," Dad said, "though the map I picked up only covers a part of them. I figure we can explore for the rest of the day, find a spot like this to spend the night, then explore some more before heading to the canoe drop-off downstream."

Ryan sensed that his mother wasn't pleased with the prospect of spending a full day—and night—in this dank enclosure.

"Come on, boys," Dad said. "Let's try some hand fishing." He'd brought equipment for that, too. Fishing line, weights, hooks, and bobbers designed for fishing with a handline. The two boys sat cross-legged in the sand and began to assemble their rigs.

Just as Ryan managed to thread a weight over his line, a deep rumbling shook the cave. He looked up in alarm, and so did Aaron. Even their father looked concerned.

"What was that?" Aaron asked.

Dad tried to wave it off. "There're some mines in the area. Someone must have set off a charge a few miles away. Nothing to worry about."

"Jared..." Mom said. "Being in a dark cave with no hot water is bad enough. I don't want the roof caving in on me."

Dad chuckled. "It'll be fine. I promise."

Ryan waited for a moment to see whether the rumbling would continue. When a minute passed without any tremors, he finally went back to threading his line.

And then the rumble returned—except this time it was *much* stronger than before. The ground shook violently. Waves formed on the water. The walls began to crack, and bits of rock began to fall. Clouds of dust blew forth from the depths of the cave.

The Riverton family did the only thing they could. They huddled together as their world collapsed around them.

ADDENDUM

For readers who are familiar with my style of book construction, the addendum is where I talk about the science of the story you just read. But this is without a doubt a fantasy novel, so there's no science, right?

Well, yes and no. I will admit that this first installment in what is a four-book series does have the least of what I'd call traditional science. This will evolve a bit in the future, but there are some things that I think are interesting to discuss that have to do with science and relate to this novel.

I should note that these addendums are intended to give very brief explanations of what might be complex concepts. My intent is to only leave you with enough information to give a remedial understanding of the subject. However, for those who want to know more, it's also my intent to leave you with enough keywords that would allow you to initiate your own research and gain a more complete background understanding of any of these topics.

So what kind of science could there even be in this fantasy novel? I'll admit, it's a challenge, but I'm up for it.

For instance, Arabelle's uncanny ability to pinpoint the direction of someone she knows well, you wouldn't consider that a scientific element, but I can somewhat correlate that to an upgraded version of magnetoreception.

"Magnetoreception? What's that," you ask.

Magnetoreception:

Well, you might have heard of homing pigeons. These are birds that can find their way back to a spot no matter where they are in this world. It almost seems like magic, but that phenomenon is very real and it's based on something called magnetoreception.

This ability is based on an organism's sense of magnetic fields around them and oddly enough many creatures can detect a magnetic field to help them pinpoint location, altitude, and direction.

It's not as rare a thing as you might expect. Even some bacteria have a sense of magnetic fields. Mollusks do too, as do many fish along with many land-based vertebrate animals. It could be argued that even humans are in some small sense sensitive to fields around them, some more than others.

Going back to the example of the homing pigeon, they have the uncanny ability to be "remember" the location where they were hatched and when taken from that spot, even thousands of miles away, they manage to be able to come back to the exact same nest they were born in.

Akin to sharks where they can sense the electrical signals of other animals nearby using an organ called the ampullae of Lorenzini, imagine such a "sixth sense" being tweaked. Or we somehow evolved the ability to sense other people at a distance.

Some things are still strictly-speaking "fantasy" but it's not as far-fetched as it may initially seem.

Infravision:

Infravision? Infravision is a loan word from a popular game that describes the ability to see things in the infrared spectrum. Is it real? Can people do that, and if so, would it be like the ability exhibited by Arabelle where she can see creatures in the dark?

Well, let's talk briefly about what does infrared even mean. What is infrared and how does it relate to the whole light spectrum?

I would hope that we're all very familiar with a jump rope, and if you wiggle one end of the rope you'll see that the rope makes wave-like shapes. The distance between each of the peaks is called the wavelength, and the slower and less energy you put into the wiggling the longer the length of the wave.

Well, light is the same way. Light also travels in a wave, however the length of the wave is very very short. How short? Well, the typical visible spectrum for humans is between 380 nanometers (violet) and 740 nanometers (red). Yes, nanometers, one billionth of a meter. Very small, but very significant.

Infrared light has wavelengths longer than 740 nanometers that's where "infravision" becomes interesting.

Why is it interesting?

Well, we normally think of light as something that is shining out of a flashlight, or maybe a TV or computer monitor. We don't think of things glowing with light all the time. Your desk, the rock on the ground, or the squirrel in the woods. The only reason we don't is because most of us can't see that glow.

I'll give you an example that will help. Most of us are pretty familiar with the stovetops that have those metal coils on them, and many of you may have some right now. If you set the stovetop's setting to "high" those coils tend to glow red. That means that there's enough energy being emitted that the glow from the coils has a short enough wavelength for us to see it enter into the visible light spectrum, and thus it looks red.

If you set it to medium or low, the coils look black, no "light" whatsoever, but we know it's still hot, right? All it means is that the energy of the light being emitted is of a longer wavelength than what we can see. It is still glowing, just the light is in the infrared range.

Well, that applies to all of us. We all glow at various levels based on our heat signatures, and there are many creatures, most of them cold-blooded like snakes, fish, and frogs, that can see into the infrared spectrum.

However, there have been some unusual cases where it's possible for humans to see flashes of light due to infrared stimulation. These are situations that are usually involving a beam of coherent infrared light shot through a laser, and a single point on the retina registers the energy of two incoming photos as one and sees it as a green flash of light, but these are not real-world applications.

I noted above that it's cold-blooded animals that have typically evolved with the ability to see infrared, and not warm-blooded ones. That makes quite a bit of sense, because you'd think that with warm-blooded animals, the animal's body gives off heat and would interfere with the animal's vision.

So, even though there isn't any inherent examples of humans seeing in the infrared spectrum, it's not impossible to imagine such a capability. And hopefully, this gives a little insight into what the whole thermal imaging concept really means.

More science to come in Heirs of Prophecy, that much I do promise.

ABOUT THE AUTHOR

I am an Army brat, a polyglot, and the first person in my family born in the United States. This heavily influenced my youth by instilling in me a love of reading and a burning curiosity about the world and all of the things within it. As an adult, my love of travel and adventure has driven me to explore many exotic locations, and these places sometimes creep into the stories I write.

I hope you've found this story entertaining.

- Mike Rothman

You can find my blog at: www.michaelarothman.com
Facebook at: www.facebook.com/MichaelARothman
And on Twitter: @MichaelARothman